Wild and Wicked

ITALIAN STALLIONS
BOOK FOUR

MARI CARR

Wild and Wicked

Gianna, queen of to-do lists, clean freak, organizer extraordinaire, has her future all figured out. Dream job at twenty-four, engaged at twenty-six, married at twenty-eight, first baby at thirty. And she's on her way to achieving that...sort of. She has a job, though it's not a dream, and she even thought she had her guy. Until he dumped her just short of that engagement ring deadline.

Enter Elio Moretti, king of the ice, the playboy hockey star who lives his life just one day at a time. When Gianna and Elio are trapped in his family's cabin during a blizzard, the concept of opposites attract is put to the test. Until the tequila comes out.

Their steamy one-night stand throws Gianna's original plan out the window—and now she only has nine months to come up with another one. Lucky for her, Elio is very good at thinking on his feet and calls a play that just might give her everything she wants.

Chapter One

G ianna was late. She'd debated not coming at all, but in the end, she decided she'd be better off spending this evening with her friends versus sitting in a too quiet, too empty apartment, alone with only her thoughts. Besides, there wasn't a damn thing left in her place to clean.

She'd scrubbed every single solitary inch of it over the past three months. Ever since Sam Mannarino, her boyfriend for the past eleven—ELEVEN—years told her he thought their relationship had run its course and they should call it quits.

For the first couple of weeks after he'd packed up his stuff and moved out of the apartment they'd shared, she'd thought maybe he was just blowing off steam. After all, you don't date someone for eleven years and not have a few fights or "we were on a break" moments that never lasted more than a week or two. But when he didn't come back, didn't respond to her occasional texts, and sent her *one* phone call straight to voicemail, she didn't get depressed— she got fucking pissed off.

And that anger hadn't abated until...

Until tonight.

"You late too?"

Gianna jumped slightly, so lost in her thoughts, she didn't

hear one of her best friends, Liza Moretti, walking up the porch steps behind her.

"Sorry," Liza added, when she realized she'd scared her. "Thought you heard me."

"I got held up. Last-minute shopping," Gianna explained lamely, as Liza opened the front door to the house without knocking. Not that anyone would hear them if they did. The music emanating from the living room had hit a volume level that had the windows pulsating in time with the beat.

Gianna's girlfriend, Keeley Gallo, had moved into this mansion with her boyfriends—plural—Gio and Rafe last fall, the three of them so over-the-top, sweetly in love, it gave Gianna a toothache.

Rafe had inherited the huge Gothic monstrosity—one they were all convinced was haunted by the ghosts of Rafe's grandparents—and he and Gio were currently renovating it. They were living here while they did the work, but Keeley had eventually put her foot down, saying the mansion was too damn big to make their forever home.

So Gio and Rafe had formed a partnership and decided to go into business together. Their plan—a brilliant one, in Gianna's mind—was to turn the mansion into an inn. Once it was ready to open for business, they were hoping to buy a reasonably sized house to settle down in.

Gianna had a degree in hotel management and, while she hadn't brought up the subject yet, she was hoping to convince Gio and Rafe to let her run their haunted inn. She just needed to clean up her resume, practice her pitch, then pray they went for it...because her current job at a basic close-to-the airport hotel was mind-numbingly tedious and boring to the extreme, presenting her absolutely zero challenges.

She'd spent the better part of two hours this afternoon adding more twinkle lights to the foyer because there'd been nothing else to do. Too many more months there, and she would turn into a legit zombie.

A few weeks ago, Keeley had decided to throw a Christmas party, and it had been all her girlfriends had been able to talk about since she'd set the date for the bash. Keeley, a party girl from way back, loved nothing more than planning a menu, decorating, creating a guest list and a music playlist, then dancing the night away.

Gianna could get behind the lists part of the planning process because there was nothing she loved more than a good list. She currently had at least five different lists she was working off, at work and at home. But the rest...well...all she could see at the end of this event was a shit-ton of cleaning to do.

Which might not be a bad thing, now that she thought about it. Maybe she'd volunteer to come back tomorrow morning to help Keeley put the house back to rights.

"You made it!" Keeley yelled excitedly when she and Liza walked into the grand foyer. "Here," she said, arms outstretched. "Give me your coats. I'll stash them in the office."

Gianna and Liza took off their coats and handed them over, both shaking a few flakes of snow from their hair. It was only flurrying, though weather forecasters were predicting a very snowy Christmas season.

Just the thought of the holidays made Gianna feel unnaturally tired. Maybe she was coming down with something. The idea of getting a cold felt more reassuring than admitting that what was *really* wrong with her was most likely depression.

This holiday was going to be a rough one, the first she'd ever had to spend alone. Growing up, she had always celebrated Christmas with Grandma Mary, who'd raised her. She and Sam had been seriously dating when her grandmother passed away, so since then, her holidays had been spent with his family, who'd always embraced her with welcome arms.

"Hey. I was starting to worry you two weren't coming," Penny Beaumont said as she ventured into the foyer.

"Oh my God. Don't even get me started on why I'm late,"

Liza said dramatically, flipping her chestnut-colored hair over her shoulder. "Matt Russo is a zit on the ass of humanity."

They all might have laughed if Matt's brother, Gage—and Penny's fiancé—hadn't chosen that moment to walk in.

Gage grinned. "I always figured he was a zit on the ball sac, but I like your version better. Allows both genders to feel the pain."

Liza grimaced, her look only slightly apologetic.

Liza was a Moretti, Gage a Russo. Putting those names together was basically a recipe for disaster because the two families had hated each other since the beginning of time for some long-past slights. The current crop of Morettis and Russos were sort of hanging onto the grudge but only half-heartedly.

As evidenced by Gage's presence here at the party.

Liza's father, Cesare, and her nonno would flip their lids if they knew Gage was in attendance, which was why they hadn't been informed. If there was one thing the Moretti kids were experts at, it was avoiding the wrath of the older generations.

For her part, Gianna didn't give a crap what anyone's last name was. She'd gotten to know Gage over the past few months since he and Penny became a couple, and she really liked him.

"So what did my dear big brother do?" Gage asked.

Liza scowled. "The Grinch insisted on a meeting with me. This evening. Like it couldn't wait. FYI—it could have fucking waited. There was nothing he wanted to discuss that couldn't have been said in January. Or in a stupid email. It's the goddamn Saturday before Christmas. What's wrong with that guy? Did he misplace his soul somewhere?"

Liza, typically good-natured, fun, and kind, had one hot button, and its name was Matt Russo, though her anger toward the man had nothing to do with the family's war and everything to do with the man himself. Liza had recently landed her dream job as Executive Director of the Philadelphia Initiative—a foundation that worked to increase philanthropic donations in the city. Her friend loved everything about the gig, except Matt

Russo, who served as the chairman to the board for the same foundation. It placed him and Liza in similar circles far too often for her friend's comfort.

Gage lifted his hands in a "what can I say" manner. "Matt doesn't do holidays. Or weekends. Every day is a workday in his world."

"That's sad," Gianna mused as Keeley returned to the foyer.

"Why's everyone still out here when the party's in there?" Keeley pointed toward the living room, which was bursting at the seams with people.

"This is the only place we can talk and actually hear what the other person is saying," Penny pointed out.

Keeley snorted. "I told Gio the music was too loud. Hey, Gio!" she yelled into the living room.

"Yeah?" he shouted back.

"Turn the music down. Nobody can talk."

Gio shouted something in reply, but Gianna couldn't hear it. Regardless, the volume of the music did dip down. A little bit.

Keeley's eyes widened in exasperation. "I swear to God, the guy's hearing is shit. Doesn't bode well for the 'growing old' part of our relationship. I'm a brilliant conversationalist. How is he going to appreciate that if he can't hear me?"

"Is it the conversation you want him to hear or the nagging?" Liza teased.

"I don't nag," Keeley replied. "Much."

Everyone laughed. Gianna joined in, but her laughter was forced. She was rethinking her decision to come. Socializing, smiling, faking happy was going to take more energy than she had to give.

"Now...what were you guys talking about?" Keeley asked.

"We were just explaining why we were late," Liza replied. "Or at least I was, and I can sum it up for you in two words. Matt Russo."

Keeley groaned. "Ugh. What a douche." Then she also recalled Gage's presence. "Sorry," she murmured.

Gage just grinned, unoffended. "I'm well aware of my brother's reputation in this particular social circle."

"Yeah, but...still." Keeley quickly changed the subject. "Soooo...why are you late, Gianna?"

Gianna considered brushing the question off but decided against it. The reason she'd come to the party tonight was because she needed her friends. "I had to stop by the mall to pick up the last part of my boss's Christmas present after work and I ran into Sam."

"Oh," Penny said, sympathetically. "That couldn't have been easy."

Gianna nodded, briefly glancing at Gage, who must have sensed her unease with his presence. She really liked Penny's fiancé, but this conversation was going to be hard enough to have with her girlfriends.

Gage, mercifully astute, gave Penny a quick kiss on the cheek. "I'll let you women chat. Toby and Rich have been holding up that back wall long enough, studying the damn quarters game. By now, they've probably worked out the physics behind it and are itching to give it a try. Time to draw my posse into the game."

"You just called the nerd circle your posse," Penny teased, grinning.

"That's right," Gage said unabashedly. "And I stand by it. Twenty bucks says I can have Toby rolling quarters off his ass into the glass by the end of the night."

"Behave yourself." Penny swatted her soon-to-be husband, looking at him with so much love, it physically hurt Gianna to witness.

Had she ever looked at Sam like that?

She and Sam had fallen in love in high school during their sophomore year. Gianna suspected that at some point, she had stared at Sam like he hung the moon, but after so many years together...the rush of first love had given way to comfortable companionship, something she'd, well...*liked*.

Sam hadn't just been her boyfriend; he'd been her best friend.

So when he left, he took a hell of a lot more than just his clothes, his old-school record collection, and stupid *Star Wars* Legos models. He'd taken her heart *and* her sounding board.

"You haven't seen Sam since he moved out, have you?" Keeley asked, though Gianna's friends all knew that. Somehow, Sam had found a way to erase himself completely from her world, ghosting her by not texting, not calling, and avoiding all their usual stomping grounds.

"No. I haven't," she confirmed.

No-nonsense Liza sliced one hand through the air. "Well, good then. It's done. The Band-Aid is ripped off, so you don't have to dread the first meeting anymore. How did it go?"

Gianna swallowed deeply. "Fine. I mean..." She shook her head. "Not fine. He was with a woman."

Keeley's shoulders fell. "Aw, babe. It's been three months. You had to know he would move on."

Her friends had been encouraging her to do the same. Trying to convince her that Sam's leaving was a good thing because they'd been fighting too much and neither of them had been truly happy the last several months of their relationship. All of that was true.

But her being alone didn't feel like a better thing. Not at all.

"I get that," she said. "I really do. It's just..."

This.

This was the part that was going to be hard to say. The part that had taken the anger she'd felt the past few months and morphed it into hardcore devastation. She could almost hear the shattered pieces of her broken heart crashing against each other inside her.

Which was weird. Because even she could admit that tonight should have only fueled her ire more.

"I was playing it cool," Gianna said. "Proud of how strong I sounded. I asked him how he'd been, he said fine and introduced me to Emma. Then stupidly, for some reason, I asked if they were on a first date. I don't know why I asked that, but I guess I was just looking for something to say."

"What did he say?" Liza asked.

Gianna sighed sadly. "He didn't answer because Emma beat him to the punch. She said no. Said they'd been dating since July."

Liza frowned. "July?"

"But you two didn't break up until..." Penny stopped talking.

"September," Gianna finished for her. "Apparently Emma didn't know about me, either."

"He was cheating on you!" Liza said hotly. "The deceitful, no-good, piece-of-shit motherfucker. Did you call him out on it? Please tell me you fucking lit into him."

Gianna shook her head. "I was too...God...stunned. I think I was waiting for Sam to correct her, but when I looked at his face, I saw it was true. Emma seemed to realize she'd said something wrong, but I could tell she didn't know what. After that, Sam was anxious to get away, so the two of them said goodbye and that was it."

While the anger Gianna had been carrying around since Sam dumped her had vanished, Liza appeared to have found plenty of it. "I can't believe he did that to you. What the fuck is wrong with him?"

Gianna had no reply to that. She'd loved Sam with her whole heart. But more than that, up until this afternoon, she would have called him the most trustworthy guy on the planet. Even after the breakup. In eleven years, he'd never lied to her. Not once.

Or maybe the truth was, she'd never *caught* him in a lie.

He'd made a fool of her, and she hated him for that. But perhaps what hurt more was that she hated herself more for being so gullible, so stupid, so blind. If she told her friends how she felt, they'd tell her she was wrong, and maybe they'd be right.

It didn't matter though.

It was still the way she felt. Right or wrong.

Emotion was rarely intelligent.

"You're better off without him," Keeley said. "I never liked him."

Gianna couldn't help it. She laughed. The first real one of the night. "You loved Sam. You spent years telling me how lucky I was to have such a great guy." Keeley and Liza had spent most of their early twenties sludging through the online dating swamp, while Gianna had been shacked up in what she'd genuinely believed was premarital bliss with the man she was going to spend the rest of her life with.

So much for her Great Life Plan.

Sam had thrown a major monkey wrench into Gianna's perfect life list.

Dream job at twenty-four, engaged at twenty-six, married at twenty-eight, first baby at thirty.

Sure, she didn't exactly have her dream job, but at least she was employed. Now, here she was at twenty-six, and she sure wasn't admiring the engagement ring she'd hoped Sam would give her on her last birthday. Instead, he'd given her a new Roomba vacuum cleaner, which probably should have shown her the handwriting on the wall.

And maybe it would have if she wasn't such a clean freak and if her previous Roomba hadn't gone on the fritz. At the time, she'd thought it was a great present, thoughtful, perfect.

She was an idiot.

"All this tells me," Liza said, placing her hand on Gianna's forearm, "is it's time."

Gianna shook her head, perfectly aware of what Liza was referring to. "No. My life is just fine the way it is."

Liza had been trying to drag Gianna out ever since Sam had dumped her. Of course, she knew that was only because Keeley had fallen madly in love with Gio and Rafe around the same time, leaving Liza without a wingman at the nightclubs and bars.

Liza scoffed. "Gianna, dammit. What you're currently doing doesn't classify as a life. You go to work. You go home. You clean. You sleep. Then the next day is just rinse and repeat."

Penny, who was the quietest—as well as the newest—in their group of girlfriends, uncharacteristically chimed in. "I've been where you are, Gianna, and trust me, while it might feel easier to avoid the dating game, in the end, it's just lonely as hell. I spent a decade of my life living on my own with only my cats because I was too afraid to take a chance on something more." Penny leaned toward her, her voice lower. "Take the chance. It will be the best thing you'll ever do."

Gianna didn't know how to respond to that. Because it sounded like very good advice. "That's easier said than done."

Penny gave her an understanding smile. "Tell me about it."

"You're going to have to kiss a lot of frogs, none of us is denying that," Keeley added. "And there are going to be a lot of disastrous dates, but when you find the one or ones," she amended, grinning like the Cheshire Cat, "you forget all the pain in an instant."

"You thought Sam was the one," Liza said. "He wasn't. But that doesn't mean there's not another—better—guy who will be absolutely perfect for you."

Keeley nodded. "Exactly. But you're not going to find your Prince Charming by hiding inside all the time. You're going to have to put yourself out there and look."

"I know it's not easy." Liza, at twenty-nine, was the single-woman record holder in their girlfriend group. "And there are going to be times when you're going to want to pack it in and adopt a cat."

"Or four," Penny said with a laugh.

Liza chuckled. "Your self-confidence will most likely take a beating, but just consider it paying your dues."

"I...I'm not ready," Gianna repeated, though even she could hear her weakening resolve. She'd been on her own since September, hating every minute of it, and part of her wondered if she hadn't run into Sam, would tonight have been the night she'd given in to Liza's demands that she set up Tinder and Bumble accounts?

Maybe.

Actually probably.

But then she'd seen Sam, and any healing—she could admit

there'd been minimal—vanished in an instant, and once more, she was left nursing the big gaping wound in her heart.

"Okay. But just so you know...I'm gonna keep inviting you out with me. Maybe you're not ready to date, but dammit, you can still have some fun. What are you doing for Christmas?" Liza asked.

Gianna had managed to keep at bay the tears she'd been fighting since leaving the mall, but Liza's question struck hard. She blinked rapidly, hoping her friends wouldn't see them.

Of course they did, all three women instinctively shifting closer.

"Gianna," Keeley said softly. "You didn't think we were going to let you spend it alone, did you?"

Gianna hadn't really considered spending it with her friends, though she wasn't sure why not. She had the greatest friends on earth, and they never failed to include her.

"You're spending Christmas Eve with the Morettis," Liza said, as if it had all been prearranged for months. "Ordinarily, I wouldn't throw someone into a Moretti Christmas Eve unprepared, but you've been to more than enough of our parties over the years to know exactly what you're getting yourself into. Just understand that we only give it about fifty percent of effort during those other celebrations. We really turn it up at Christmas."

Gianna just barely managed to hide her horror. She'd grown up an only child in a house that contained her and her grandma. She remembered being shell-shocked the first time she'd attended a Moretti family summer picnic, stunned by the sheer number of people and the volume, everyone seemingly talking at once. There was no way that was only fifty percent.

It belatedly occurred to Gianna that it was no wonder Gio's hearing was crappy. It had probably been impaired by a lifetime of Moretti parties.

Penny shuddered at Liza's warning, while Keeley grinned. "Kayden and I have been spending Christmas Eve with the

Morettis since our parents died. It's a great time, but yeah...it's a lot."

Keeley had been raised by her older brother, Kayden, after their parents died in a plane crash. It made sense that she and Kayden would be included in the holidays, given Kayden and Liza's brother, Aldo, had been best friends since birth. And even more so now, considering Keeley was dating Gio, Liza's cousin.

"Are you going?" Gianna asked Penny, who quickly shook her head.

"Dear God, no. I'm spending Christmas morning with my very quiet, non-Italian family, and Christmas Eve at some bougie restaurant with Gage and his brothers."

"It doesn't matter if Penny is there or not," Liza said assuredly. "You will be. I have spoken, thus it is so."

And that was when Gianna realized arguing would be futile.

That was also when it occurred to her...she didn't want to argue.

"Thank you," Gianna said, truly grateful not to have to spend Christmas alone.

"Alright. Let's get this party started. Our girl Gianna needs wine, and lots of it," Keeley said, leading them into the living room. "It's in the kitchen."

Penny glanced across the room. "Damn. Gage did exactly what he said he'd do." They all looked and saw Penny's two IT workmates, Toby and Rich, bouncing quarters off the coffee table with several Moretti men. "I'm going over there. Don't want to miss it if Toby does try the ass-bounce."

Keeley laughed, until she spotted a nearly empty platter. "Better top up the plates before Joey starts a mutiny. I swear to God that guy's stomach is a bottomless pit." She started to grab the platter, but she was intercepted by Gio, who'd pulled her into a circle of people who were dancing their asses off.

Gianna looked at Liza. "I'm going to pour myself a glass. You want one?"

Liza nodded. "Yeah. In a minute. I want to finish our conversation."

Gianna didn't realize they *hadn't* finished. "What's left to say?"

"I'm worried about you."

Gianna was touched by Liza's concern. "I appreciate that. I really do. I just...I know it's been three months, but after tonight, after hearing that Sam..." She couldn't make herself say the words.

"Cheated on you." Liza, meanwhile, had no problem speaking the truth.

"It's going to take me some time to wrap my head around that."

"Maybe so, but in the end, what would wrapping your head around it change?"

"Not one damn thing. God, Liza, I've been with one guy my whole life and that relationship started when I was fifteen years old. I might be the most clueless woman on the planet when it comes to the dating scene."

Liza gave her a sympathetic grin. "So let's take the first baby step tonight."

"How?"

Liza gestured around the room. "You are surrounded by at least a dozen hot, single guys. Tonight, you practice flirting in a secure environment."

Gianna laughed. "You call the Morettis secure?"

Liza didn't share her humor. "Actually, yeah. They'll flirt back without letting it go too far, and they'll keep an eye on their buddies at the same time." Her friend looked around the room, her gaze landing on Joey and a man Gianna didn't know. "Joey's home, and the guy with him is his cohost from *ManPower*, Miles. I went out to dinner with them last night and had a blast. Miles is funny, nice, and really hot."

Gianna agreed. "He is super-hot. Maybe too hot for me to start with?"

Liza dismissed that argument with an irritated sniff. "Girlfriend, I'm going to let you get away with that this one time because you took it on the chin tonight, thanks to that dick of an ex. But you're going to have to accept that you are gorgeous. Period. End of discussion. So go flirt with Miles. Then..." Liza spun around, exploring the rest of the available men. "Flirt with Toby and Rich, Penny's IT buddies. Give the nerd circle a thrill. And finally, I think you should wrap up the practice session with a couple of the guys Luca brought from the construction team. Check out the guy in the blue flannel shirt." Then, after a pause, "You know what, leave him for me. I wouldn't mind running my hands over those muscles."

"Jesus," Gianna muttered. "You seriously expect me to spend my night flirting with all these guys?"

"Yes."

"You're not asking for much, are you?" Gianna said sarcastically.

"Just do it. And then, right after Christmas, we'll go out and—"

Gianna cut Liza off before she got too carried away. "I took the week after Christmas off from work. I had so much unused vacation time, my boss pointed it out. I was thinking I might go somewhere. The walls of my apartment are starting to close in on me."

"Hey, that's a great idea. If I didn't have two can't-miss meetings at work, I'd go with you."

Gianna gave Liza a sad smile. "I'd be shitty company."

"You're never shitty company. Where are you thinking of going?"

Gianna shrugged. "Somewhere cheap," she joked. She had money in the bank, but she was by no means rich. Even less so, now that she was paying the rent on her own instead of splitting it with Sam.

Liza considered that for a minute, then lit up. "I have just the place."

"You do?"

"Yep. My family owns a small cabin in the Poconos. It's nothing fancy, and when I say small, I mean tiny. The whole cabin is just one big room, if you don't count the bathroom. When we were kids, my parents took us there once every couple of months. In the summer, we would fish in the pond, hike the surrounding trails, make s'mores over the firepit. In the winter, we'd all snuggle up in front of the fireplace, play games, ice-skate on the pond. It is, hands down, one of my favorite places to be."

"How in the hell did six of you sleep in a one-bedroom cabin?"

Liza was the youngest of four kids and the only daughter in her family. Two of her brothers, Aldo and Elio, were here tonight. Bruno, the oldest, was married with kids of his own.

Liza laughed. "That was the magic of it. My brothers and I all piled into the middle of the living room area with sleeping bags, while my folks slept in the bed. We would tell scary stories, joke around, and wrestle, until my dad would finally lose his shit and threaten to whoop our asses. He never did, but the way he said it usually had the desired effect, and we'd all calm down and go to sleep."

Gianna had to admit, the way Liza described the cabin did make it sound awesome. Of course, there was a big difference between going there with a huge, rambunctious, fun family and going alone.

"Bruno used to take Vivian out there when they were just dating, for romantic getaways, and then even after they got married. I'm pretty sure my nephew Billy was conceived in the cabin. I've gone there a few times alone, usually whenever I'm stressed out as fuck and just need to get out of the city. It's so peaceful and beautiful. I take a stack of romance novels, a few bottles of wine, a ton of comfort food, my hiking boots, and by the end of the trip, I always feel a thousand times better."

Gianna had a bunch of books she'd been wanting to read, as well as a couple of puzzles she'd been meaning to put together. She loved puzzles, the more challenging the better. While she'd taken the time off with the intention of getting out of town, she hadn't put any serious thought or effort behind making the plans, too worried about spending the money.

What Liza was offering sounded like the answer to a prayer. She'd go to the cabin for a few days, take long walks in the woods, read in front of the fire, and figure her shit out. "Are you sure your family won't mind me staying there?" Gianna asked, aware that she was starting to get excited about the prospect.

"My parents will be glad someone's using it. As we've all gotten older and busier with our jobs, we don't go there as much as we used to. Go to the cabin. Clear all the Sam bullshit out of your head. You should shine at that. You're an excellent cleaner. Then come back with a blank slate, ready to be filled with my stellar advice and dating expertise. Okay?"

Any regret Gianna harbored about coming to the party tonight was gone in an instant. Liza had offered her a plan, and she loved having a plan.

And while she was away, she intended to make a new life list. She could do this.

Gianna nodded. "Okay."

"Good," Liza said, pointing to Miles. "Now, go flirt."

Chapter Two

"How much longer until you can lose the damn sling?" Aldo asked him.

Elio sighed heavily. "I have an appointment two days before Christmas down in Baltimore. I'm hoping the team doctor gives me a clean bill of health so I can get rid of it. It's seriously cutting into my fun time."

Aldo laughed. "I forgot you were left-handed. You know, sometimes I like to use the less dominant hand. Feels like a piece of strange."

Elio narrowed his eyes. "You're hilarious."

"You're a creative guy and in good shape. Are you telling me you can't figure out how to fuck a woman with your arm in a sling?" Aldo asked.

"This thing has the wrong effect on women. Makes them want to take care of me, not...*take care of me*," he said, wiggling his eyebrows as he emphasized the last reiteration.

"Been a long time?"

"Nine brutal months."

"Jesus." Aldo frowned. "You realize you've only been in the sling eight weeks."

"I'm aware."

"What happened with Paula? Thought she might be the one."

"No. We were cool when it was a no-strings-attached thing, but toward the end, she was hinting that she wanted more. A hell of a lot more. Something that began with a ring and ended with vows. I'm not stepping into that trap."

Aldo rolled his eyes. "Never met a guy more averse to commitment than you."

"Says the guy who's five years older than me and still a bachelor."

"It's not for lack of trying, believe me," Aldo insisted. "Besides, how do you know that's what she wants?"

"For a year or so, we only contacted each other when we were horny and wasn't like it was an exclusive thing. The last six months, she's started texting at random times, just general chitchat. And she has this annoying talent for 'running into me,'" Elio finger-quoted, "at all my usual hangouts."

"So that's it? No more hookups?"

Elio shrugged. "Yeah. I broke things off. She knew going in I wasn't looking for a relationship, and she assured me she wasn't either."

"Sounds to me like she thought she could wear you down," Aldo said with a grin. "Woman doesn't know just how stubborn you are."

Elio lifted his red Solo cup, toasting to the truth of that statement.

"Bet you'll be glad to get back to work," Aldo said, changing the subject.

Elio nodded because that was the response his older brother most likely expected, but the truth was...he wasn't in any big hurry to return to the team. Which was probably the answer to a question Elio had been turning over in his mind for the better part of a year.

He'd signed with the professional hockey league when he was just eighteen, though he spent his first year playing in the minors before being drafted to the Baltimore Stingrays.

Eleven years—ELEVEN—spent on the ice, on the road, riding in busses and planes, rooming with other players in the big league.

Always in motion.

Constant motion.

The last two years, he'd suffered some injuries—a couple of concussions and this damn broken collarbone. After each injury, he'd been placed on the reserve list, forced to slow down.

His family, teammates, and friends all assumed he'd hated the downtime because in truth, the old Elio would have been climbing the walls, bitching and moaning and chomping at the bit to get back on the ice.

But that hadn't been the case at all. He'd been shocked to discover he *loved* having the time to stay home and simply sit still.

More and more, he found himself jealous whenever he spoke to someone in his family, and they shared all the stuff happening at home. He'd missed over a decade of birthdays, holidays, picnics, fall firepits, and parties like this one tonight. All because he'd been out on the road. None of that had ever bothered him...until recently.

"I have to admit," Aldo said, "it's been cool having you around more the last couple of months. Going to miss you when you rejoin the team. I'm running out of single guys to hang with."

Elio glanced around the room, acknowledging the truth of his brother's statement. It seemed that in the last year, quite a few of his cousins and buddies had found love and settled down. Tony and Rhys had fallen hard for single mom, Jess, while Gio and Rafe had shocked the hell out of him when they admitted their love for Kayden's little sister, Keeley.

Elio had made more than a few jaunts to Philadelphia during November and December, something he'd never had the opportunity to do before. When the team was home, he remained in Baltimore with them, working out as much as he could with his injury, but when they hit the road, he did too, traveling to spend time with his family. In a lot of ways, the broken collarbone had felt like a blessing.

He hadn't mentioned his changing attitude toward his job to anyone, but now...it felt as if his brother had opened a door he didn't want to close. "I liked being back here too. Been thinking maybe I'd like to come back to Philly permanently."

Aldo's brows furrowed, either in shock or confusion. Elio hadn't given any indication of the idea before now. "You mean you could transfer to the Flyers? Or you want to quit altogether?"

"The latter."

Aldo didn't bother to mask his surprise. "Wow. I gotta admit, I didn't see that coming. Is it because of the injuries? You *are* better, right? Concussions are nothing to fuck around with and if you're having issues with headaches or—"

"I'm not," Elio interjected. "Not at all."

"You still get a lot of playing time," Aldo mused, and Elio hid his grin. Aldo tended to think out loud, talking his way through things in a way that didn't require responses. "So it's not like you're bored as a benchwarmer. Hell, even after a couple months out, you're still one of the scoring leaders on the Rays."

"I've spent a lot of years on the road, away from home," Elio said. "At what point should I just say I'm getting too old for this shit?"

Aldo scowled. "You're nowhere near too old. There are some guys who've played the game into their forties. You're only thirty, for God's sake."

"I'm going to be thirty-one next month. And while I know that realistically, I have at least a few more good playing years in me; it's not a question of the body being able."

"You're not sure the mind is willing."

Despite the five-year difference in their ages, Elio had always felt closest to Aldo, who'd never treated him like an annoying little brother but had instead taken their sibling relationship and expanded on it, offering him close friendship as well. Sure, they still gave each other shit, teasing, wrestling, blackmailing whenever a situation called for it or if it was just funny.

Elio had his own apartment in Baltimore, which had been his home for over a decade, but when he came back to Philly, his "room" was in Aldo's apartment, the two adding roommates to the brothers-and-friends relationship.

"Is that what's been curtailing your extracurricular bedroom activities, prior to the busted collarbone?"

"Probably," Elio admitted. "I've been distracted and out of sorts. Debating whether or not I want to keep playing the game."

"Are you talking about hockey or booty calls?" Aldo joked.

Elio chuckled. "Maybe a bit of both. It might shock you to know...I haven't really missed not having sex. It was starting to feel like more hassle than it was worth."

No muss, no fuss. That had been his dating motto up until last summer, when he realized he was bored with...fuck...with everything. Hockey, sex, his life.

"What are you thinking about doing? Quitting right now?"

Elio shook his head. "Hell no. I'd finish the season. There's no way I'd screw the team like that."

"Then what?" Aldo asked.

Elio shrugged with his good shoulder. "That's the million-dollar question, isn't it? All I've ever done is skate, play hockey."

Aldo took a sip of beer. "Would you want to coach or something?"

"I don't know. Not professionally. Because that would defeat the whole purpose of quitting so I can finally come home."

"You're a young guy, Elio. Smart, driven. I don't doubt for a second you could find a second career, something you might even like more than hockey. Besides, it's not like you're hurting for money. I know you've been socking away a shit-ton of that very healthy paycheck of yours."

"I have. I wouldn't have to find another job for a long time if I didn't want to, if ever." Elio appreciated Aldo's support and encouragement. "Hey, listen, man. Right now, this is all a hypothetical thing. I'm not a hundred percent sure I want to hang up my skates. Do you mind keeping this just between us?"

"Of course. But don't you sort of have to decide soon? Let management know?"

Elio nodded. "Yeah. The clock is definitely ticking on that."

"When do you have to go back to the team after you get the clean bill of health?"

"Two days after Christmas," Elio lied. He wasn't due back quite that soon, but he wanted to take some time for himself. He planned to go to his family's cabin in the Poconos for a couple days, but he was keeping that information on the down-low because he knew if he told his brother, Aldo would take some time off and join him. Hell, knowing Aldo, he'd invite the rest of the guys, and suddenly Elio would be in a sleeping bag on the floor surrounded by a bunch of bourbon-swilling, cigar-smoking cousins, friends, and brothers. Ordinarily, he loved the camaraderie, but not now.

What he needed now was peace and quiet and a chance to sort out his thoughts. Things always had a way of becoming clear after some time in the crisp mountain air.

His brother caught sight of someone over his shoulder. As Elio turned, Aldo called out, "It's about time you got here."

Elio smiled as their kid sister Liza approached.

"I was starting to wonder if we should send out a search party," Elio said, bending over so Liza could give him her standard kiss-on-the-cheek greeting. "You're usually first to arrive, last to leave when it comes to parties."

Liza offered the same buss to Aldo, then launched into a long-winded complaint about Matt Russo.

Ordinarily, Elio was all in on the Russo bashing, but it felt like lately, all Liza did was bitch about Matt. He was trying to convince himself the "she doth protest too much" vibe he was starting to get wasn't there. Because God help her if it was, given the way their family felt about the Russos.

He glanced across the room at Gage, begrudgingly admitting

to himself that the second Russo son was a decent guy. He was obviously head-over-heels devoted to Rhys's sister, Penny, something that would have had the old Elio cracking the imaginary whip above his head, complete with sound effects. But tonight, he wasn't feeling it. Gage looked happy. And that was an emotion Elio had been struggling to find for far too long.

Liza continued to bitch, and Elio decided Gage Russo was one thing.

Matt was another thing entirely.

He tuned out Liza's complaints as he studied the other party guests. It was just as Aldo said. Lots of love in the air. Tony and Rhys flanked Jess on the couch, the three of them bent close, talking like they were the only ones in the room. Gage was standing behind Penny, one hand on her waist, the other on her wrist as he tried to teach her the proper way to bounce a quarter into a glass. Keeley was slow dancing with Gio in the corner, while Rafe leaned against the wall, drinking a beer and chatting with Luca. He could tell Rafe was only giving the conversation about ten percent of his attention, the rest locked on Keeley and Gio.

Elio was starting to feel like the odd man out surrounded by all these happy couples.

"So what were you guys talking about?" Liza asked, drawing his attention back to her.

"Life, death, taxes," Aldo teased. "The usual."

"Actually, Aldo was going on and on about how much he's going to miss me when I go back to Baltimore. You know our brother can't function a single day without me around," Elio joked.

Aldo rolled his eyes. "Yeah. That's what I was saying. More like I'll be glad when you and your smelly running shoes vacate the apartment again. I'm going to have to fumigate the place."

Elio lifted his cup and drained it. "I'm going to go get a refill. You guys need anything?"

Aldo shook his head as he tilted his cup slightly, showing him it was full.

Liza glanced around. "Gianna was supposed to grab me a glass of wine, but it looks like she took my advice. Homegirl is getting her flirt on."

Elio looked across the room and spotted Gianna Duncan talking to his cousin, Joey, and his cohost, Miles. "Her flirt on?"

"I'm determined to drag her into the dating scene with me, but she's got zero experience. Thought tonight might be a good place for her to practice her flirting skills. I gave her a list to work from, eligible guys to bat those baby blues of hers at."

Elio frowned. "Jesus, Liza. Why would you encourage her to do that? What if she gets the wrong idea and thinks I'm interested when—"

He stopped midsentence when Liza laughed loudly. "Dear God, El. I didn't put *your* name on the list."

He frowned harder. "Why not?"

His question only made her laugh harder. "Sorry," she said between giggles. "You're going to have to choose a side. Are you pissed that she might flirt with you or pissed that I told her to steer clear?"

"You told her to steer clear? Of me?" Elio wasn't really sure why that bothered him so much.

Liza shook her head, looking far too amused. "No. But I'm thinking I should have. I only included the names of guys she might stand a chance with. There's no way in hell I'd send the queen of committed relationships—you realize she dated Sam for eleven years—to flirt with the world's biggest commitment-phobe. Give me a little credit, bro."

Elio looked back at where Gianna stood with Joey and Miles. Both guys were talking at the same time, clearly telling one hell of a story. Gianna was laughing and, at one point, she reached out to put her hand on Miles's forearm. It was a casual touch, one that could pass as friendly or, as Miles appeared to take it, flirting. He shifted a bit closer to Gianna, and there was no denying the guy was interested.

"Damn," Liza murmured. "Maybe she doesn't need the practice after all."

Elio watched Gianna interact with Miles for a minute longer, aware his sister was right.

Gianna had been friends with Liza for years, but his path didn't cross hers very often. Regardless, Elio felt as if he knew her fairly well, simply because his sister was a fan of long phone conversations, and for some reason, she felt it was her God-given duty to share all the news of home with him whenever they talked.

He used to find those long-winded calls annoying, but like everything else lately, his attitude on that had changed. Nowadays, he enjoyed hearing the gossip from home. And as such, he knew that Gianna had been dumped by her longtime boyfriend, Sam, whom Elio had met a handful of times over the years.

"She ran into Sam tonight. Found out he'd been cheating on her," Liza said, still observing her friend's interactions with Miles and Joey.

Aldo frowned. "Seriously? What a dick! And to think, I actually liked that guy."

Liza shrugged. "He had us all fooled."

"She looks like she's doing okay now," Aldo said.

Liza shook her head. "She's faking it. I can tell. But sometimes you just have to fake it 'til you make it."

Elio considered the truth of that statement, surprised to discover it described his actions of late. His family only knew the Elio who lived and breathed hockey day and night, and who'd never had a relationship because he was fully focused and wholly committed to just one thing—his career. As his love of the game began to fade, he found himself struggling to figure out who he was without it...without letting anyone realize.

Watching Gianna put on a brave front felt a bit like looking in the mirror, and he experienced an unexpected connection with the woman.

Elio shook off the heavy feelings. It was a fucking party, and he was getting too bogged down in his shit. He'd always prided himself on his ability to go with the flow. So it was time for that guy to take the wheel. "Red or white?" Elio asked, ready to turn things up a notch and join the quarters game. For that, he needed more beer.

"Red," Liza said. "I'll be over there," she said, pointing to the same game he'd been eyeballing. "Teaching those guys how it's done."

Elio shook his head, amused, as he walked to the kitchen, filling his cup from the keg in the corner with one hand, thanks to the damn sling. "Mad skills," he said, when he saw Keeley watching him.

"Impressive," she acknowledged with a snort. "Came in to reload the food platters." Keeley took a tray of bacon-wrapped hot dogs from the oven.

"Hot damn," he said. "I was hoping there were more of those. What the hell are they and why are they so good?"

Keeley laughed. "Jess shared the recipe with me. I'm not sure who thought wrapping hot dogs in bacon, stabbing them with a toothpick, sprinkling with brown sugar, then baking them was a good idea, but whoever it was is a genius as far as I'm concerned."

"Amen." Elio grabbed one of the bite-sized treats off the platter and popped it into his mouth. "Heart attack on a plate. And I'm still going to eat a half dozen more."

"Need any help?"

Elio turned toward the doorway at the sound of Gianna's voice as she walked into the kitchen.

Keeley shook her head. "Nope. Got it all well in hand."

"Oh, hi, Elio. Nice to see you again," Gianna said with a smile that was nothing but friendly. Liza really *had* left him off the flirting list.

"Same," Elio said. "How are you doing?"

"Fine," she replied, giving the standard answer, even though Elio sensed she was anything but. Gianna reached for a glass. "I came for wine. Got waylaid by Joey and his cohost, Miles. He's a really nice guy. He and Joey seem thick as thieves already."

"That's good to hear," Elio said. "I haven't had a chance to meet him yet. Need to go introduce myself."

"I just opened a new bottle of red," Keeley said as she ripped into a bag of potato chips and filled a bowl.

Elio looked around the kitchen and chuckled at all the food. "I can see Gio's Italian roots are rubbing off on you, Kee. You've got enough food in here for an army."

"You Morettis are a bunch of vultures," she joked. "You'd think half the people out there hadn't eaten in weeks."

Gianna poured herself a glass of pinot noir. "It's the holidays. The one time of the year when the word 'diet' is deleted from everyone's vocabulary."

"Only to return in January with a vengeance," Keeley said.

"Diet, you say? Can you define that word?" Elio asked, popping another of the hot dogs into his mouth. "I'm not familiar with it."

Keeley laughed. "You don't have to be. For one thing, you skate about a gazillion miles a week, and for another, you have the Moretti genes."

Elio shrugged casually. "We like good food. No crime in that."

Keeley, who begun stirring meatballs in the Crockpot, pointed the spoon at him. "You've been spoiled by your aunt Berta and Nonna."

"And the other aunts and my mom as well," Elio agreed. "We Morettis learn from the cradle that food is love."

"That didn't hold true in my home," Gianna said, taking a sip of her wine. "Food was sustenance, nothing more. If we were hungry, we ate, and sadly it was nothing special. Since it was just me and Grandma, we pretty much lived on soup and sandwiches."

"That sounds terrible," Elio said, suddenly aware that he knew very little about Gianna's childhood. Liza was a few years older than Gianna, who'd been friends with Keeley in high school.

After Keeley's parents died, she began hanging out with the Morettis more, dragged along for the ride by her brother Kayden.

But Gianna's friendship with Liza didn't really begin until after he had joined the NHL, so apart from the occasional socializing when he was home, they hadn't spent much time together, and all of that had been amid family or their large group of friends.

She smiled, though it looked forced. "It wasn't so bad."

Elio recalled he was supposed to grab a glass of wine for Liza. Gianna must have remembered the same thing as she picked up another glass and filled it.

"For Liza?" he asked.

She nodded. "She's probably wondering what's taking me so long."

"Joey has the gift of gab," he said, walking back toward the doorway that led to the living room.

Gianna followed, laughing. "You're not kidding. How's your collarbone?"

He drew her attention to the cup he was holding with his injured arm by lifting it slightly. "Almost completely healed. Hoping to get out of this sling right before Christmas."

"That's great news. I can't imagine it's been comfortable wearing it all this time. We were here the night you got hurt, actually, watching the game," Gianna said.

Liza had called him shortly after he'd been helped off the ice, after he'd gotten word from the team doc that his collarbone was broken. She'd told him about the hockey viewing party, and he'd hated knowing that most of his family had watched him take that hit.

"It's a rough game," Gianna added.

"It can be."

"Guess I'll go deliver this wine to Liza," she said. They'd paused in the threshold between the kitchen and living room, both about to return to the party when Keeley stopped them.

"Freeze!" she yelled, capturing their attention.

"What's wrong?" Gianna asked.

Rather than respond verbally, Keeley pointed to a spot above their heads.

Gianna and Elio looked up at the same time.

"Seriously, Kee?" Gianna said. "Mistletoe?"

"You know the tradition. Don't bring bad luck into my house by snubbing your nose at it."

"You don't consider a haunted house bad luck already?" Gianna joked.

Keeley snorted. "We have friendly ghosts. And I'd like to keep it that way."

Gianna gave Elio an apologetic look that he didn't understand. "Sorry," she muttered.

He tilted his head. "Why?" He could see his question had taken her aback.

"I..." she started. "Well, uh...I'm sure you don't want to...um..."

"Kiss you?" he finished for her.

She blushed, the innocent look surprisingly endearing.

Elio's teammates claimed he had a type, but they'd been wrong about what it was. They'd made their assumptions based on the women he always went out with, but his dates weren't driven by genuine attraction so much as by...well, availability. He was no stranger to beautiful, bold, sexually experienced women, the rink bunnies who went out of their way to attract the attention of a well-paid professional athlete. Paula had definitely fit that mold.

He was used to being sought after and approached by the fairer sex. The women he slept with almost always made the first move, and he was fine with that. It meant he didn't have to work that hard to get laid. A woman would flirt, bat come-hither eyes at him, and he'd take her to bed.

For one night. He never stuck around for sleepovers, never got phone numbers, never pursued anything more than the sexual release.

The only reason Paula stuck around as long as she had was because she'd played the game better. Until she didn't.

Gianna, however, was *not* that type. And there were too many parts of him not only noticing that fact but appreciating it.

"I'm just saying," Gianna stammered, none of the casual flirting he'd seen her laying on Miles apparent at the moment. "It's just a silly tradition, so..."

She planned to walk away. He could see it.

And for some reason...it pissed him off. "Gianna?"

"Yeah?"

"It's not silly."

Before she could protest, he lowered his head, intent on following through on the mistletoe tradition, on wiping away some of the vulnerability he saw in her eyes.

She raised her face, clearly ready to offer him a quick, platonic kiss. In fact, that was exactly what she gave him, but just as she began to back away, Elio wrapped his free hand around her waist and pulled her closer.

"I think we can do better than that," he murmured—before giving her a much less platonic kiss.

Her lips were soft and warm against his, and she startled briefly when his tongue made an appearance. He stroked it along the seam of her lips, inviting hers to come out to play.

Elio wasn't the type to do anything half-assed. Not hockey and certainly not kissing. And while he could tell she wasn't as experienced as his past lovers, she was certainly making up for it with enthusiasm.

She parted her lips, offering him entry, and he didn't hesitate for a moment, his tongue darting out to meet hers. She tasted like the wine she'd just taken a sip of, sweet and tart at the same time.

He was sorry her hands were occupied, holding the two wineglasses. He wouldn't mind having them on him, feeling her fingers stroke his chest, maybe wrap around his shoulders. It had been too long since he'd had a woman in his arms, and he wasn't sure he'd ever had one whose kisses impacted him quite like Gianna's. Though he couldn't put his finger on why.

There was an openness to her that he found himself responding to. Which was strange. He'd always felt like the one Moretti who didn't quite fit, the one the stork most likely dumped at the wrong house. His family was tight knit, always together and in each other's business, and while he was feeling that pull to belong lately, it hadn't been very powerful the first thirty years of his life. Unlike his brothers and cousins, he'd also never felt the need to exert that overprotective gene around the women in his life. Probably because he hadn't been around enough to see all the shitheads Aldo claimed Liza seemed to attract.

Gianna felt like the kind of woman he'd want to shelter, to defend, to...

Keep.

She sighed softly as he deepened the kiss, running his tongue along her lower lip. He wasn't sure how much time passed before he recalled they were standing within plain view of everyone in the party. He pulled away, regretfully, forcing himself not to go back for seconds.

Gianna blinked several times as if to clear her vision. He took pleasure in realizing he hadn't been the only one to lose his head.

Elio gave her a quick wink, hoping it would work at dispelling whatever the fuck it was that had just passed between them. He'd heard the term chemistry before, but he'd always chalked it up to female fantasy, a flight of fancy or whatever. But now...he wasn't so sure it wasn't a real thing.

Gianna's cheeks were flushed an even brighter shade of red, though this time he knew it was driven by heat, not embarrassment.

They still stood close, her gaze locked with his, and he could read the confusion and desire there. He wasn't sure how she was pulling off that combination, but that was definitely what he was seeing.

Elio had never taken the time to look at Gianna very closely, but now that he was, he had to admit she was very pretty with her shoulder-length blonde hair. She was medium height, which meant she was about a foot shorter than him. She was quite slim, almost *too* thin, which seemed to indicate her simple eating habits hadn't changed. Her skin was fair, like porcelain, and her nose and cheeks were dotted with a light smattering of freckles that added to the wholesome air about her.

It occurred to him it was that wholesomeness that had probably kept him from noticing her before. That and the fact she'd had a serious boyfriend for as long as he'd known her.

"Whoa," she breathed, not hiding the impact of that kiss.

After too many years spent with women who were accomplished in seduction, she was a breath of fresh air.

"I think we did the mistletoe proud," he said.

"I'll say," Keeley chimed in, fanning herself, eyes wide. "Holy shit."

Elio laughed, then turned his attention back to Gianna, and while she was the one who was supposed to practice flirting, he was the one doing it. "So...meet you back here in about an hour?"

Gianna rolled her eyes, responding to his words like they were a joke, when he wasn't entirely sure they were. "You're shameless. All you Moretti men got in line twice when they were handing out charm, didn't you?"

"Three times," he corrected, then decided it was probably a good idea to step away from...whatever this was. He hadn't lied to his brother. Now was the time to focus on making decisions about his career, his future. There wasn't room in his head for anything else.

"Merry Christmas, Freckles."

She giggled softly, shaking her head in amusement at his nickname for her.

"Merry Christmas, Elio," she replied. "Thanks for the kiss. I needed that," she admitted, before walking away to deliver the wine to Liza, who—mercifully—had been too wrapped up in the quarters game to see him kissing her friend senseless.

Then he considered her comment...and realized something unexpected.

He'd needed that kiss too.

The only thing he couldn't figure out was why.

Chapter Three

Gianna leaned forward, shifting slightly to alleviate the pain in her knees from holding the same position for so long. She'd put a towel down, kneeling on it, rather than the hard tile floors, but she probably should have grabbed a pillow instead.

Stretching, she fought hard to scrub the back corner of the oven. She was fairly certain it had never been cleaned. Not once in its very, *very* long life.

She sang along with Spotify, belting out one of her favorite P!nk songs, "Fuckin' Perfect," as she worked. Liza had told her to take this time at the cabin to work her shit out, and Gianna figured her best chance at doing that was letting her girl P!nk build her back up and help her find her feet again.

She had arrived at the Moretti cabin in the Poconos a few hours earlier, and she'd known in an instant that Liza had given her a true gift. The place was so quaint, so inviting and cute, that she'd fallen in love with it within seconds of walking through the front door.

Her holidays had also been surprisingly great. A Moretti Christmas Eve was everything Liza had promised and more, but rather than feeling overwhelmed and out of place, Gianna had gotten, perhaps for the first time in her life, a true sense of family.

Not that she'd grown up without a family, but it had always just been her and Grandma Mary in a quiet apartment that had been devoid of any sort of life or liveliness or...God, even joy. The holidays she'd spent with Sam and his family had also been fairly low-key and relatively uneventful.

None of that held true at Nonno and Nonna Moretti's house. She'd been welcomed with open arms and a lot—holy shit, *a lot*— of hugs and food and music and presents and laughter and wine.

Jesus. So much wine.

The Morettis were huggers, the whole bunch of them, and she'd found those friendly, caring, warm embraces filling her well in ways she hadn't even realized she'd needed.

Elio had been there—of course, it was his family—but because of the huge crowd, she hadn't had the opportunity to do more than wish him a Merry Christmas and accept his friendly sling-free hug, which had been very much like the ones she'd received from his brothers and cousins. Not that those hugs had produced the same reaction as Elio's. None of the others had left her feeling so tingling inside.

Unfortunately, there'd been no repeat of the mistletoe kiss, more's the pity.

She had never really noticed Elio in the past, beyond acknowledging that he was sex-on-a-stick hot. She may have had a boyfriend, but she wasn't blind. All of Liza's brothers and male cousins were hot. It was just a fact of life.

But on Christmas Eve, she'd found her gaze traveling around the room to find him, to watch him interact with his family, her newfound fascination driven by that kiss.

God almighty.

That. Kiss.

Prior to the holiday party, she'd kissed one guy in her life. Sam. And while she'd always found Sam's kisses very sweet and sometimes even sexy, she realized now her opinions were misinformed and inaccurate because she had not done *nearly* enough research in that area.

She had tossed and turned in her bed the night of the party, not due to sadness over Sam as she might have expected, but because Elio had turned something on inside her that she could not turn back off.

Not even now, nine days after the party.

Gianna tried, once again, to push it out of her mind, which was easier said than done. She was such a glutton for punishment, constantly fluctuating between sadness over Sam and lust for Elio, the most unavailable man on the planet.

She'd been friends with Liza enough years to have heard all about Elio Moretti's aversion to anything even remotely approaching a relationship or even dating. His sister had dubbed him King of the Booty Calls, claiming Elio was married to hockey and that was it. End of story.

Sex wasn't in the cards for her in the near future, so it was best to stop obsessing over that damn kiss. That, or maybe she should break down and try out her new sex toys.

Elio was on his way back to Baltimore, and she most likely wouldn't see him again until the hockey season was over.

Besides, she thought, internally wagging a finger at herself, *what the hell do you think is going to happen the next time you do see him?*

Nothing. Not one damn thing.

It wasn't like mistletoe was always hanging in doorways, or Elio was interested in her. It had been one kiss.

For him, it had probably been a run-of-the-mill, nothing-special kiss, which meant she was the idiot making way too big a deal of it. Simply because it had been a long time since she'd been kissed, and it was probably going to be a very long time before she was kissed again.

"That's fucking depressing," she muttered aloud. She talked to herself a lot these days. She had hated the utter silence of the apartment in the weeks after Sam moved out, so she'd started talking aloud in an attempt to fill it.

She was starting to think there might be some value to Liza and Penny's suggestion that she get a cat.

Wait. Had that been a suggestion? Or a warning?

"Oh, fuck it. It doesn't matter. You're not getting a cat," she told herself, shuddering at the thought of the mess a litter box would make.

She pushed a strand of hair out of her face with the back of her hand, silently chastising herself for what she was doing. She hadn't come here to clean. She'd come to relax.

The problem was, when she had something on her mind, something that was bothering her, her go-to was to clean. Grandma had taught her that. Told her countless times that there was no worry so big that it couldn't be scrubbed away with elbow grease.

In the past, Gianna had always found that to be true, but she'd been scrubbing her ass off since September and her worries weren't fading this time. Between her broken heart, her loneliness, and her dread of entering the dating pool, her no-fail stress reliever was—well—failing her.

"Just keep scrubbing," she muttered in her best Dory voice, doubling her efforts to chisel her way through what looked like decades worth of grease splatters, overflowing pies, and God only knew what else.

Upon arriving at the cabin, she'd unpacked her clothes in the small dresser near the bed. She'd made the bed with clean sheets, unpacked the groceries she'd brought with her, then carried in a load of wood and started a fire in the large fireplace.

It had been her intention to pour a glass of wine and start one of her jigsaw puzzles before dinner, but then she'd started thinking about Sam and the way he'd lied to her, then she'd relived that kiss from Elio for the millionth time, then she'd tried to figure out what the hell she was going to put on her online dating profile if she gave in to Liza's nagging, and then...before she knew it, she was on her knees, scrubbing the oven.

The song changed to "Try," and Gianna felt her chest grow tight, the words reminding her too much of shit she'd come here to forget. When the chorus started, she sang along, trying to let the lyrics bolster her.

She had a terrible voice, which was why she saved her sing-alongs for times when she was alone.

"What the hell?"

"Shit!" Gianna jerked up, banging her head hard on the top of the oven at the sound of a male voice behind her. She rapidly pushed herself out of the oven, rubbing the back of her head as she twisted around on the floor, armed with nothing but steel wool. Her knees were killing her, so rising was going to take some effort.

"Gianna?"

She blinked a few times to clear the gray spots behind her eyes and figure out if she was seeing what she thought.

Elio stood a few feet away from her with a hockey stick raised in his hands.

"What's the stick for?" she asked.

"It was the only thing in my car that I could use for a weapon."

"Why did you need a weapon?" she asked, confused. She must have knocked herself senseless. The back of her head was throbbing.

"I thought I was going to have to come in here and drive out whoever was squatting in my family's cabin. Didn't expect to find another car in the driveway and smoke coming from the chimney when I pulled up," he explained.

"Oh. Gotcha. Sorry about that. What are you doing here?"

He frowned. "That's what I was going to ask *you*." His gaze traveled from where she was still sitting on her ass on the floor to the stove. "Are you..." He paused, looking at the dishwashing gloves on her hands. "Are you cleaning the oven?"

She hastily stood up, stripping off the gloves as she did so. "Yes. But please don't tell Liza."

"I..." Elio appeared to struggle with the request for a moment. "Okay, I won't. Why are you scrubbing the oven in my family's cabin?"

Gianna thought about it and realized she didn't have an answer to that question that didn't make her sound like a bit of a lunatic. "I'd rather answer the other question."

Elio grinned. "Okay. Go for it."

"Your sister loaned me this cabin for the week. I had some vacation time from work that my boss told me to use, and I wanted to get out of town because I'm so fucking sick of my apartment. It's just, I don't have a lot of extra money for travel, now that I'm paying the rent by myself, so Liza suggested I come here." Gianna was aware she was rambling, but Elio's presence in the cabin had taken her off guard.

Elio nodded slowly. "I see. This is obviously what I get for keeping secrets from my family."

"Secrets?" Gianna asked.

"I told everyone I was going back to Baltimore, but the truth is I was hoping to steal a few days alone here."

"Oh. Shit," Gianna said. "I'm sorry."

"You apologize a lot."

She thought about it and realized he was right. She'd never really noticed. But now wasn't the time for self-reflection. It looked like her vacation was going to be cut very short. "If you'll just give me a half hour or so, I can pack all my stuff up and clear out of here."

"What?" Elio asked. "No. I'm not telling you to leave."

He was being a gentleman, and very nice, but it was his family's cabin. Obviously, he had the right of way. "It's fine, Elio. Seriously. It's your cabin. I'll just gather my things and head back to Philly."

"Thought you were sick of your apartment." He leaned his hockey stick against the wall.

"Yeah, but it's not like I wasn't going back there eventually. I wasn't escaping forever."

Gianna grabbed the tote she'd carried her groceries in and started to open the refrigerator. Elio stepped behind her and closed it.

She glanced over her shoulder, trying to ignore the way her body woke up and paid attention whenever Elio got close to her. She wondered if there was some sort of pheromone he was releasing that caused this reaction in her. Tight nipples, butterflies in her stomach, and damp panties. The whole shebang. Not that she was getting banged.

"Elio," she said, clearing her throat. "I'm not crashing your alone time."

"You're not leaving," he stressed, still holding the fridge closed. "Actually, neither one of us is." He followed that pronouncement by pointing at the window above the kitchen sink.

Dusk was falling, but it wasn't full dark yet, so there was enough light left to show her that at some point while she'd been cleaning the oven, it had started snowing. Heavily.

"Oh," she breathed.

"The roads are already covered and getting slick as the temperature drops. I fishtailed a couple times during the last mile up the mountain. There's no way either one of us is driving out of here in that."

She kept looking out the window, not because she was fascinated by the snow but because she needed a minute to compose herself.

She was spending the night in the cabin. With Elio.

"Um…" she finally said when the silence had drifted into that awkward stage. "Okay. Just for tonight. I'll sleep on the couch."

He studied her face for a moment, then said, "We'll revisit the sleeping situation later," which was decidedly noncommittal. "I'm going to go grab my stuff from the car." Elio turned and walked to the front door of the cabin.

"Need help?" she offered.

He glanced over his shoulder. "Yeah. I'd appreciate that. Unless you have plans to start scrubbing the kitchen floor and washing the windows. Wouldn't want to keep you from your housekeeping duties."

She narrowed her eyes at his joke, then piled on. "No worries. I was saving those chores for you."

Gianna tugged on her boots and coat as he chuckled, the two of them walking to his car together. He grabbed a duffel from the backseat of his car and a few bags of groceries.

"Only other thing I need is on the passenger seat," Elio said as she opened that door. She shook her head as she picked up the bright green box of Patron Silver.

"The last thing you need is tequila. There's a liquor cabinet in there that's already overflowing with bottles." Gianna had been dying to combine some of the bottles to clean it out. The cabinet was something out of her nightmares with three open, nearly empty bottles of vodka, four open bottles of bourbon, and two bottles of tequila with just a couple shots left in each. What kind of lunatics opened a new bottle before the old one was finished?

"The liquor is required," Elio said as they climbed the three stairs of the porch. He hadn't lied about the snow turning to ice and becoming slippery. She had to hold on to the rail to steady herself on the slick surface.

"Required?" she asked as they walked back into the cabin and stripped off their coats. Elio dropped his duffel by the front door, then walked to the kitchen area to start unloading his groceries.

"I'm surprised Liza didn't tell you. You can't come to the cabin empty-handed. This place requires payment."

"And you pay with liquor?" she asked, amused.

Elio nodded, his face solemn as if he was explaining some religious rite. She might have thought him serious if not for the laugh lines around his eyes betraying him. "The cabin demands it."

"Well, then it's a good thing you came, or I might have been in trouble. All I brought was wine."

Elio feigned a shudder, then crossed himself.

She placed his bottle of tequila next to the other two and tried to shut down the part of her head that told her she could reduce the number of bottles in that cabinet by half in less than ten minutes. She'd intended to tackle that task tomorrow, but now that Elio was here, she suspected he'd look at her like she was six eggs short of a dozen if she tried. She was already on shaky ground, considering he'd caught her scrubbing the oven.

Gianna followed him to the kitchen to help him unpack his groceries.

She blushed slightly when she realized he was standing by the refrigerator looking at the weekly menu she'd printed out before leaving home and hung up there with a magnet. Oh God. All her crazy was showing right now.

He glanced back at her curiously.

"I like to plan my meals. It helps me make a grocery list."

"You do this every week or just when you're on vacation?" Elio appeared to accept her explanation, which was a relief.

The weekly menu had been a bone of contention between her and Sam the last couple years of their relationship. So much so, he'd become passive-aggressive about it, cooking things that weren't on the list, and telling her he wasn't going to eat macaroni and cheese on Tuesday just because it was written on her damn menu. The truth was, she wasn't that committed to the actual days as much as she just liked knowing she had every night covered. But...well...she hated passive-aggressiveness, so whenever Sam hit her with it, she dug in her heels and pushed the issue in retaliation.

"I make a menu every week. I guess you probably think that's a bit silly," she said.

"Not at all. I'm a disaster at the grocery store." He reached into his bag. "Case in point," he said, as he pulled out taco shells, refried beans, and taco seasoning. "I went to the store with no list. Thought tacos might be good one night while I was here. Got halfway up the mountain before I realized I forgot cheese and sour cream. And hamburger."

Gianna laughed as she pointed to her menu. "You're in luck. Because I'd planned a burger night *and* a baked potato night. I have all those things. We can combine."

"Perfect. Tell you what, let's finish unloading all this stuff, and then we can sit down and revise the menu to incorporate all our food. Maybe you can teach me how to meal plan, because I don't want to tell you how many times I either have to go back to the store, order Instacart for forgotten shit, or wind up just saying fuck it and getting pizza delivered."

She grinned, touched that he not only wasn't making fun of her list, but he seemed impressed by it. Then she considered what he'd just suggested. "We don't need to figure out more than tonight. I really am going to head home tomorrow," she reminded him.

Elio reached into his back pocket and pulled out his phone. He tapped on the screen a few times, then turned it around to show her what he'd opened.

A weather app.

One that predicted eight to twelve inches of snow tonight.

Holy. Fuck.

Chapter Four

"I think we might want to go ahead and figure out a few days' worth of menus," Elio suggested, as she tried to wrap her head around the fact they were going to be trapped here together for *days*.

"When I checked the weather yesterday, it was only calling for a light dusting of snow here," she said stupidly.

Elio nodded. "Forecast updated this afternoon. I almost considered changing my plans and driving back to Baltimore. Glad I didn't. I wouldn't like the idea of you up here alone in a snowstorm."

"You wouldn't have known I was here," Gianna pointed out, surprised when Elio looked almost angry about that fact.

"Does anyone know you're actually here—safe and sound?"

"I texted Liza earlier to let her know I made it." Gianna expected that to appease him, but it didn't seem to, so she continued. "Liza said she comes up here on her own sometimes too."

Elio sighed. "I'm aware of that. Doesn't mean I like it."

Gianna grinned. "Careful, Elio. Those overprotective Moretti genes are creeping out."

Rather than reply, he finished unpacking his groceries. "I'm going to go bring in enough wood to keep the fire going tonight.

Temperatures are supposed to plummet, and without that fire burning, it gets pretty chilly in here."

"Okay. While you do that, why don't I figure out dinner?"

"Sounds good." Elio put his coat, hat, and gloves on and ventured back outside. Gianna shivered as a burst of frigid wind rushed through the cabin when he opened the door. He hadn't lied about it getting colder.

She had to admit that she was glad he'd shown up too. She'd felt perfectly fine staying here on her own, but that was when she thought she'd be able to leave whenever she wanted. The idea of being trapped on the mountain in a snowstorm, alone, was something else entirely.

Gianna rummaged around the kitchen, amused by Elio's contributions to their food stores. He wasn't kidding about not working from a list. He'd hit the snack aisle hard, more than covering them when it came to popcorn, potato chips, pretzels, peanuts, and Doritos. And as he'd said, he had managed to bring half the ingredients for three meals. In addition to his partial taco meal, he had bought spaghetti sauce but no noodles, and steaks and potatoes but no vegetables. He also had a loaf of bread and some sandwich meat, without condiments.

He had fared better in the drinks area, managing to remember water, beer, coffee, and soda.

She decided the steaks looked the best, and she wished she'd thought to put that on her own menu. She'd combine his mouthwatering rib eyes with the baked potatoes and the salad fixings she'd brought. Elio made a couple trips with his arms loaded down with wood that he placed in a box next to the fireplace. She was sorry he was wearing the thick flannel shirt and a coat because she wouldn't mind getting a better look at his muscles straining with the weight of the wood.

God. She really needed to get a handle on her hormones.

Before heading out for a third load, Elio glanced over, checked out what she was making, and smiled.

"I was hoping you'd go for the steaks."

"You packed no vegetables," she said, adopting a stern mom voice.

"Yeah...I remembered that around the same time I recalled forgetting the cheese and sour cream. I got a later start than I'd planned and wound up rushing through the store so that I could beat the snow. You probably can't tell from what I packed, but I usually eat very healthy meals."

"Truth is, I didn't pack much in the way of fun snack food. I can't believe I forgot to bring chips and dip."

"We make a good team then." Elio grinned. "Let me go get one more load and then I'll cook the steaks."

God. He was going to help her cook. Why did the idea of Elio Moretti in the kitchen get her motor revving? She and Sam had cooked together a million times and it hadn't been foreplay. It had just been dinner.

"Down girl," she muttered under her breath. She played around with her Spotify, choosing the Happy Hits channel, then dancing in place to Justin Timberlake's "Can't Stop the Feeling!" as she sliced carrots. She had just finished putting the salad together when Elio joined her.

"Good music," he said, shaking his ass in time with the beat and making her laugh. "JT's got nothing on me."

Gianna was not about to argue with that, but she rolled her eyes because she felt like she should try to keep him humble.

Elio reached for a frying pan, adding oil and turning on the heat.

"I have some mushrooms and onions we can sauté if you'd like," she offered.

"Hell yeah. Sounds great."

They worked in quiet efficiency, Elio pan-frying the meat as she washed, then microwaved the potatoes.

"Those smell so good," she said, stepping next to him as he pulled the steaks from the pan, wrapping them in foil to rest for a few minutes.

The two of them worked together to set the table, then

carried the food over before sitting down to eat. It was strange how unpacking the groceries and cooking dinner felt natural and easy, but right now, sharing a meal together like this felt intimate.

She was suddenly struggling to think of something to talk about. It was safe to say that she and Elio were closer to acquaintances than friends. They had a similar social circle, but their interactions always happened in the larger group, so they'd never had a serious one-on-one conversation or been alone together, until now.

"So," she started, before realizing she didn't have a damn thing to say after that. "This is awkward."

Elio laughed. "I'll admit this wasn't how I envisioned the next few days."

She opened her mouth to apologize, but Elio raised his hand to cut her off.

"And before you apologize again, I'm not saying I'm disappointed. Not at all."

"Yeah, but you came here to be alone and... Why *did* you want to be alone?" she asked, then tried to backtrack. "Sorry, that's none of my business, is it?"

Elio sliced off a chunk of steak. "I'll answer your question if you answer one of mine first."

Gianna nodded before thinking better. "Okay."

"Why were you cleaning the oven?" he asked, before eating the steak.

She leaned back and groaned. "God. I can't believe you caught me doing that. I must look like such a weirdo."

He shook his head. "Not really."

"I clean when I'm upset."

Elio frowned. "You were upset?"

Gianna shrugged. "I'm a lot of things right now. So many, I should probably start a list."

He grinned. "You like lists, don't you?"

"Yeah. There's nothing more gratifying than drawing a line through something you've accomplished."

"So give me the rundown on the things bothering you. Let's see if we can figure out how to start marking some of them off the list."

She was touched by his desire to help her. "I guess you know Sam and I broke up."

"Liza mentioned it, yes."

"I found out a week or so ago...the night of Keeley's party, actually...that he was cheating on me." She could tell by the lack of surprise on his face that Liza had shared that tidbit as well. "Which you apparently know."

"The two of you dated a long time."

"Eleven years," she added.

"And he was your first boyfriend?"

She nodded.

"I'm sorry he cheated on you. That was an asshole move."

"Yeah. It was," she agreed sadly.

"So I'm guessing if we really were making a list of all the shit going on inside you, you'd be feeling sad, pissed, hurt, and betrayed."

"Those things exactly. And I'm also lonely and stressed out."

"Why stressed out?" he asked.

"Because your sister is dragging me into the dating scene, which is a place I haven't been since I was fifteen."

Elio cut off another piece of steak, holding it aloft on his fork as he looked at her. "I think it's safe to say you've *never* been there. Not sure you can call it a dating scene at fifteen."

"Which just helps me make my point. Plus, the idea of online dating feels so..." She couldn't quite come up with a word, so she settled for, "Icky. Judging someone based on looks, their job, or how clever or funny they sound in just a few words seems so shallow."

"Yeah. It does."

"So you've never gone on any of the dating sites? Tinder or Bumble or whatever else there is?"

The look he gave her, a combination of arrogance and over-confidence, had her chucking a carrot at his head.

"Don't say it," she warned.

"I don't hurt for dates, Gianna. Not. At. All. Haven't had to resort to the online tactics yet."

She sighed. "You said it. Cocky bastard."

He chuckled and wiggled his eyebrows at her in response.

"According to your sister, what you engage in isn't called dating."

Elio raised his hands. "She's probably right. What I do is less dating and more hooking up."

"Ah. Well, I have zero experience with hooking up. And very little with casual dating. So...I'm screwed."

He chuckled, but she noticed he didn't disagree. They fell silent for a moment or two, both of them eating.

She took a bite of her baked potato, startled a second later when he reached across the table to wipe a smear of sour cream from her lower lip. She was even more surprised when he licked his finger clean. Everything he did felt so sexually charged. Liza called him her "player" brother, the one women flocked to and threw themselves at. Something he'd just admitted himself.

The thing was, she'd never had that kind of sexy predator attention directed her way.

Until Elio. First with that kiss. And right now.

Nervousness had her talking again before she could think better of it, her rambling breaking the sexual tension simmering between them. Dammit.

"Anyway, I think my cleanliness was a learned behavior," she said. "My grandma raised me, and money was always tight. She worked as a cashier at a department store during the week, then she cleaned newly vacated apartments for a rental company on the weekends. She took me along when she was cleaning. At first because I was too young to stay home alone, and she couldn't afford a babysitter. Then, as I got older, I kept going so that I could help."

"Every weekend?" he asked.

"All the way through high school. We needed the money," she explained. "You should have seen the way some of the renters left the apartments. Absolutely disgusting. It's incredible to me how some people can live in filth. Toilets and showers that were black with mildew. Moldy refrigerators that stunk so bad it would take your breath away when you opened them. Torn blinds. Holes in the walls. Cigarette burns in the carpet."

"Jesus," Elio murmured.

"We'd clean what we could, then make a list of things that needed to be replaced or repaired for the company. I always swore that when I got my own place, I'd never live like that."

"It's no wonder you clean all the time. PTSD. I didn't even see those places, but now I feel the need to give my apartment a good scrub."

She grinned. "Grandma always said cleaning is a good way to relieve stress, to distract you from things that are upsetting you," she said, repeating her grandmother's thoughts on elbow grease.

"Did cleaning the oven help?" Elio asked, and she could tell it was a sincere question, not him laughing at her idiosyncrasies.

"It did," she lied, unable to tell him that her stress vanished when he showed up. One look into his cocoa-brown eyes and the anxiety drifted away. She looked at them again now, and all the awkwardness she'd felt when they'd first sat down to eat faded too. Elio was easy to talk to, a good listener.

"But that's enough about me," she said before he could press her on that response. "I'm monopolizing the conversation."

"I don't mind," Elio said. "It occurs to me we don't know each other very well."

She thought the same thing. "No. We don't. Which leads me back to my original question. Why are you here?"

Elio fell silent for a moment, and she wondered if he was going to answer.

"I have a lot of stuff on my mind too, work concerns, and I

thought I'd come here to decompress. Little did I know all I needed to do was clean my apartment."

She laughed. "Missed opportunity on your part."

He shrugged. "Maybe. Maybe not. You finished?"

She nodded, rising when he did, the two of them carrying their plates to the sink.

Elio washed them while she cleaned the rest of the kitchen.

"So," she said once they'd finished. "Here's another question. Are you a clean-up-right-after-dinner guy or one of those who just piles the dishes in the sink until you run out of them?"

Elio chuckled. "Can I plead the fifth?"

"You can, so long as you realize that's pretty much an answer in itself."

"True. I wouldn't say I wait until there are no dishes left, but I'm also not super familiar with what my sink looks like empty." He tossed the dishcloth into the sink, proclaiming, "Two points!" Then he grabbed another beer for himself before topping up her glass of wine. "Want to put a dent in that puzzle you brought before bed?"

She nodded, butterflies fluttering in her stomach at the thought of bedtime. She followed him to the living room, sitting down on the couch, while Elio pulled the large, overstuffed recliner closer to the coffee table. They worked together, flipping all the pieces picture-side up, then started searching for end pieces.

She was relieved he wasn't one of those people who just picked up a random piece and started anywhere. She was the type who did the border first, not even bothering to touch the center pieces until it was in place.

As they put the puzzle together, they talked more. Elio told her stories about past hockey games and some of the crazy adventures he and his teammates had when out on the road. She shared some funny snippets about the guests at her hotel, either things they'd demanded, left behind, or weird complaints they'd lodged.

Two hours passed quickly, and as Gianna yawned, glancing nervously at the bed again, she realized just how long her day had been. She'd risen at dawn to pack her suitcase, getting on the road to the Poconos by nine this morning.

"Okay," Elio said, putting down the puzzle piece he'd been trying to place. "Let's get the sleeping situation out of the way. I can tell you're tired. It's a king-size bed, Gianna."

"I know that."

"And you're sitting on the couch. What do you think about it?"

"Why is it so hard and uncomfortable?" she asked, prompting him to laugh.

"Because it was cheap."

She pointed to the plush bearskin rug in front of the fire. "That looks comfy. I could—"

"You're not sleeping on the floor. We're both adults. And I can promise you right now, I won't venture onto your side of the bed. Unless, of course, you ask me to."

She snorted. "I'm not going to do that."

Elio raised his hand. "Don't feel like you have to give me an answer now. Take some time to decide."

Gianna laughed, enjoying his easy sense of humor. "Fine. We can both sleep in the bed." She raised one finger at him sternly. "But I'm trusting you to be a gentleman. Don't make me call Liza."

Elio raised three fingers, giving her the Scout's Honor promise, though she was ninety-nine percent sure he'd never been a Boy Scout.

Gianna walked over to the dresser and grabbed her pajamas. "I'll just go get changed and brush my teeth."

Elio nodded as she walked into the bathroom and closed the door, aware her hands were shaking slightly. Not out of fear or nervousness but because she wasn't all that certain she could resist issuing Elio the invitation to join her on her side of the bed.

She shook her head at herself in the mirror. "You are not having sex with Elio," she muttered under her breath. And then, to solidify that thought in her mind, she made a mental list of all the reasons why.

He's Liza's brother.

He's a player from the word go.

You are not a one-night stand girl.

He's experienced and you are...a lot less so.

The list worked its magic, so she brushed her teeth, put on her pjs, then walked back into the living space.

Elio grinned when he saw her pajamas. "Cute."

Yeah, she thought sadly. That's exactly what they were. She might have rethought her bedtime attire if she'd known Elio was coming, certain these long fleece pants adorned with dozing teddy bears and the long-sleeved pink tee that said "Time to hibernate" wouldn't have been tossed in her suitcase.

And there was another item for her list of why she and Elio would never have sex. He was no doubt used to sexy women, and the best she could pull off was cute.

"I built the fire up. I'll get up a couple times tonight to add more wood to keep it going. Otherwise, it's bound to get cold in here. The wind is really whipping out there."

"Yeah. Turning out to be quite a snowstorm. Blizzard-like." She walked to the far side of the bed and crawled beneath the covers as Elio took his turn in the bathroom.

When he emerged, she sucked in a rough breath.

Holy. Shit.

Like her, he was wearing lounge pants, but his were a solid navy blue and hung low enough to give her a wee peek of those V-shaped abdominals she'd always figured were reserved for body-builders or male models. Her view of the muscles was unhindered because Elio was shirtless, his bare chest chiseled from stone, the very definition of six-pack abs.

It took a second before she realized she was staring. And another second more before it occurred to her, he was staring back. Amused.

"I forgot to grab a shirt," he said, pointing to his duffel, which was still near the front door. "Should I go get one, or do you need more time?"

She laughed because what else could she do. He'd busted her. Big-time.

Gianna rolled over, putting her back to him—though it hurt her to do so. "I don't care what you do. I'm going to sleep."

"Well," he drawled. "Since you don't care..." He walked to the other side of the bed. She felt the mattress dip as he climbed in.

She should have told him to put the damn shirt on.

Because now she was sleeping with a half-naked Elio, and she was suddenly struggling to recall the reasons on that list. Something about Liza...and a one-night stand.

"Gianna?"

"Yeah?"

"You can relax. You're safe with me."

Until he said the words, she didn't realize how tightly she'd been holding herself. Or how close she was to the edge of the bed. Or the fact that she was barely breathing.

"I...know," she whispered, aware that she *did* know that, and she felt her body loosen.

"Good night, Freckles."

She grinned, loving the nickname—her first one, unless she counted Gee, which was just boring, so she wasn't. "Good night, El."

Chapter Five

Elio blinked a few times, trying to see in a room that was way too dark. He'd spent most of his adult life waking up in strange hotel rooms while on the road with the team, so he wasn't alarmed.

Instead, he was confused.

Because something had woken him up from a very sound sleep.

Then he felt it again. A slight tremble next to him.

He shook himself awake, recalling he was at the cabin. Given the blackness surrounding him, it was still very late. The utter darkness also meant he'd let the fire burn out.

Which was why Gianna was shivering.

He moved slowly, standing up. He winced when his bare feet hit the ice-cold hardwood floor.

"Fuck," he muttered to himself, gingerly picking his way across the room, taking care to avoid walking into any of the furniture. The fire wasn't completely out, but the last few embers were about to give up due to the lack of fuel. He tossed a bit of kindling on the fire, trying to stoke the flames back to life. Once the kindling caught, he added two large logs, waiting until he was certain they were going to burn.

He tiptoed back to the bed, grabbing an extra blanket on the way, before slipping beneath the covers once again.

Gianna's sleepy whisper broke the silence when he gently lay the blanket on top of her. "Thanks. You weren't kidding about it getting cold without the fire."

"I always forget how dark and quiet it is out here. It means I tend to sleep the sleep of the dead. I didn't mean to let the fire go out."

"It's unbelievably dark and quiet," she agreed. "I'm a city girl through and through, so this feels weird. I was sleeping so soundly there for a while, I didn't even dream. That never happens. Then it got cold."

"It's not usually quite this quiet. The snow is muffling a lot of the normal sounds. Ordinarily, you'd hear insects chirping or leaves rustling."

"Wonder if it's still snowing."

He felt her shiver again. "Guess we'll find out in the morning. It'll take a little while before that fire warms the cabin back up."

"The extra blanket is helping. Don't you want to share it?" she asked.

The two of them lay on their sides, facing each other. He could see her face, in shadows, now that the fire had begun to grow. He would have expected it to feel strange, lying in bed with her like this, but instead it felt comfortable, even nice. "I'm warm enough like this. I work on ice, so I've built up a pretty high tolerance for cold."

"Must be nice. Meanwhile, I could give Olaf and Frosty a run for their money, temperature-wise," she said, as he watched her trying to burrow deeper under the duvet.

He reached out, then cursed as he took her hands in his. "Damn. You're not kidding. Your hands are freezing." He began to rub them briskly, trying to help warm them up.

"Yeah. I'm definitely wearing socks to bed tomorrow night. I'd go get a pair, but I'm pretty sure I live in this bed now. There's no way I'm getting out from under these blankets. Ever."

He closed his hands around hers, shifting slightly closer. "Slide your feet over here. Put them under my legs."

She shook her head. "No, I couldn't do that to you. Seriously. Blocks of ice would be warmer."

He released one of her hands to reach down and tug her knee, pulling her leg up so that he could grasp her foot.

"Jesus, Freckles. We're talking frostbite levels. Where are the socks? I'll go get them."

"I'll be fine. It's already getting warmer in here."

Elio glanced toward the nightstand. According to the clock, it was four a.m. "Roll over and face away from me."

"Why?"

He grinned. "Just do it."

She turned to face the wall, and again, he noticed how slim she was. No wonder she was cold. The woman had zero body fat insulating her.

She jerked slightly when he gripped her waist and pulled her back to his chest.

"We can share body heat until you're warm again."

"Oh. Is that what you're calling this? I thought you were going to wait for an invitation," she joked, though she wasn't pulling away. There was no denying the tiredness in her voice. If she were a little more awake, he wondered if she'd put up a bit more resistance. She'd been nervous about crawling into bed with him in the first place.

"That invitation was in regard to your side of the bed. Technically, we're both still on our own sides. We're just meeting in the middle." He'd been amused when they'd first gotten into bed last night. Gianna had clung to the very edge of the mattress, and he'd been worried she might fall out of the bed.

Sometime during the night, she'd moved closer and closer to him, which was why her shivering woke him up.

She settled in, sighing heavily. "I'd argue with you, but you're so freaking warm."

He chuckled, then went for broke, wrapping his arm tightly

around her middle. She sank even deeper into the embrace. Her blonde hair tickled his nose, but he enjoyed the smell of her citrus shampoo.

Gianna moved her feet until they rested on his—they were fucking freezing—yet he let her do it, giving her another way to steal whatever warmth she could from him.

He sure as hell didn't mind. She felt good in his arms.

They fell silent, and it was only a few minutes more before her breathing slowed and he could tell she'd fallen back to sleep. He listened to the soft, easy sound and let it lure him back to dreamland as well.

The next time Elio opened his eyes, he knew exactly where he was and who he was with. The cabin was much brighter, though it wasn't because of sun but rather snow. The world outside the window was awash in vivid white, everything buried under mounds of snow. It was still falling, though not as hard as the previous night.

The cabin was much warmer now. Actually, it was bordering on hot. Thanks to the fire and Gianna. She'd rolled over at some point, draping herself over half his body, his own personal hot water bottle. Her head rested on his shoulder, her arm wrapped around his waist, and one of her legs was lying across both of his.

His body responded to the embrace in ways that would most likely make her uncomfortable if she were awake. His cock was rock hard, tenting his lounge pants in an obvious way.

He tried to will it away, but his attempts were pointless. Especially when Gianna sighed softly. He felt her eyelashes flutter against his bare chest. He glanced down because he wanted to see her face when she woke up.

Her expression didn't disappoint. At first, she stilled, like a cornered animal. No doubt she was trying to determine if she could extract herself without waking him up. But that look was fleeting when she lifted her eyes and saw him looking back at her.

"Good morning," he said, his voice husky from sleep.

She flushed a bright red, and he grinned. God. He'd never been with such an innocent woman. Not even when he was younger and new to sex himself.

Gianna slowly removed her leg and lifted her arm, intent on shifting away from him. Elio knew he should be a gentleman, should let her make her escape, but fuck that jazz.

She felt good and warm and...like she belonged right where she was.

He tightened his arm around her shoulders, tugging her back into place.

She resisted. "Elio."

"Let's just relax a little bit longer. Even with the fire, it's going to be cold when we crawl out of this bed. Besides, we're on vacation. It's not like we have anything to get up for."

He expected her to continue the fight, so he was surprised when she resumed her previous position, going soft in his arms.

"It does feel nice. I miss sleeping next to someone," she confessed.

"I wouldn't know," he said.

She lifted her head, giving him a look that said she didn't believe him for a minute.

"Seriously," he insisted. "Sex and sleeping aren't the same thing, you know."

"Yeah, well, it's been three and a half months since I've done either."

"Nine months for me...on the sex part, so I win," he said, laughing softly.

"Number one, you're too competitive. And number two, I don't really think you can call that a win."

"Good point."

"It's really been that long?"

He wasn't surprised by her question. Liza had obviously done a very good job painting a picture of him as a shameless playboy. Gianna probably thought he had a different woman in his bed every night. "I was seeing a woman, Paula, off and on, but that fell apart at the end of last season when she started pushing for more."

"What's more?"

"Sleepovers."

"I thought you were joking about that. You mean you *really* never spent a night with her?"

He shook his head. "Never."

"Never had a broken heart?"

Gianna was clearly functioning with one, which bothered him. He hated to think she was still so hurt.

"No broken hearts," he reassured her.

"Hmpf."

"Paula saw our relationship going somewhere I didn't."

"Where?" Gianna asked.

He gave her a crooked grin. "To the altar."

She giggled quietly.

"After I called it quits with Paula, I decided to take a break from women. And sex."

"Liza's told me all about your aversion to anything even slightly resembling a relationship. So Paula's been your only girlfriend?"

Elio was amused by her question because Gianna clearly had very black and white ideas of what to call sex partners. "You're not listening. She wasn't a girlfriend, Gee. She was a steady booty call. One that's having a hard time letting go."

"What's that mean?"

He hadn't meant to get into a conversation about Paula. Primarily because he meant what he said. The woman never registered on his radar as anything more than a few hours of fun between the sheets.

But Gianna was surprisingly easy to talk to, so he went ahead and answered her question. "It means that while I've told Paula countless times and in countless ways that we're through, she's harboring under the delusion that I'm either kidding or going to come to my senses."

"Damn. Sounds like you've got yourself a stalker."

He chuckled. "Nothing that dramatic. More like a minor annoyance. When I get back to Baltimore, I'm going to reiterate that it's over, and—hopefully—that will be the end of it once and for all. It's past time for her to move on."

"As easily as that," she said, more to herself than him. Gianna was struggling with the moving on part when it came to her ex.

"Yep. The truth is, the only commitment I've ever made is to my career. Even if I had the interest, it's not that easy to start a relationship when you're traveling most of the year. And during the off-season, there's conditioning, exhibition games, volunteer work with the team, stuff like that. I'm away from Baltimore as much as I'm there. I've never had the time to invest in dating someone seriously."

"Sure," she said sarcastically. "Time is the only issue."

Elio bopped Gianna on the tip of her nose with his finger. "Liza really has given you the full rundown on all my perceived bad habits, I see."

"Your sister knows no secrets."

"I'm aware."

"And she loves the sound of her own voice. The only one to give her a run for her money on that front is Keeley."

Elio laughed. "You're not wrong there."

They lay in companionable silence for a few minutes.

"So, should we make a plan for the day?" she asked.

"You like a schedule, don't you?"

She nodded. "I'm pretty sure I'm OCD. Because the truth is, I like to know what I'm doing and when. I kind of get stressed out if I don't have a plan. I know that's weird and annoying. It used to drive my grandma and Sam crazy."

Elio liked Gianna's openness, even when sharing things that might be embarrassing or unfavorable. It shone a light on something he'd always suspected but never thought too much about in terms of the women he slept with. They'd all been playing games, saying things they thought he wanted to hear, never revealing anything real about themselves.

There was none of that with Gianna.

"I'm a professional athlete," he said, "so I'm no stranger to schedules."

"Yeah, but those are made up for you. If you'd come to the cabin and I hadn't been here, what would you have done?"

He could lie, could tell her he had a game plan for each day, but Gianna had offered him honesty and he wanted to give her the same. "I would have gone with the flow, done whatever I felt like. But I like your idea better."

She narrowed her eyes suspiciously.

"So I say we start with a big breakfast. I saw bacon in the fridge."

"I am kind of hungry. I brought eggs too." She pushed away from him, sitting up.

He sat up as well. "I can whip up some hash browns."

"Perfect."

"After that, I'm going to go out and start moving some snow. Figure I need to shovel a path to the woodpile at least. And it probably wouldn't be a bad idea to start shoveling out at least one vehicle."

Gianna glanced out the window. "That might be an act of futility. It's still snowing."

"True, but it's only going to get heavier and deeper. Best to try to stay ahead of it if we can."

"I'll help."

"Sounds good."

"And after that," she said, eyes bright as they plotted out their entire day. "If you want, I brought the ingredients to bake cookies."

"That'll be fun. I brought some hot cocoa so we can eat and drink ourselves into sugar comas while we work on that puzzle some more."

"And then...tacos for dinner?" she asked.

Elio climbed out of bed and walked over to his duffel bag, pulling out a long-sleeved T-shirt. "Hell yeah. I'm declaring it taco and tequila Tuesday."

She laughed, crawling out of bed as well. "Let me go get dressed and we can start on breakfast."

Elio threw another log on the fire and decided Gianna might have the right of it when it came to making plans.

Her way gave him a lot to look forward to.

Chapter Six

The day had gone exactly as they'd planned, and Elio struggled to recall when he'd had such a good time. He and Gianna cut a decent path from the cabin to the woodpile. Or at least they had. Until it devolved into an epic snowball battle.

They'd also made serious progress on the puzzle and plowed through at least half a dozen large chocolate chip cookies.

Now, Gianna stood by the sink, washing the dishes while he wiped the table. The entire day had felt completely domestic, something he'd always figured would be boring, a sign that he'd basically given up all hope of leading an exciting life. The truth was, nothing had been boring at all. Only fun and relaxing and comfortable.

And another fact had revealed itself to him somewhere in the middle of the snowball fight.

His attraction to Gianna was now off the charts.

He wanted her. So much so, he'd tried to take a page from her book, creating one of those lists she loved so much. His list was reasons why he shouldn't have sex with her.

Unfortunately, he'd come up with a lot more than he'd wanted to.

For one thing, Liza would kick his ass if he seduced her recently dumped friend. For another, the more time he spent with her, the more he could tell they were quite different people. Gianna was very structured, focused, much more serious than he was. He considered himself a fly-by-the-seat-of-his pants, go-with-the-flow, always-looking-for-a-good-time kind of guy. Plus, she was a relationship girl from the word go, and that was the last thing he was looking for.

Then, for the first time ever, he found himself tacking the words "right now" onto that thought.

What the hell?

He couldn't figure out his career issues right now, so why the fuck would he add another wrinkle?

"Want some hot tea?" she asked, once she'd finished the dishes.

He shook his head. "Nope. We still have one more thing on our schedule."

She groaned. "I was hoping you'd forget about that. Me and tequila don't mix. The last time I did shots was with your sister, Keeley, and Jess."

"What happened?"

"Let's just say I lost a couple of hours at the end of the night. Sam had to pick me up at the bar. Apparently, I insisted on stopping for Big Macs on the way home and serenaded him with every Jimmy Buffett song I knew...or even didn't know. He said eventually I just started making up words."

"Sounds hilarious to me."

Gianna giggled. "Yeah, Sam said it was quite a show, but he wasn't mad about it. That year for Christmas, he gave me Jimmy Buffett's Greatest Hits and told me I should brush up on the lyrics before my next tequila night."

"Have you practiced?" Elio asked. "Because I'm going to want that concert later."

She followed him to the living room area, her heavy sigh

drawing his attention as he grabbed the fifth of tequila he'd brought with him, along with two shot glasses.

"If you'd rather not—" he began, but she cut him off.

"Oh no. It's not that. It's just…" Her words trailed off, and he got the sense she was hesitant to finish her thought.

"What is it?"

"You realize there are two open bottles of tequila in that cabinet. We could…um…"

Elio recalled her comment about being OCD. "Want to finish those two first?"

She nodded. "It might help. The cabinet really is overflowing. The idea of opening a new bottle when there are two open already makes my brain itch."

Elio knelt in front of the cabinet, amused by her comment, then realized she was right. The cabinet was out of control. "You know, it would take a joint effort on our part, but I think we could clean the whole thing out this week."

Her eyes lit up. "I think so too. All we have to do is combine the bottles and then—"

He shook his head. "Nope. That's not what I mean." He pulled out the two tequila bottles that were already open. "There are only a couple shots each in these. But if we move from tequila to vodka shots, we could clear four bottles out just tonight."

"I'm not singing Jimmy Buffett," she insisted, and he laughed.

"The night is young. You should never say never." He placed the four partial bottles of liquor on the kitchen table, then grabbed a deck of cards. "You ever play blackjack?"

"Yeah. Why?"

"Thought we could play. You beat me, I take the shot. I beat you, you drink. If it's a draw, we're both spared."

"We'll be trashed in ten minutes," she said, digging in her heels.

"No, we won't. I'll deal first." Elio shuffled then dealt their cards, one facedown, the second face up. "Queen for you. Ten for me."

Gianna looked at the facedown card, considering. Then she tapped once. "Hit me."

He dealt her third card face up. "A five."

"I'll stop there."

He looked at his cards, then said, "Dealer is holding. Whatcha got?"

She flipped over her cards to reveal her third card was a six. "Blackjack."

"Damn." Elio turned his over to reveal his cards added up to twenty. He poured himself a tequila shot, lifted the glass in a silent toast to her, then drank it down.

They played several more hands, both of them evenly matched when it came to shots. They'd polished off the two open bottles of tequila and had moved on to the vodka.

"My head is starting to spin a little," she admitted.

"Should I fire up Spotify? How do you feel about 'Margaritaville'?"

She laughed. "God no. I can't carry a tune in a bucket. Sam used to cover his ears, called it noise pollution. And believe me, he wasn't wrong."

Elio leaned back in his chair. "You mention Sam a lot."

"Shit. Yeah. I do," Gianna said. "It's not because I'm still hung up on him. But..."

"You dated a long time."

"My entire adult life has included him, so now it feels like I'm trying to figure out who I am without him."

"I get that."

She gave him an incredulous look, and he knew why. He'd talked about his lacking relationship history, but he still understood where she was coming from.

"I do get it," he insisted. "You spent your adult life with Sam. I've spent mine on the ice. When I leave the game...who am I?"

"Oh," she breathed. "Yeah. God, you do understand."

Elio dealt another hand. Gianna lost. After the first couple of shots, she'd made a disgusted face when the liquor hit her tongue. This time, she tossed the vodka back like it was water.

He lost the next two hands and realized it wasn't his head spinning so much as the room. "Shit," he muttered, as he counted two empty tequila bottles and three empty vodka ones.

Gianna giggled, weaving in her chair. She was drunk.

"Come on," he said, standing up on unsteady feet. "Let's go sit by the fire."

Gianna took the hand he proffered, the two of them stumbling across the room together. She dropped down onto the bearskin rug, a little more heavily than she might have if she'd been sober.

"Oopsie-daisy," she said, just barely catching herself from falling to her back.

Elio laughed as he joined her, his descent not much steadier than hers. "Oopsie-daisy? What are you? Five."

Gianna laughed and Elio did too.

"I'm shit-faced," she admitted.

"Yeah. Me too. It was probably a bad idea to switch from tequila to vodka."

She laughed again, louder. "Yeah. It was switching liquors that really did us in. Not the number of shots we took in a very short time frame."

Elio winked.

"Can I tell you something?" she asked, slurring the "s" on *something*.

"Of course."

"I liked the way you kissed me under the mistletoe."

Elio leaned closer. "Oh yeah?"

She cut the distance between them by half. "Did you know you're only the second guy I've ever kissed? In my whole life?"

He hadn't considered that, though he probably should have. "So you haven't gone out with anyone since Sam?"

She shook her head.

He could feel the heat from her breath on his face. Three more inches and his lips would be on hers.

"I made a list," she confessed.

"Another one?" he murmured, his gaze dropping down to her lips. Aware that it was the alcohol doing the thinking and the talking for both of them.

"It was a list of reasons why I shouldn't sleep with you."

He considered his own attempts at convincing himself to keep his hands off her. Right now, he was struggling to remember what was on his list. "So did I."

Gianna's eyes widened. "Seriously? Was Liza on it? Like you couldn't sleep with your sister's friend or something?"

Elio snorted. "Yeah. She was number one."

"She was number one on mine too," Gianna said, giggling. "That bitch!"

The two of them fell away from each other, laughing so uncontrollably and hard that Gianna dropped to her side, clutching her stomach. "Stop making me laugh."

Elio lay down next to her, facing her, the position reminding him of the wee hours of morning, the two of them talking in bed. "Okay," he said, gripping her waist to pull her body against his. "I will."

He sealed his lips to hers, kissing away her giggles. Gianna's hands rested between them, gripping the front of his T-shirt.

The kiss was a hungry one, the two of them clinging to each other as their lips and tongues danced, stroked, took.

Gianna's grip loosened on his shirt, drifting lower, her fingers tickling his abs as she sought the hem.

Elio broke the kiss, sitting up briefly to pull his shirt over his head. He started to lay back down next to her, but Gianna stopped him. Pushing herself up, she knelt in front of him, her gaze locked on his chest.

"God, you're so sexy," she breathed. "I really want to have sex with you."

"I want that too." Elio thought he should say more, but he couldn't for the life of him figure out what. The liquor was impairing his ability to think, so he kissed her again. "You taste good."

"We taste like tequila. And vodka. If I wasn't already tipsy, I think I could get drunk off your kisses."

He'd been seduced by some of the sexiest women on the planet, but none of those experienced lovers had ever turned him on as much as Gianna was right now.

"Gianna?"

"Yeah?"

"Take off your sweater," he demanded.

She didn't hesitate. She pulled the sweater off in one fast motion, dropping it to the floor next to her. She wore one of those sexy push-up bras, the kind that showcased a woman's tits to perfection.

He ran his fingers along the tops of her breasts, watching as the blush on her face crept lower, her chest going pink as well.

Elio lifted his gaze, taking in her expression. One look into her pretty blue eyes and he saw everything he needed to see.

She was beautiful, funny, and so damn sexy, she took his breath away. How had he not noticed for so many years?

"I've never had anyone look at me like that," she whispered.

"Like what?"

"Like they could devour me whole."

He cupped her jaw with one hand as the other wrapped around her waist, their eyes locked. "That's exactly what I want to do," he murmured, his lips moving against hers.

Gianna's hands found their way to his shoulders as they kissed again. He could kiss her all night and never get his fill.

He reached around her, unfastening her bra with skilled fingers. Gianna slipped the straps down herself, stripping it off completely.

Elio broke the kiss, dragging his lips and tongue along the side of her neck. Gianna tilted her head, her eyes closing, her expression one of pure bliss when Elio cupped her breasts, lifting them so that he could suck one of her tight pink nipples into his mouth.

"God," she breathed, her head falling back when he increased the pressure, the suction.

She was so inexperienced. Just one lover. He had no idea what her sex life with Sam was like, and it occurred to him that a smart —sober—man would probably ask for some clarification on that.

Elio was neither smart nor sober.

He sucked harder on her nipple as Gianna's fingers flew to his head, her fists closing around strands of his hair, pulling it roughly. It stung, but that sensation only pushed him to go further. He lifted his head, retaining his grip on her breasts. He watched her face as he pinched her nipples, loving the way her breathing became more rapid, ragged, the little squeaks and moans that told him without words to keep going.

"Elio," she said, her head falling forward, her forehead resting on his shoulder. "Please. God. I need..."

He gripped her waist, lifting her more fully to her knees, so that he could unbutton and unzip her jeans.

"Yes," she hissed, helping him tug the denim as well as her panties over her hips. Elio watched as she twisted onto her back, pushing her ass off the ground so that she could draw them off completely.

She started to sit back up once she was naked, but Elio pressed down on her shoulder, holding her in place.

He knelt next to her, his gaze sliding down her body, from the top of her head, all the way down to her feet.

"Say something," she whispered when the silence drifted a bit too long. It was the first touch of shyness he'd seen from her this evening.

Elio threw his leg over her hips, bending until his face was just above hers. He still wore his jeans, aware that once they came off, there was no way he could stop himself from taking her.

He didn't want to do that—not yet—because there was no way in hell he was going to rush this.

"You are the most beautiful woman I've ever seen."

She started to shake her head, but Elio tucked his finger under her chin, held her still.

"The most beautiful," he stressed, holding her gaze as he spoke.

She blinked a couple times...and then she gave him a breathtaking smile.

He kissed her then because he had to. Needed to.

Gianna ran her fingers along his chest, toying with his nipples, drawing her nails along his pecs, his abs. He broke the kiss and pushed away when he felt her trying to unfasten his jeans.

He shook his head. "Bad girl."

"I want to see you."

"You're going to get the full tour, trust me. But not yet. There's something you have to do for me first."

"What?" she asked.

"Come."

She frowned until he ran his fingers along her slit. She was soaking wet, more than ready for what came next. Regardless, he wanted to make tonight good for her.

Elio was the king of one-night stands, but he knew without a doubt that wasn't what this was going to be. They were going to be trapped in this cabin for at least three more nights. And he intended to put every single one of them to good use.

He ran his tongue through the valley between her breasts as she took an unsteady breath, one that turned into a giggle when he pushed the tip of it into her belly button.

"That tickles," she said.

He continued his southerly journey, lifting one of his legs. "Open your legs, Gianna."

The second she spread her thighs, he shifted, kneeling between her them, pushing them open even more.

He lowered his head, not stopping until he reached his destination.

"God," she whispered, when he used his thumbs to open her

labia. He wasted no time sucking her clit into his mouth, giving it the same treatment he'd just employed on her nipples.

"Holy shit!" Gianna's hands found his hair again, gripping it as he ran his tongue along her slit. He pressed his tongue inside her pussy, and Gianna reared up, in surprise or perhaps excitement. Elio lifted his head, capturing her gaze.

"Sam didn't really...like to... He didn't do that very often. Or like...ever."

Elio nodded slowly. "Gianna?"

"Yeah?"

"Sam was an idiot."

The pleased smile she gave did funny things to his heart. He found himself wanting to find more ways to put that smile on her face, to make her happy.

He lowered his head once more, and this time Gianna was prepared as he thrust his tongue in and out of her, as far as he could reach. With his thumb, he rubbed her clit, increasing her arousal, loving the way Gianna didn't hold anything back. She told him with her words and her moans everything he needed to know.

She was close, so he lifted his head, replacing his tongue with two fingers.

"Oh my God," she breathed, her hips rising and falling in time with the thrusting of his fingers. She was so tight, and Elio went light-headed as he imagined how fucking good she was going to feel around his cock.

"El!" she gasped, reaching for his wrist, trying to stop him. "Too good."

"Let go," Elio said, driving his fingers in deeper, faster.

"I...it's too much. I'm...*fuck*!" Her back arched as she came, her pussy muscles clenching hard against his fingers.

Elio didn't let up, determined to draw every ounce of pleasure he could from this orgasm. She needed it. She fucking deserved it.

She jerked at the initial impact of her climax, then shuddered several times more as the aftershocks pulsed through her. Finally, he slowed his motions when he felt her body go limp.

Gianna groaned when he pulled his fingers out, her gaze locked with his as he licked her juices off each digit.

"Fuck," she whispered. "How are you so hot?"

Elio chuckled. "Let's move this party to the bed."

Chapter Seven

Gianna was too boneless to move, let alone stand up. Not that Elio was giving her a choice in the matter. He reached for her hands, pulling her to a sitting position, then to a standing one. He wrapped his arm around her waist, offering some much-needed support.

The effects of the alcohol were waning, so it wasn't the tequila that had her stumbling. It was that orgasm.

All she could think was *what the fuck was that*? She'd come before...loads of times. But it had never—NEVER—hit her like that.

"You okay?" Elio asked, looking equal parts concerned and pleased. He knew exactly what he'd done to her.

She nodded. "So okay."

Elio gave her a quick, sweet kiss on the cheek. "Good. Because we're nowhere near finished."

The two of them moved to the bed as one, stopping when they reached it. Elio cupped her cheeks and kissed her. For such a gentle touch, it packed a punch. Gianna slipped her arms around his waist when he deepened the kiss. She fell into it, into him, as minutes passed, the two of them simply kissing, tasting, sharing each other's air.

"I love kissing you," she confessed, when they finally parted.

Elio pulled back the covers, then gestured for her to climb in.

She did so, surprised when he made no move to follow her. Or to even to take off his jeans.

"Elio?"

"I need to ask, Gee. We've had a lot to drink tonight. I love kissing you too. And if you want, we can just keep doing that. This doesn't have to go any further. I don't want to do anything you might regret tomorrow."

It was kind of him to ask, and she respected him for trying to be a gentleman, but she sure as fuck didn't want one right now. She was kind of hoping for a bad boy. Who knew when she'd get another opportunity to sleep with a sexually experienced, built-like-a-brick-house hockey star?

Actually, she knew the answer to that.

Fucking never.

She was calling this a late Christmas present for herself.

"I've wanted you since the holiday party. Tequila isn't making this decision. I am. And I want this more than I can say. Please don't stop."

He hesitated a moment longer...and that was when she wondered if he wasn't stopping because of her inebriation but because he didn't want to have sex with her. She recalled her list. She was nothing like the women he usually took to bed. What if it was just as she suspected and she really wasn't his type?

"Unless...oh. I'm sorry, Elio. I didn't mean to pressure you. I realize I'm probably not like Paula, or your other...well...I understand if you're not inter—"

"Don't finish that sentence," he said, his voice deep and almost angry. "Jesus, Gianna. Do I look like I'm not interested? Like I don't want to fuck you six ways to Sunday?" He gestured to his jeans, to the obvious bulge constricted within the denim.

The bulge was...significant.

"Whoa," she breathed.

"That," he said, pointing to her. "*That's* what I mean. You've only slept with one man. I've had more lovers than I can count. I don't... Fuck...I don't want to hurt you."

"Hurt me how?"

"Physically. Emotionally. You name it."

"You won't hurt me," she said, more certain of that than she'd been of anything in her life. "I trust you."

"That's nice, but—"

She cut him off. "My eyes are wide open. I know you aren't looking for a relationship, and to be honest, right now, neither am I. I've wasted years with a man I loved, who I'd planned to spend the rest of my life with. And in the end, he lied to me, cheated on me. All I'm capable of right now is casual dating." Then, before he could get the wrong idea, she quickly added, "And one-night stands. Do you know how many experiences I've missed in the last eleven years?"

She didn't wait for him to answer.

"All of them," she said. "Fucking *all* of them. Pretend I'm just like all the other women you've taken to your bed. One night. Give me one night, and I promise I won't ask for another."

Elio took a long, deep breath...then he unbuttoned his jeans and slid down the zipper.

She didn't move, watching, concerned when he didn't push his jeans down.

"Please," she whispered.

"I'm going to take you, Gianna," he said at last. "But I want to make some things very clear before I do. You are *nothing* like those other women, and I don't want that fucking promise. You can ask me for anything."

Before she could figure out how to respond to that, he pushed his jeans and boxers over his hips, bending down to strip them off completely.

Gianna froze, her gaze locked on his dick. "Oh!"

Elio gave her one of his standard cocky grins, which helped her find her bearings...a little. "Change your mind?"

She narrowed her eyes, certain she should knock him down a

peg or two. Unfortunately, her self-preservation was stronger than her smart-ass nature at the moment. "I want to be impressed by..." She waved her hand toward his cock. "That. But intimidation is sort of winning out."

Elio climbed into the bed, chuckling. "I'm trying to think of something humble to say, but I like the idea of coming out on top when it comes to dick comparisons."

The effects of the alcohol were waning, but she still felt drunk, light-headed, thanks to that orgasm he'd just given her. She had seriously thought the top of her head was going to blow off, and every orgasm she'd ever had in her life, now—in hindsight— seemed lukewarm at best.

"Lay down," Elio said, and she complied, reaching to pull him down for a kiss. His body was propped next to hers, supported by his elbow. She was thrilled when he kissed her again, taking his time, giving her a few minutes to get her bearings. She was so ready for the next part, but she also wanted to savor the moment.

She'd never considered kisses foreplay. With Sam, they'd been more an act of affection, of caring, but Elio's kisses would get an X-rating from the Motion Picture Association, his lips driving her thoughts down all sorts of sinful, kinky avenues.

He ran one hand down the side of her neck, her shoulder, her arm, before resting on her hip.

Gianna wanted to touch him too. She drew her fingertips along his chest, silk over steel, but she hesitated when her hand reached his stomach.

Elio took over, grasping her wrist, pulling it lower. "Wrap your hand around my cock," he demanded.

Elio's bedroom tone drove her wild, and she wondered if there was anything he could request in that deep, low voice that she would refuse.

She was pretty sure there wasn't.

She curled her fingers around his dick and cursed, recalling her lack of sexual research wasn't just limited to kissing. She'd only seen Sam's penis before tonight, and it had seemed perfectly respectable.

Elio's was a bit longer and thicker—God, way thicker.

Liza and Keeley had been sending her links for vibrators and dildos ever since she and Sam broke up, but she'd only hit the buy button on one of them and that was because she'd been three glasses of wine into a pity party.

Most of the links her friends had sent were for toys Gianna had considered so big, they had to be jokes. She'd honestly thought they were just teasing, so most of the time she'd just responded to the texts with the eggplant emoji, along with the shocked-face one.

Then she and that half bottle of Malbec purchased what she'd considered a huge dildo, one that was in her suitcase, still in the package, along with the vibrator Penny had given her for Christmas.

Now, the toys her friends had been suggesting didn't seem so big at all.

"Still intimidated?" he murmured, though not in a way that felt like he was laughing at her, but more like he was concerned about her.

"A little. But I don't want to stop," she hastily added.

"Then we won't stop." He shifted his grip from her wrist to her hand, holding it around his thickness. He began moving her hand up and down, showing her just how hard and how fast he liked it.

She heard his breath quicken, a low moan coming from deep in his throat, and she was thrilled to know she could have the same impact on him that he had on her.

As she stroked him, Elio's lips slipped from her cheek to her ear, nipping the lobe before venturing downward.

He released her hand, leaving her to continue stroking him on her own so that he could cup her breast and suck her nipple into his mouth again.

One second, he was gentle, the next rough. He kept changing

the tune, alternating the pace, keeping her on her toes. The contrast was heady, exciting.

"Harder," she whispered.

Elio stopped sucking on her nipple, releasing it with a pop. "You like the hint of pain, don't you?" He pinched her nipples as if to prove his point.

Her pussy clenched and she nodded. "I didn't know I did until now. Everything you're doing is driving me crazy. In a good way."

Elio studied her face for just a split second, as if he was trying to decide if she was telling the truth, before placing his lips back around her nipple and giving her exactly what she'd asked for. He sucked hard. Sparks flared to life, flashing beneath her closed eyes, igniting a trip wire that had her entire body pulsing and throbbing with need.

"Please," she cried out. "God, El."

He lifted his head, and she saw the same overwhelming desire she felt reflected in his eyes.

Gianna had always been the good girl, the responsible, toe-the-line friend. She'd never done an impulsive, reckless, crazy thing in her life, but with Elio, she felt out of control, wild, wicked.

And she liked it.

He pushed her legs open, kneeling between them just as he had on the floor in front of the fire. She still held his cock in her hand. Elio gently pulled it away, lifting both her hands until he was pressing them to the pillow beneath her head.

"Leave your hands there," he demanded.

"I want to touch you."

"And I want you to surrender to me. So that's what you're going to do."

There was that voice again. And just as she suspected, she responded to it, giving him exactly what he asked for.

"Surrender?" she murmured.

"Have you ever been tied up in bed?" he asked.

Gianna shook her head. She and Sam had established a solid sex routine early in their relationship, and no part of that routine ventured into kinky areas.

"Ever been spanked?"

"No," she whispered, though she liked the idea of that a lot.

"Sixty-nine?"

"We tried that a few times, but it was kind of awkward."

"Anal?"

"God no," she exclaimed, and he chuckled.

"Did the two of you use toys on each other?"

"No. Sam and I didn't really stray too far from the missionary or doggie-style positions. I bought a dildo after we broke up, but it was a totally wine-fueled purchase," she confessed, wishing she could suck the words back in. She was honest-to-a-fault, something Grandma said would be an admirable quality if it wasn't so damned annoying. Of course, it wasn't like Gianna had much of a choice. She was the world's worst liar—blushing and stammering and failing to establish eye contact. She'd learned early on it was easier just to tell the truth.

"Is that right?" Elio said, way too interested in what she hadn't meant to say. "You didn't by any chance bring it with you, did you?"

"I'm pleading the fifth on that," she said, perfectly aware that her face was probably blood red and answering the question without her having to confess. Because she *had* brought it. A last-minute, impulsive act, driven by the fact it had been sitting on top of her dresser for over a month, taunting her, daring her to try it. Since she had viewed her trip to the cabin as her chance to turn over a new leaf, she'd decided the new and improved Gianna should be a sex toy girl.

"Okay," he said, letting her off the hook easier than she expected. Until he added, "But we're revisiting that question later."

She decided to lead them back to safer territory. "I should add that while I don't have a lot of experience, I would like to try *all* those things you just said. Except for the, you know, butt stuff."

Elio gave her a quick kiss on the cheek. "Tonight, we're going to stick with what you know."

She grimaced. "That sort of defeats the point of going to bed with you."

Elio laughed. "I'll try to make it memorable for you without all the bells and whistles."

Before she could persuade him to at least consider the spanking or the bondage—she'd packed a couple of scarves that would work great—Elio gripped his dick, running the head of it along her slit, up and down her opening, without giving her what she wanted, what she needed.

"Push inside me," she said, issuing her own demand.

He continued teasing her as if she hadn't spoken at all. "You're so wet, so hot. God, do you know how good you're going to feel? How do you want it, Gianna? Slow, hard, rough, gentle...?"

Her response came easily because she didn't need to think about it. She'd spent eleven years in a comfortable relationship that she was just now realizing was completely passionless.

Elio could offer her so much more.

She was facing a lot of long, lonely months, despite Liza's best intentions. So this had to count. "I want to feel it. Not just now, tonight, tomorrow, or next week. I need you to take me hard enough to last until..."

"Until?" he prompted.

"Just until," she said, uncertain what she was waiting for exactly.

"Until," he repeated, thrusting inside her, one hard, deep drive that took him to the hilt.

She winced because it hurt, filling her well past her limits, until it didn't. Her body adjusted as he held still within her.

Hell, her body didn't just adjust. It took over.

Her pussy clenched around his thick flesh, and the world

around her turned as white as the snowy woods outdoors. "Oh my God," she gasped, when she started to come. One pulse, then another, then...

"Fuck." Elio withdrew as quickly as he'd entered, his breathing ragged.

"No!" she yelled when her orgasm sputtered and faded away without being fully realized.

Elio was shaking his head like he'd received some sort of electric shock and it rendered him senseless. "Jesus."

"Elio?" she asked, confused by his tone. Something had shaken him up. Why would he pull out like that? Was he still worried about hurting her? "It didn't hurt, I swear."

"No. I forgot the condom. *Fuck*," he repeated, and suddenly she understood his remorse. "I'm sorry, Gianna."

"It's okay," she said. He'd been inside her less than ten seconds, and he hadn't come. Then she panicked, but not for the same reason he had. "Wait. You *have* condoms, right?"

"I do. A whole box, brand-new."

"Thank God." She expected him to go get one, but instead, he remained where he was, caging her beneath him.

His gaze locked on her as if he was trying to wrap his head around something. "You were about to come, weren't you?" he asked.

Gianna felt her cheeks go warm. She hated how often she blushed around him. "Um..." She bit her lower lip.

"One thrust." He grinned, shaking his head in amazement. "Fucking hell, that's hot." Elio looked over his shoulder, toward the front door. "Condoms are in my duffel bag."

"What a shame," she joked, "that they're allllll the way over there." He'd yet to move his bag away from the front door, grabbing shit from where it sat, like a heathen—which was what she'd teasingly called him earlier today—instead of unpacking like the civilized human she had proclaimed herself to be.

Elio snorted, then his eyes lit up. "Actually, if we're lucky..." He stretched out toward the nightstand, reaching beneath it.

"Paydirt." He lifted his hand, revealing a condom. "Bruno used to bring Vivian up here when they were dating."

"Liza told me."

"He always hid a stash of condoms under the drawer. There's a little ledge there. I'm stealing his last one." As he spoke, Elio slid the condom on. "Now, where were we?" he asked as he gripped his cock and placed it at her pussy. "Oh, that's right. You were about to come on my dick after one thrust. Because I'm such a stud."

She started to laugh, but the sound morphed to a breathy cry when Elio reentered her with the same force and speed as the first time.

This time, he didn't pause, didn't give her time to think or adjust.

The only thing she was capable of was feeling. And dear God, she was feeling it. Everything.

Within three thrusts, she was coming, but Elio didn't acknowledge her orgasm, didn't give stop. She gripped his arms, trying to find something to hold onto, to keep herself from flying away, splintering apart.

He'd told her to keep her hands on the pillow, but he may as well have asked her to stop breathing. There was no way she could remain passive when he fucked her so roughly, took her so hard. If he wanted that, he should have tied her up.

"More," she gasped, as pleasure and pain, delight and fear ebbed and flowed, one taking precedence, then the other.

Her nails pierced the skin on his shoulders and Elio winced. She eased her grip, but he said, "Scratch me again. Leave your mark. I need this to last too."

She lifted her head, intending to kiss his chest. Instead, she bit him.

Elio clasped the back of her head, holding her against him, then made the same demand she had. "Bite harder!"

She sank her teeth in deeper, and Elio gave her the same,

nipping at a spot between her shoulder and her neck. At this rate, they would tear each other apart.

Elio fucked her harder, and the orgasm she'd thought had passed flared to life once more. Her head flew back on the pillow as she fought for air, all semblance of control ripped from her hands.

She was his. He owned her, every part of her.

Elio slowed his thrusts, allowing her to come down, kissing her, soothing her. "You're perfect," he gasped.

Perfect? All her life...no one had *ever* called her perfect.

Practical? Yes.

Organized? Also, yes.

Responsible? Sadly, another boring yes.

But perfect? Never. Not once.

She lay there for a moment, letting it soak in, fighting not to tear up in the face of such a beautiful moment.

"Elio," she whispered, running her fingers along his face, enjoying the roughness of his five-o'clock shadow. Everything about him was so masculine and sexy. Which was why she couldn't believe he was here with her...calling her perfect.

"Back with me?" he murmured. "You looked a little lost in thought."

"I'm here," she said.

"Good. Now pay attention."

She frowned briefly, confused—until he touched her clit.

She reached for his hand, like she had on the rug, and once again he shook it off. "Hands on the pillow, Gianna. You're not finished surrendering."

"I don't think I—"

"You can," he interjected. "And you will."

It took more willpower than she expected to put her hands on the pillow next to her head, her palms up in a way that screamed of submission.

She was glad she'd made the effort when she saw the heated, hungry look in his eyes. "Good girl," he whispered.

Oh fuck. Why was that so hot?

He continued to stroke her clit as he picked up the pace, fucking her harder and harder until her back arched and she screamed.

"Fuck me!" she yelled, the orgasm so strong, it hurt. Everything he did was fierce. Ecstasy.

She never wanted this night to end.

As the climax waned, Elio withdrew, only for as long as it took to flip her over and draw her onto her hands and knees before him. "Grip the spindles of the headboard. Hold on."

She had just closed her fists around the wooden spindles when Elio was there, inside once more, fucking her with complete and utter reckless abandon.

"You're going to come again," he said, the words feeling more like a threat at this point.

"I can't!" she complained. "One more time will kill me."

He chuckled darkly. "No, it won't."

She jerked when he spanked her ass, a stinging swat that caught her off guard. "You're going to come with me, Gianna." He accentuated that point by peppering her ass with a half dozen more smacks.

It was just as good as she'd thought it would be.

She didn't bother to deny his words. At this point, she couldn't. Her body was responding despite her exhaustion, his spanking the extra impetus she needed to reach the peak again.

"I'm close," he said, reaching around to touch her clit. It was far too sensitive, so his first touch flashed hot, an electrical spark that sizzled, burned. She dropped to her elbows, her strength deserting her. The new position only allowed him to go deeper.

She gasped out his name, over and over, as he came with her, his cries mingling with her own.

"Elio! Yes. *God*."

"Jesus. Gianna. Fuck! Never. Felt. So good."

Neither of them moved as the last vestiges of their climaxes rumbled through them. Even after they'd faded completely away, they remained there, locked in place, the only sounds in the room the crackle of the fire and their gasping breaths.

Gianna stirred first; her strength completely gone as she fell facedown into the pillow, their bodies disconnecting. She missed the feeling of him inside her in an instant.

She expected Elio to join her—God, he had to be exhausted too—but he remained where he was, kneeling between her legs.

"Gianna," he said, his voice low.

"Mmm," she hummed.

"Are you on the pill?"

It took a second before her brain engaged enough to understand the question and form an answer. "I was getting the shot. Was due for one in October, but after all the shit that went down with Sam, I didn't bother."

He was quiet.

"El, if you're still worried about before, you were only inside me a few seconds and you didn't come. I'm sure it's fi—"

"The condom broke."

Gianna lay still, trying to let the words sink in. As she did so, she noticed something she hadn't before...the sticky dampness between her legs.

"Oh."

Two minutes earlier, she didn't have enough energy to lift her head, certain she was on the brink of twelve exhausted hours of dreamless sleep. Now, her heart was racing, and she suspected she could run a marathon if asked to.

She pushed herself up, climbing off the mattress. "I'm going to go to the bathroom to clean up," she said, hating how small her voice sounded. Her gaze was locked on the edge of the bed because she was too afraid to look at him, to see Elio's expression. "I might jump up and down a couple thousand times too. Just for good measure." It was a weak joke at best, but God, what could she say?

She grabbed a T-shirt from the dresser next to the bed, pulling it over her head, too aware of her nakedness all of a sudden. She started to walk toward the bathroom, but she didn't manage more than two steps before Elio's hand snaked into view. Before she realized his intent, he'd grasped her wrist, stopping her.

She looked at his hand, wrapped around hers, recalling the way he'd done the same thing when he'd guided hers to his cock.

"Gianna, look at me."

She closed her eyes briefly, his request harder than he realized.

"Look at me," he said again, slowly, almost sternly.

She lifted her eyes to his.

"Go do what you need to do, then come right back here."

"Okay," she said.

"Don't hide in there," he added. "And don't start scrubbing anything."

She barked out a loud, unexpected laugh. "I can't make any promises."

"I'm giving you five minutes. If you're not back, I'm coming to get you."

"I'll be right back."

He released her and she walked to the bathroom, shutting the door. She cleaned herself up as best she could, waiting for the panic attack that should be coming.

It didn't make an appearance.

She stared at her reflection in the mirror, but she didn't recognize the woman looking back. It wasn't that she looked different. It was that she *felt* different.

Before she could consider how, there was a knock at the door. "It's been five minutes."

"I'm done," she replied.

Elio didn't wait. Instead, he opened the door, his gaze locking with hers in the mirror.

"Okay?"

She nodded twice, then stopped, shaking her head once, before stopping again. In the end, she just shrugged.

Elio reached out for her, tugging her into his arms, into one of those warm, caring, amazing Moretti hugs. He'd pulled on his lounge pants, but he was still shirtless, his skin soft against her cheek.

"I love your hugs," she admitted. "They feel so..." She struggled to find the right word. In the end, she landed on the one that felt right for reasons she wasn't sure she could explain. "Safe."

"You *are* safe with me, Gianna. I..."

She waited for him to say more, but he fell silent.

Gianna tightened her grip around his waist. She wasn't sure how, but Elio, a man she'd spent less than forty-eight hours alone with, seemed to understand her on a level she'd never achieved with Sam.

"Come on," he said, wrapping one arm around her waist. "Let's go back to bed. We need to talk."

She followed him, the two of them climbing back into the bed. She attempted to crawl to her side, but Elio gripped her ankle.

"Nope. We're not going back to that your side, my side bullshit again." He lay down on his back, then lifted his arm. "Come here."

She shifted into his embrace, her head pillowed on his shoulder. He wrapped his arm around her, tucking her even closer.

"Have you ever heard the expression 'don't borrow trouble'?" he asked.

She lifted her head, giving him a self-deprecating grin. "I've been a worrier from way back. My grandma used to say it to me all the time. Always said it was pointless to worry about stuff I couldn't fix or change."

"I think I would have liked your grandma," Elio said.

"She would have liked you too. So what are you saying, Elio?"

"I'm saying there's not a damn thing we can do right now to change what happened. Well, I mean, apart from me apologizing for being such a fucking dumbass and not going to get one of the new condoms. I'm so sorry, Gianna."

She shook her head. "I don't need that apology. It was an accident, and it wasn't anybody's fault."

He looked like he wanted to argue that point but didn't. "We're going to be snowed in for at least two, maybe three more days. Nothing we do during that time will change the fact the condom broke. So, here's what I'm proposing...we don't borrow trouble."

"Don't worry about it?" she asked. "You realize that doesn't sound like me at all."

"All I'm asking for is three days, Gianna. When we leave, you'll go home and take a pregnancy test. If it's negative, no harm, no foul. If it's positive, you're going to call me and we're going to figure it out. We'll have all the long conversations and we'll come up with a plan. Together."

"Together?" She hated the way her voice cracked on the word. She'd spent the last few months feeling very alone and lonely. The idea of having someone to go through any part of her life with felt like a gift.

Elio scowled. "Of course, together. You and me. We're going to figure it all out. I'd never leave you to do this alone."

She knew that. Knew it all the way to her bones. It was why his hugs felt so safe.

"So we just go on like normal while we're here?"

He nodded. "Except for one thing. We're not cleaning the fucking cabin. Not scrubbing the floors, the toilet, the sinks, or the windows. None of that."

She laughed, then pointed upward. "Those ceiling fans are coated in a layer of dust. All I need is a ladder and five min—"

"No cleaning," he stressed, smiling.

"How else am I supposed to shut my brain down, push the worries away?" She'd intended the question to sound like a joke, but it came out too sincere, too serious.

Elio never missed a beat. "I'm going to distract you."

"How?"

He kissed her forehead. "It's a surprise. I'll tell you tomorrow."

"In other words, you don't know."

He chuckled. "I have all night to figure out something that doesn't require me using a mop."

She sighed, surprisingly content—happy even—then rested her head back on his shoulder. The two of them lay there in the silence so long, she thought perhaps he'd fallen asleep.

"Elio," she whispered.

"Yeah."

"Up until that twist ending, tonight was one of the best nights of my life."

Elio cupped her cheek, lifting her face up to look at his. "Mine too."

She read the sincerity, and it warmed her all the way through, touching the places that had been damp and cold since Sam told her he didn't love her anymore.

"Good night, Elio," she whispered.

"'Night, Gianna."

Chapter Eight

Elio grinned as he opened his eyes, forced to admit this was probably the greatest way to start the day. Gianna had twisted away from him at some point in the night so that he was now spooning her, one of his arms wrapped around her, his hand cupping her breast.

He lay there for several minutes, listening to the soft, gentle sound of her breathing. He was just a few short weeks away from thirty-one and he'd never woken up with a woman in his arms. Now he was on day two of waking up with Gianna and—dammit—he was starting to realize he'd been depriving himself all these years.

His one-night stands had always been about sex. Sleeping never played a role in that. Paula had asked him to stay one night after they'd had sex, telling him it was too late to be on the road. He hadn't even considered the invitation, getting dressed and using one of his countless standard excuses for leaving.

Paula had always taken his middle-of-the-night departures in stride, but that night, she'd pushed back, getting angry with him, proclaiming he was in no danger of catching feelings if he spent one damn night in her bed. She'd accompanied the complaint with her so-called "teasing" nickname for him—Tin Man.

When he'd reminded her that he wasn't looking for more than sex—something she'd claimed repeatedly to be okay with—he suggested they call it quits. And that was when she had backpedaled fast, claiming she was tired and talking nonsense. She hadn't asked him to stay the night again after that, but things still ended a few weeks later. Because Elio knew she wasn't happy, just as he knew he couldn't give her what she wanted.

Now Elio considered Gianna...wondering, had they indulged in a one-night stand, one where he could have gotten in his car and driven away, if he would have gone home last night.

Something told him even if there'd been no snow, nothing to stop him from doing his usual cut and run, he'd still be in bed with this woman wrapped up in his arms.

Gianna sighed in her sleep, snuggling closer. Her ass brushed his crotch. Mr. Morning Wood made a rapid appearance. The sun streamed brightly in the front window. They'd slept much later today than yesterday, which stood to reason, given their very late night.

Elio lay there, replaying the evening from beginning to end. Gianna had been a goddamn revelation—sexy innocence and a passionate wildcat, all rolled into one. There was a dull pain in his chest where she'd bitten him, and the scratches she'd left on his back still stung. The sex had been hot as fuck, and all he could think about was how much he wanted a repeat.

But he wasn't sure Gianna would be willing.

Perhaps she would have agreed before the condom broke, but now, knowing her penchant for worrying, she likely wouldn't want to tempt fate again.

His promise to her last night had been sincere. If she was pregnant, there was no way he wasn't going to be right there with her, every step of the way.

Jesus.

If she's pregnant.

Those words kept rolling around in his head, and while they were sticking, they weren't producing the right response.

Maybe he was still drunk. Because that was the only way he could explain to himself why he wasn't freaking the fuck out.

After they'd both come, Gianna had fallen facedown on the bed, exhausted after too many orgasms, and his cock had slipped out. He'd reached down to pull the condom off...and that was the moment when the bottom *should have* fallen out. Not only on the night but on his whole goddamn life. Because marriage and kids weren't something he'd ever thought about. There hadn't been time. He'd been too focused on hockey, the game, the records. He loved his career to the exclusion of everything else. So much so, he'd missed over a decade of family time, and he'd never given his heart to any woman because his was already spoken for, claimed by hockey when he was just a young boy.

Now there was a chance he'd gotten Gianna Duncan pregnant.

So why wasn't his heart racing, his chest tight? Why wasn't he panicking, swearing off sex forever, making deals with God to get him out of this?

None of that was happening. Not now, and not even last night when he'd calmly asked her about birth control, then talked her off the ledge.

Though, in hindsight, he didn't think she'd been on any ledge because he hadn't sensed a great deal of anxiety in Gianna either.

When he'd walked into the bathroom, he'd expected to find her sobbing, devastated, terrified, not standing calmly in front of the mirror. He'd gone in there ready to offer comfort, a shoulder to cry on.

Hell, he probably should have been shedding a few tears of his own.

Instead, they'd hugged, crawled back into bed, and then he'd pushed off the "what-if" conversation, proclaiming they could have it after they knew for sure.

Elio suspected that probably wasn't the smartest decision. This was a big fucking deal, so they should definitely sit down and spend some serious time talking about it. He'd initially pushed it off because they'd still been under the effects of the tequila. He could broach the subject today.

But he wouldn't.

Because what he'd thought last night, and what he was still thinking today, was so fucking foreign to him, he couldn't make peace with it...

If she was pregnant, he wanted to marry her.

Wanted to marry a woman he barely knew after spending two nights stuck in a cabin with her.

Those words had been on the tip of his tongue when he'd hugged her in the bathroom, and they were the reason why he'd shut up so quick.

He'd figured sober Elio would come to his senses.

He hadn't. Which meant he wasn't talking about what happened last night until he'd gotten the hell back home and managed to get his head screwed back on straight.

Gianna stirred again, and he recognized the moment she woke up. She stiffened slightly in his arms, then, to his delight, she went soft once more. He gave her breast a squeeze to let her know he was awake too.

"Good morning," she said, her voice husky with sleep as she turned over to face him.

He smiled, then moved forward, giving her a quick kiss. Her brow creased, with confusion or surprise. Had she expected him to stop touching her? Kissing her?

God, he hoped not.

"How's your head?" he asked, wondering if she was hungover.

"Fine. I think we burned off most of the alcohol before we fell asleep. Nothing like orgasms and panic to sober a body up."

Elio got hung up on the word *panic*.

"Are you panicking?" he asked.

She considered that, then shook her head. "No. Which is weird because I should be."

"I feel the same way. Feeling the urge to clean the entire cabin?"

She gave him an adorable grin. "Nope. Not yet anyway. Ask me again after a cup of coffee."

They lay there for a few minutes, neither in a hurry to get out of bed.

Gianna was the first to break the silence. "So, you're going to have to explain the morning-after protocol for one-night stands. Does it involve breakfast? Awkward conversation?"

Elio shrugged one shoulder. "We're going to have to figure it out together because I've never done a morning after."

She waited for a moment, perhaps expecting him to add a "just kidding" to his pronouncement. He didn't.

"You know, you keep saying you've never spent the night with a woman, but I find it very hard to believe," she admitted.

"I'm not sure why. It's exactly as I said. Sex is sex and sleeping is sleeping. I've never found a reason to mix the two."

He watched as she tried to let the dust settle on that information.

"Okay. Well, I guess we'll just play it by ear." She glanced over his shoulder to the window. "The snow stopped but looks like the wind has picked up. Looks cold as shit out there."

She was clearly thinking he wanted to break out of here like a bat out of hell. After all, wasn't that what he'd admitted to always doing?

"We're definitely not leaving today. And probably not tomorrow either. I'm going to have to call my coach later and break the news I'll be a couple days later getting back than expected. You okay with being stuck here with me a bit longer?"

She nodded. "Yeah. Because you promised to distract me." Gianna shifted a bit closer, letting the duvet slip lower. She'd put a T-shirt on after the condom incident but no panties, no pajama bottoms. And since the shirt was riding up, he was able to see her stomach. An inch or two more, and he'd have a good view of the top of her pussy. His fingers itched to push the covers down.

He pushed that thought away, his eyes lifting to meet hers. Elio studied her face, certain there was no way he was seeing what he thought he was. But the mischievous twinkle in her eye told the tale. She was flirting with him, and she knew exactly where'd he'd been looking and what he'd been thinking.

"You're right," he said, his voice deep with the desire to take her again. "I did make that promise."

She shook her head, gripping the covers to pull them up, as if suddenly aware of what she'd just done. "God. I shouldn't still be horny, right? I mean, for one thing, that was a fuck-ton of orgasms. And for another, the condom broke, so you would think my girl parts would be all 'hell no'."

Elio didn't interrupt her, let her continue her adorable rambling.

"Maybe I'm still drunk?" she pondered. "Maybe that's why I'm not freaking out." She paused, looking at him, waiting for some sort of response.

"I'm sorry, what?" he joked. "I stopped listening after horny."

"Idiot," she teased, punching him on the shoulder before attempting to rise, intent on getting out of bed.

Elio shifted closer, wrapping his arm around her waist, unwilling to let her go just yet. "I'm sober as a stone, and you are too. I don't know why we're not freaking out, but I'm happy to roll with it."

"Speaking of stone," she said, her cheeks flushing as her gaze drifted to regions south. "I'm getting poked."

Elio wiggled his eyebrows suggestively. "Morning wood. It's a fact of life when you're a guy."

"So...what are you going to do with it? Leave it alone or..."

Elio's cock thickened even more. "I suppose that depends on you."

"Me?"

He gave her a wicked grin. "You have first right of refusal."

She laughed. "Oh my God. You can't seriously want to have sex with me again after last night."

Elio didn't laugh. Because it wasn't funny. "Gianna, I want you so much right now, I can't see straight."

"You do?"

He nodded.

"So...this would be morning-after-a-one-night-stand sex?"

Elio didn't like that label any more than her thinking that last night was a one-off. Maybe that had been his initial intention, but somewhere in the midst of it all, he'd known all the way to the depths of his soul that one night with her wouldn't be enough. "It can be whatever we want it to be. Gianna, the ball is in your court. *I'd* like to continue this affair for as long as we're here, but if you don't want that, say the word, and we go back to snowed-in friends, doing puzzles and hanging out. I promise you, I'm cool with whatever you decide."

Gianna was a thinker, and he respected that. Especially now. She was the one with no experience when it came to casual sex, so she was the one who was going to have to figure out if a short-term affair was something she wanted.

"I really want to have sex with you again. But do we have to stick to the standards? I'd like to try some of the kinky stuff too."

Elio was torn between laughing and flipping Gianna over his lap to give her exactly what she asked for. He was dying to spank her perky little ass again.

"Don't move." He climbed out of bed, sprinted across the chilly hardwood floor, and picked up his entire duffel bag.

Gianna sat up, grinning as he carried it over to a chair near the bed. He rifled through it until he found what he was looking for. He tossed the box of condoms on the bed, amused when she picked it up to study it.

"Only twelve?" she complained.

She was going to be the death of him. And he couldn't wait to put his life in her hands.

He started back toward the bed, but she held up her finger, stopping him. "You still haven't unpacked."

He jumped onto the mattress, and she giggled as she bounced. "You can help me do that later. After I spank you. I specifically told you not to move."

Her eyes widened, but there was no denying she wanted what he offered.

Elio grasped the hem of her T-shirt and pulled it over her head, so she was naked in an instant.

"Your turn," she said, reaching for the waistband of his lounge pants. He shoved them away.

"Always so impatient." He gave her a quick, hard kiss, then before she could react, he twisted her, pushing her facedown on the mattress.

She tried to push back up, but only until the first slap landed on her ass.

"Ouch," she said, but there wasn't a hint of pain in her tone.

He spanked her again, just twice, before squeezing her ass cheek, adding pressure to the heat.

"Why does that feel so good?" Gianna murmured, though her question was clearly rhetorical.

He spanked her again, her ass turning the same delightful pink of her cheeks whenever she blushed.

She groaned when he lowered his head and nipped at her ass. Gianna tried to skitter away playfully, but he tightened his grip, holding her in place. He spanked her again, but this time he didn't pause, didn't give her time to adjust.

Soon, Gianna's hips were rising to meet each slap.

"Please," she gasped at last.

Elio rose briefly so that he could push his lounge pants off. Gianna remained on her stomach in the middle of the bed, watching him out of the corner of her eye.

She started to push up, but when he shook his head, she dropped back down. "Stay just like that. Let me look at you."

She wiggled her ass impishly, and he gave her one last spank because he couldn't resist. Then, he grabbed a condom from the box, wishing he'd sprung for the jumbo thirty-six pack. Something told him he'd be hard-pressed to limit himself to just twelve more times with Gianna. He rolled the condom on and sent a silent prayer to the gods that this one didn't break. Then he climbed on the bed, kneeling between her legs.

He gripped his dick and ran it along her slit, from clit to ass. He grinned to himself when he recalled her wanting everything except the "butt stuff." He was tempted to try to change her mind about that.

Fuck it. He was definitely going to change her mind on that.

Gianna kept trying to catch him, to force him inside every time he got close to her opening, but he shifted away, simply stroking the wet heat. She pleaded, then threatened, then cursed, but he didn't give in. He liked playing with her, liked her breathlessness, her pink cheeks—ass *and* face—and the way she never held back her emotions, sharing them with him through words, adorable squeaks, and expressions.

She was an open book, one that he didn't want to stop reading.

"Roll over, Gianna," he said at last, when his teasing was becoming too painful even for him. "I want to see your pretty face when I slide inside you."

She shifted, wincing slightly when her sore ass hit the mattress. He grasped her thighs, parting then lifting them until the back of her knees rested on his shoulders.

She reached down, gripping his cock, guiding it to her opening. "Please don't tease me anymore. I want you inside me."

"You still want to feel it?" Her request last evening had caught him off guard. She'd offered nothing but open honesty as she asked for exactly what she wanted.

He'd started to press her about her "until" comment...but stopped when he became aware that he didn't want to hear the response.

What if she wanted to feel it *until* she fell in love with someone else? *Until* she met the one? *Until* she found the man who could make her forget all about her cheating ex...and him?

He hadn't asked what it meant because he didn't want to imagine any of those possibilities.

"Yes," she breathed. "Please."

He thrust into the hilt as Gianna cried out his name.

"Elio!"

He gave her only a second or two to adjust. It was all the time he could spare before he fucked her in earnest. She felt like heaven on earth.

Like she was made for him.

Elio shoved that thought out of his head. Stress about his looming decision was clearly causing him to crack up. That, combined with the fact all his relatives and buddies were walking around with damn hearts in their eyes, was screwing with his head.

He wasn't this guy. Wasn't the type to fall for a woman in a matter of days.

He wasn't the type to fall at all.

It had to be the work situation. He was frantically seeking for something to latch onto because once hockey was gone, he was a man without a country.

Then he looked at her and realized that wasn't true. Because here he was, pounding into Gianna's body like a man possessed, on the brink of coming and knowing that two seconds after his release, he'd want her—need her—*again*.

He touched her clit, and Gianna came almost instantly. He slowed down, only so that he could observe her, watch the myriad of emotions that flashed across her face, in her eyes.

"Holy fuck," she gasped. "So good! El...God...El. Please tell me the condom didn't break."

He knew it hadn't, but he withdrew so that she could see for herself. "All good. So what do you say we get serious now?"

She lay beneath him, her body flushed, a light sheen of sweat shimmering on her skin. Her chest was rising and falling rapidly, and despite it all, her eyes lit up with desire. "Oh good. I was afraid we were just going to do missionary again."

Elio barked out a loud laugh. She was hilarious. She made sex fun, which was a novel experience for him. He grasped her hand, drawing her out of the bed. "Okay, kinky girl. Feet on the floor, bend over the mattress," he directed.

"That sounds a lot like doggie style," she teased, even as she did what he'd demanded. Her cheekiness earned her another spanking, this one with a bit more bite. He wanted to prove to himself that what he'd suspected last night was true. Gianna liked her pleasure laced with pain.

She glanced over her shoulder, looking at him with the sexiest bedroom eyes he'd ever seen. "More."

He shook his head, then pushed two fingers inside her wet pussy.

"Oh!" she said, with a hint of surprise in her voice. She'd expected him to get right back down to business, given how hard his cock was. It was throbbing and making some of its own demands, but he was nowhere near finished with Gianna.

He coated his fingers with her arousal, slowly fucking her, building her desires back up until she was gasping for air. She shuddered when he finally pulled them out.

Then she jerked when he pressed the tip of one to her anus.

"Elio," she said. "I thought—"

"Shhhh. Just a finger. You dismissed the *butt stuff* too quickly." He didn't bother to hide the amusement in his voice as he used her terminology, his grin growing when she shot him a dirty look over her shoulder.

"If it hurts—" she started.

"You say so, and I stop. There's no point of no return, Gee. Everything we do should bring us both pleasure. If it doesn't, it's off the table. Okay?"

She nodded, her features smoothing out until she looked like a woman without a care in the world.

Trust.

Gianna trusted him.

It felt good, made him want to make sure he didn't do anything to lose it.

Elio chastised himself for yet another wayward thought. Too

much more of this mushy-gushy shit and he'd start composing poetry for her.

He pushed his finger into her to the first knuckle, then went for broke and started working it all the way in, with a slow in-and-out motion, going deeper with each return.

Gianna's head hung low, the weight of her upper body supported by her forearms on the bed.

Once his finger was fully lodged, he stopped. "You like it? Want more?"

She nodded.

"Let me hear you say the words, Gianna. Ask me."

"You were right. I like it. I want you to..." She was shy about asking for what she wanted. The way she hesitated and blushed was endearing.

"Yes?" he asked, deliberately being obtuse.

She groaned. "God. I want you to do the butt stuff, okay? But just your finger," she added.

He chuckled. "As you wish."

Elio thrust the single finger in and out, and within seconds, Gianna was adding to the motion, moving in time.

On one forward motion, he added more fuel to the fire, lining his cock up and pushing it back into her pussy as his finger continued to breach her ass.

Gianna started to fall forward, surprised by the dual penetration and looking to escape, but he was ready, prepared. He used his free hand to grip her shoulder. To hold her in place as he fucked her roughly.

Her orgasm built back up quickly and while he wanted to draw this out, wanted to hold off as long as he could, there was no way Gianna wasn't taking him down with her this time.

She let out a high, keening cry, her pussy muscles clenching around him until he saw stars. His balls tightened and then he was there, calling out her name along with every religious deity he knew of, collapsing against her.

Now, like last night, neither of them sought to separate for a few minutes, both too starved for air, for strength.

Finally, he forced himself to stand up and withdraw.

She didn't lift her head from the mattress. "Still good?"

He knew what she was referring to. "The condom held."

Elio crossed to the bathroom to throw it away, then he walked back to the open doorway. Gianna remained where he'd left her.

"Wanna get a shower with me?" he asked.

For a woman who appeared to be on the verge of sleep, his invitation woke her up quickly.

She pushed up off the bed. "Yeah. Sure."

Elio gave her a quick smack on the ass when she walked by him to enter the bathroom. "Then how about we make some breakfast and discuss our plans for the day?"

"Can I suggest today's theme?" she asked.

"Sure. What do you have in mind?"

She gave him the sexiest smile he'd ever seen. "I think we should dub today Wild and Wicked Wednesday."

He shook his head. "No. I think we're going to make that the overall theme. Wild and Wicked Week."

"Oh, hell yeah," she breathed. "The whole week."

And just like that...he was rock hard again.

Elio stretched out on his back on the bearskin rug, naked as the day he was born, staring at the ceiling, more relaxed than he'd ever been in his life. Gianna, also nude, was lying next to him but in the opposite direction, her knees by his shoulders, her head next to his thighs.

The entire day played over in his head. When Gianna made a plan, she fucking made a *plan*.

After their sexy shower—where they'd taken turns scrubbing each other—and breakfast, he'd lifted her up onto the kitchen table, eating her for dessert before they used condom number two.

And while he hadn't wanted to leave the warmth of the cabin, he'd suggested they shovel more snow because it was either that or remain trapped in the cabin until first thaw. Which didn't sound as bad as he might have expected.

The snow had stopped coming down, but the wind had blown hard enough throughout the night to cover the paths they'd dug out yesterday with deep drifts. They'd spent a good three hours redoing a lot of what they'd done the day before.

When Gianna declared her arms "officially Jell-O," they'd returned to the cabin for hot cocoa and some downtime, working on the puzzle.

Puzzle time ended when Gianna had dropped to her knees, crawled around the coffee table, reached into his jeans, pulled out his very interested, very erect cock, and took him into her mouth.

She'd intended to give him a blow job, but Elio had recalled her comment about her past attempts at sixty-nine being "awkward." He'd decided to show her how that position was done. He'd stripped off the rest of his clothing, then hers, before pushing her to her back. She took his dick back into her mouth, unaware of his plans until he shifted his body the opposite direction. Elio had fucked her with his tongue and teeth, driving her to her orgasm, slowly, with lots of teasing intermingled with rough touches. Throughout it all, she gave him the blow job of the century. It was so good, he feared he'd climax before her. He hadn't, but it had been a close call.

After they'd both come, they had fallen to the floor, in these positions, and neither of them had moved or spoken since.

"You still with me?" he asked at last, curious if she'd fallen asleep.

"Yeah," she said softly.

"Still think sixty-nine is awkward?" He reached out and linked his fingers with her, overwhelmed with the need to touch her.

She laughed in reply. "Not even a little bit. I must admit, there's something to be said for having sex with an experienced lover. Sam and I learned about sex with each other, both of us virgins. I'm starting to understand..."

Her words drifted away, and he realized that he hadn't been the only one lost in thought as they'd lain there. Elio sat up, then used his grip on her hand to pull her up as well.

"You understand what?" he pressed.

"Maybe Sam realized there was something missing in our relationship. Something we wouldn't ever find together."

"Are you trying to make excuses for that asshole cheating on you?" Elio's temper flared at the idea of her defending Sam for anything.

"Jesus Christ, no. That's not what I meant. I was just lying here thinking how young we were when we first fell in love, then we hung on to it because it was safe and easy. We never had to risk being alone or lonely because we had each other. What if Sam figured out that wasn't enough?"

Elio shook his head. "You're giving him too much credit, Gee. Guys don't think that fucking hard. Trust me, Sam wasn't suffering from any deep introspection over your relationship. Twenty bucks says Emma walked by, he flirted, she flirted back, he got flattered *and* hard, and then...he made a bad fucking decision."

"It *was* a bad decision," she agreed. "Cheating is a shitty way to go about breaking things off, but what if he knew our relationship wasn't working, and he was hoping to find something... someone...bet—?"

"Don't say better," he interjected, certain that was where her thoughts were headed. "Or I'll get very pissed off."

She gave him a guilty smile. "Someone else," she amended.

He cupped her cheek affectionately, hating the sadness he saw lingering in her eyes. "The reason he slept with someone else doesn't matter. Unless...does it matter to you? Do you need to assign some sort of reason to this? Some explanation?"

She shrugged. "I don't know. Maybe it would be easier if I could understand why he would throw away what we had."

"All you need to understand is that he lost you, Freckles. Trust me when I say it was the worst decision of his life, and he's going to figure that out somewhere down the line."

Gianna looked doubtful, and it bothered Elio. Because he wasn't sure her thoughts were taking her down a smart path.

"Gianna, you're beautiful and intelligent and funny. He's going to wake up one day and realize just how stupid he was."

Gianna smiled. "You're good for the soul, Elio. I don't want you to think that I'm lacking self-confidence or anything. It's just taken a bit of a beating the last few months and I'm struggling to build it back up."

"We'll add that to our to-do list for the rest of this week."

She laughed, leaning forward to give him a very sweet kiss that was too short in his opinion.

He considered wrapping his arms around her shoulders and expanding on it, but this conversation didn't feel finished. There was something uncomfortable kicking around in the back of his brain that he couldn't dismiss.

"So," Elio said, "when Sam figures it out and comes crawling back—"

"He won't," she interrupted.

He held up one finger and forged on. "Are you taking him back?"

"No," she said hastily.

He shook his head. "Don't answer that quickly. You're a thinker, Gee, so think about this."

She fell silent, and he could tell his words had landed, that they were having an impact.

"Eleven years is a long time," she said quietly. "He wasn't just my boyfriend. He was my best friend."

"Is that the answer?"

She shook her head. "No. Just the facts."

"Do you think you could forgive him for cheating on you?"

This time, she took her time before responding. "No."

Elio wasn't completely satisfied with that answer because of her hesitation. He wasn't entirely sure it was the truth. He considered pushing her on it, but no matter what they said here, if—when—the day came that Sam walked back into her life, the decision to forgive him was Gianna's and Gianna's alone.

And, for some reason he couldn't fully explain, he hated that.

Chapter Nine

Gianna sighed and snuggled deeper into the pillow, keeping her eyes closed against the ever-brightening sun. She wasn't ready to wake up yet. The bed was so soft and warm, she considered staying there all day.

Yeah, she thought. *I'm staying in bed because it's warm, and not because of Elio.*

Last night, after a sixty-nine that was a thousand miles away from awkward, they'd lain in front of the fire for hours, just talking. It felt strange to Gianna that as little as a week ago, Elio had been nothing more than an acquaintance who occasionally traveled in the same social circle she did. He'd been one of Liza's big brothers, the one she rarely saw.

She wasn't sure if it was the forced proximity or the fact she'd been basically living alone for a few months with only herself for company, but she found him easier to talk to than his sister, in some ways. And Liza was one of her very best friends.

Gianna appreciated his guy's perspective on the Sam situation, though she'd made a promise to herself that she was NOT going to talk about her ex anymore.

For one thing, what guy wanted to hear about a woman's ex-boyfriend right after they'd had sex? She'd been kicking herself for starting the conversation at all.

Not that Elio had seemed bothered by it. The reason they'd talked about Sam as long as they had was because he'd kept asking her questions. Of course, it stood to reason that Elio wouldn't mind the topic. It wasn't like the two of them were embarking on anything that would last longer than this week.

Her first casual affair.

She was a fan.

The other reason she wasn't going to mention Sam again was because she didn't want to give Elio the impression she was still hung up on her ex. Because in truth, she wasn't. Or at least she wasn't anymore.

Before this week, Gianna had been looking at the world through a very narrow lens, certain she'd never find what she and Sam had shared with someone else. But these past few days with Elio had been every bit as comfortable and easy and fun as her previous relationship had been in the beginning.

Lightning *could* strike twice. So she was going to do what Liza had demanded of her at the holiday party. She was waving goodbye to Sam through the rearview mirror, and she was putting herself out there. If that meant drudging through the online dating sites until she found the one, then so be it.

She stretched her arm across the mattress, wondering if Elio was still asleep and if she could entice him into expanding on their wild and wicked week. There were still some things she wanted to try—mainly the toys she'd brought with her—and time was running out.

Her eyes flew open when she realized the bed was empty, Elio's side cold enough that it was clear he hadn't been there for a while.

She sat up just as the door to the cabin opened.

Elio walked in with an armload of wood, grinning when he saw her. "Morning, sleepyhead. Talk about a sound sleep. I was planning to put a mirror under your nose to see if you were still breathing."

"How long have you been up?"

"Long enough to plan our day for us."

Gianna thought Elio had just been humoring her when they'd made the new menu, and then the first day's plans, but since then, she'd gotten the sense he liked knowing what the day was going to bring as much as she did.

"Oh yeah?" she asked, a little disappointed as she really *had* wanted to convince him to go into overtime on the sexcapades.

"Yep. Thought New Year's Eve needed a special theme, so today is Throwback Thursday."

She'd forgotten it was New Year's Eve. She'd been dreading the holiday a week ago, aware that for the first time ever, she'd have no one to kiss at midnight. Now that no longer seemed to be a danger. "What does Throwback Thursday involve?"

"If you can pull yourself from that bed," Elio said, as he placed the wood in the box by the fire before throwing one of the logs onto the dying embers, "I'll tell you all about it while I make you Margaret Moretti's world-famous Poconos breakfast."

Gianna's stomach chose that moment to growl, and she recalled that they'd eschewed dinner last night, pigging out on chips and dip and Doritos and Oreos. "Oooo. I am hungry. World famous, huh?"

"Yep. I brought part of the ingredients, but—"

"Forgot some," they both said in unison.

Elio chuckled. "I remembered the ingredients for the pancake mix but not the syrup. This morning, I was digging around in the cabinet and found an unopened bottle of maple syrup."

"That sounds wonderful." Gianna climbed out of the bed, reaching into the drawer for clean clothes. She and Elio had adopted a naked sleeping arrangement ever since tequila night.

She shivered when he wrapped his arms around her from behind, taking her by surprise.

"Oh my God." She tried to bat his arms away, but Elio just tightened his grip. "You're freezing."

"That's why I'm holding onto you. You're going to warm me up."

Gianna continued to struggle, squealing when he cupped her breasts with icy hands. She tried to pull them away, calling him every name in the book, but Elio, mischievous from the word go, enjoyed teasing her too much.

Or at least, that was how it started. When he pinched her nipples with that perfect amount of pressure, she became less aware of his cold hands, and more aware of the heat growing in her body.

"Turn around, Freckles. I need my good-morning kiss. Figure we should spend as much time as possible practicing for midnight." He loosened his hold enough that she could spin within his embrace, his lips right there, ready to claim hers.

She wrapped her arms around his waist, his jacket chilly from the outside air too. Not that she cared about that anymore.

"Come back to bed," she invited him. "And I'll warm you up for real."

She could feel Elio's erection, straining against the denim of his jeans, against her stomach, so she was surprised when he didn't take her up on it.

"I have a better idea. Crawl in and wait for me. I need to grab something."

After his frosty hug, he didn't have to ask her twice. She dove beneath the duvet, then watched as he walked back to the front door. There were several hooks on that front wall, from which hung an assortment of scarves and old coats. Beneath it was a basket overflowing with hats and gloves.

Elio grabbed several of the scarves before returning to the bed. "I'm not sure we fully explored as much as we could have yesterday."

Gianna fought to restrain a laugh. She and Elio shared the same one-track mind. At least where this week was concerned.

She'd never been this...well...wanton. This unrestrained. For the first time in her life, she was going off the Gianna script. She wasn't overthinking, wasn't worrying, wasn't questioning every little thing.

Nope.

For this one short, magical week, she was going to do exactly what she wanted without worrying about what came after.

Elio was a no-strings-attached guy. Hell, he'd admitted to breaking things off with Paula, the closest thing he'd ever had to a girlfriend—though he would argue that terminology—because she'd wanted him to spend the night.

All he was offering was here and now, which made it easier for her. She didn't have to worry about what came next because... nothing did.

For a second, she wondered what kind of relationship they would forge if she was pregnant, but she shoved that thought away. Every single time the memory of the condom breaking flashed through her mind, she shut it down because Elio was right. There was nothing they could do to change it.

So if she went home, took a test, and discovered she was pregnant, THEN the two of them could sit down and decide their next step. Until that time, she was treating this as exactly what it was...a break from real life, one that was going to end come Saturday morning, if the weather kept improving the way it had been.

Elio placed a knee on the edge of the mattress, twirling the end of one of the scarves in a way that screamed playful as much as threatening.

"I'm going to tie you up, Gianna."

Her pussy clenched and before she could consider her actions, she lifted her arms, sliding them along the pillow until she offered him that surrender pose that never failed to have his eyes going dark with desire.

Elio chuckled. "Wow. Really putting up a fight, aren't you?"

He was so funny, so easy to be with.

Since she'd given her consent, he didn't bother to draw things out. One second, she was free; the next, he'd bound her wrists together before securing them to the headboard. She tested the bonds, curious if his knots were for show or for real. The scarves held.

Elio noticed her slight struggle. "If you decide you don't like it, all you have to do is say 'untie me'."

"I know that." This wasn't the first time he'd offered that reassurance, but she didn't need it.

While they might not have known each other personally before now, she felt like she knew him well enough simply through Liza's comments. Liza had spent the entire decade of their friendship telling Gianna countless stories about her brothers and cousins and all the times they'd gone out of their way to stand up for others.

More than that, Gianna had witnessed those same actions herself. She considered the way Tony Moretti and his roommate, Rhys, had taken Jess in when she'd been homeless, giving her and her adorable son, Jasper, a safe place to stay when they needed it most. She recalled Keeley telling her about the night her parents had been killed in a plane crash, how Gio and Rafe had helped her and Kayden through their grief that night and in the weeks and months that followed.

Gianna had come to understand that the Moretti men were born protectors, kind, considerate all the way to the core.

With that promise out of the way, Elio got down to the good stuff. While he'd shed his jacket and boots when grabbing the scarves, he hadn't taken anything else off. It felt strangely sexy to be lying beneath him, naked, while he remained completely dressed.

Elio lowered his head, giving her a kiss that ensured whatever lingering chill remained was burned away in an instant. His tongue found hers as he cupped her cheeks, holding her still, making it perfectly clear that he was in control.

After several minutes, Elio broke the kiss, shifting farther down her body, his tongue exploring all the other pertinent parts. He sucked her nipples into his mouth, placed hot kisses on her stomach, then—sweet Jesus—he gave her the kiss she really wanted.

Elio didn't have any reservations about going down on her...at all. She sent up a silent prayer that was true of most men, because it was quickly becoming her favorite thing ever. She'd originally planned to create a new Life Goals list while here at the cabin, but instead, she'd found herself composing a different one in her head.

One she'd tentatively titled Things My Future Boyfriend Has to Do in Bed.

Elio pressed the flat of his tongue against her clit, wiggling it in a way that made her see stars.

Aaaaand that particular move had just claimed the top spot on her sex list.

Elio knew exactly how important her clit was to her arousal, and he used that information to his advantage in spectacular fashion. She tugged at the scarves around her wrists, not because she wanted freedom but because it drove home just how helpless she was to his ministrations, and it made her so much hotter.

He played with her for hours—days, years—sucking, licking, stroking, biting. Everything he did felt amazing, but none of it was enough to push her over the edge. And he knew it.

"Goddammit, Elio!" she cried out, not for the first time, when he pulled away...just before she could jump over the cliff.

He'd ignored every curse, every plea, every dirty name she'd called him, but this time he lifted his head.

She expected him to look pleased with himself, for some of that cocky swagger of his to emerge. What she didn't anticipate was the almost aggressive look in his eyes.

"Who do you belong to, Gianna?"

Fuck. Hottest question ever.

Her voice was rough, hoarse even, from her groans, her moans, her cries of sexual frustration. Regardless, she gave him what he asked for, aware nothing she'd said had ever felt truer.

"Yours," she whispered. "I belong to you."

He frowned for a split second, the expression one she couldn't read. Was he confused? Angry?

Had she given him the wrong answer?

The look was there in a flash, then gone again, wiped away by the slow, sexy smile that spread across his face. She didn't have more than a moment to acknowledge it before her eyes closed, blinded by the powerful orgasm that struck as Elio slammed two fingers inside her, crooking them against her G-spot.

"Ahhhhh!" she screamed, her back arching, her body trembling roughly as a million currents of electricity raced through her.

Elio continued to thrust in and out, giving her no chance to land, to recover.

She was hurtling through space, and gravity had no intention of letting her go.

"Jesus," she heard Elio mutter, when he finally began to slow his pace. "You are the sexiest woman I've ever fucking seen."

His words soaked in deep. Liza called Elio a player, but when he said things like that...she believed him. Perhaps it was her inexperience that had her falling for what could very well be his standard lines, but she genuinely didn't think so. Elio didn't strike her as the type of man to offer false compliments just to get laid.

"Good for the soul," she whispered, repeating what she'd said last night, meaning it with all her heart.

Elio didn't respond. Instead, he rose from the bed, stripped off his clothes, untied the scarves around her wrists, then crawled on top of her. Slipping on a condom, he pushed into her pussy, one long, slow, deep slide. Buried to the hilt, he gave her a passionate kiss.

"Mine," he murmured, his lips still touching hers, so she felt the word as well as heard it.

Then, he proved exactly how much.

· · ·

Gianna pushed her plate away with a groan. "I can't eat another bite."

They'd dozed in bed an hour after the last orgasm faded away, so that their breakfast was more accurately lunch.

Elio had mastered his mother's recipe, and the two of them had gluttonously worked their way through a huge plateful of pancakes.

"Time to work off those calories," Elio said, after dropping their plates into the sink.

"Oooo," she purred. "What did you have in mind?"

Elio tapped her under the chin with his finger. "Not that, you sex maniac. What size shoe do you wear?"

She frowned at the question. "Um...an eight. Why?"

Elio walked to a large trunk under the front window, opening it. "We're in luck. Liza wears the same size."

She shook her head when he produced a pair of ice skates. "Hell no."

"What?" he asked, aghast. "You don't like skating?"

"It's not a question of liking it. I've never done it. Never been compelled to risk broken bones or slashed skin by strapping on knife shoes."

"Knife shoes?" Elio repeated, laughing.

"Shoes with a sharp blade. What would *you* call them?"

Elio ignored her complaints as he tugged another pair of skates from the trunk, looking at them fondly. "Damn. I haven't worn these in years."

He placed the skates near the door, then took her hand, guiding her to the dresser before opening the drawer. He rifled through her belongings, pulling out the pair of long johns Liza had loaned her—declaring she'd want them if she decided to take a hike—as well as a thick cable-knit sweater, jeans, and a couple more pairs of socks.

"You're going to want to layer up. It's cold as a witch's tit out there."

"I'm not ice skating," she repeated. "I'm clumsy *barefoot.*

117

There's no way in hell I can stand up on that thin blade on ice. No way, no how."

"I won't let you fall," he reassured her.

"You aren't listening to me."

Elio gave her a kiss on the cheek. "You're right. I'm not. Now get dressed." He walked around the bed to his duffel bag, pulling out extra layers for himself.

Gianna didn't even bother continuing the fight because one, she wasn't going to win, and two, he was basically guaranteeing she'd be wrapped up in his arms for the next hour or two.

"If I do this, you owe me."

Elio brightened up. "Oh yeah? I think I like the sound of that."

"You don't know what I'm going to ask for," she taunted.

"Is it sexual?"

She gave him an *are you kidding* look. "Of course it is."

"Then I don't need to know. Deal."

Gianna gasped when they made it down the short path to the pond. Elio had been a very busy boy this morning, shoveling a narrow lane so they could get to the water. It was larger than she'd expected and—as he'd reassured her several times on the walk here—completely frozen.

"A bench?" she asked, when Elio ran his gloved hand over the wooden bench, clearing off the snow so she could sit down.

"Yeah. When we were kids, we'd fish this pond a lot in the summer." Elio pointed to several downed logs by the edge of the water. "We used to sit there, but then one year, my dad decided he was tired of getting a sore ass while fishing and declared we needed a bench. For him in the summer to fish from. And for my mom in the winter, so she could watch us skate."

"Your mom didn't skate?" She sat on the bench, pulling off her boots to put on the skates she'd carried from the cabin.

Elio shook his head, dropping down next to her to put on his skates as well. "Not much. Used to insist she'd break her neck."

Gianna narrowed her eyes. "How come she got a bye and I don't?"

"Because she'd at least done it a few times before. You can't live your entire life without trying new things, Freckles. And this is an easy one because you have me, as your teacher and your spotter." He finished lacing up his skates, then rose, kneeling in front of her to inspect her work.

"The laces are too loose," he said, as he untied them, pulling them much—much—tighter.

"I think you're cutting off the circulation."

He shook his head. "No, I'm not. You need them that tight to support your ankles."

Once he was satisfied with his work, he stood and grasped both her hands, helping her up on very wobbly feet.

"Holy shit, this is hard," she said. "And we're not even on the ice."

Elio helped her walk to the edge of the pond. He slipped onto the slick surface, never letting go of her hand.

"This is so scary," she murmured, as she tentatively—and oh-so carefully—stepped onto the ice. She felt her feet starting to go out from under her, but Elio's grip was tight, resolute, as he helped her regain her footing.

For several minutes, she merely kept her feet still, allowing him to tug her across the surface like a tractor pulling a trailer. She was already feeling some screaming in her calf muscles as she worked overtime to keep her ankles from buckling.

Elio, meanwhile, glided with ease, never stumbling, even with Gianna wobbling and using him for support.

"Okay. Now you need to learn to propel yourself," he said, shifting until he was behind her, his hands no longer holding hers, but instead gripping her waist.

She started to panic, but he remained true to his word, never once letting her fall.

He instructed her on how to move her feet, how to turn, how to stop. He was a patient teacher. Thank God. Because she wasn't sure how long they'd been outside. She would have expected to freeze her ass off, but instead, she was starting to work up a bit of a sweat.

"I did it!" she exclaimed when she mastered a turn without wavering once. Of course, there'd been no danger of falling because Elio still held her, though his hands were loose, left there just in case she needed him.

Elio grinned. "You're a natural. Now..."

She felt his hands leave her waist. "Oh shit," she muttered.

Elio came up next to her, clasping one of her hands with his. "We're going to skate together," he announced. "You've got the rhythm. You can do it."

She followed his lead, the two of them skating several circles around the pond, hand in hand. She only stumbled once, but Elio had been right there, catching her before she went down.

As her confidence grew, so did his antics. He shifted, releasing her hands completely, skating backward in front of her.

"Show off," she said, though she was impressed—and turned on—by his skating skills. She hadn't admitted to him that she didn't really consider herself much of a hockey fan. She and Grandma had never watched sports when she was growing up. Like, no sports. At all.

Sam's chosen sport had been football, but he had a standing Sunday date with a bunch of his buddies in the fall to watch at one of the other guys' houses—the friend with the big screen TV —so she gotten away without having to sit through many of those games as well. She'd always looked forward to those autumn Sundays because she got the house to herself to listen to music or watch whatever she wanted on TV. Sam had been a total remote hog, his interests running toward mystery series and true crime, while she preferred sitcoms.

She hadn't been exposed to hockey until she became friends with Liza. And while she'd joined in with their watch parties, she'd never paid that much attention to the game, typically chatting with her girlfriends or offering to grab drinks or snacks, to keep from getting bored.

Something told her she wasn't going to be able to look away from the game once Elio was back on the ice.

"Come on," he said, still skating backward, as he took both her hands in his. "Let's pick up the pace."

Before she could veto that idea, he had them flying faster across the ice. His grip was firm, steady, and like in bed, she realized that she trusted him completely here too. The cold wind was flying, blowing the hair not covered by her hat, away from her face. He wasn't holding back, and it felt like a thrill ride at an amusement park. She screamed loudly, though it wasn't one of fear but utter delight.

"We're going to crash!" she cried out when Elio got closer and closer to the shore. She should have saved her breath. With an ease that proved the man wore skates more than regular shoes, he managed to bring them to a perfect stop.

"Elio," she said breathlessly.

"Fun?"

"God, it was terrifying. Exhilarating. I loved it!"

He drew her close, giving her a long, passionate kiss. She struggled to keep her feet steady, but it didn't matter that she couldn't. Elio held strong, keeping her upright and in place as he kissed her senseless.

"Ready to go in?" he asked after a few minutes.

She nodded as he helped her back to the bench. "Do you think we might have time to do this again tomorrow?"

"Hell yeah. It's good for me to be out on the ice. I'm going to be in the doghouse when I get back to Baltimore, for failing to keep up with my workout routine."

"You do those chin-ups three times a day," Gianna pointed out, not bothering to mention watching him do what felt like an ungodly amount of pull-ups was her favorite pastime at the cabin.

"Yeah, but I'd only planned to stay here for a couple days

before returning to Baltimore to practice with the team. I'd gotten that much cleared by my coach. He wasn't too pleased when I called yesterday to say I would be stuck on the mountain at least two more days." Elio changed from his skates to his snow boots as he talked.

"Will you get in trouble?"

Elio shrugged. "Let's just say I foresee a lot of wind sprints in my immediate future."

"I have no idea what those are, but they sound bad."

Elio chuckled. "I'll demonstrate when we get back. You ready?" He stood, reaching down to help her up. The two of them strolled back to the cabin hand in hand, and as they approached the front porch, Elio handed her his skates and showed her what wind sprints consisted of.

And while they weren't something she would ever want to do, she sure as hell didn't mind watching *him*.

After doing a couple, he took his skates back from her. "Hot cocoa?"

She nodded. "Sounds perfect. And then...I plan to cash in on my favor."

"Freckles, you might be the only person I will never mind being in debt to."

Chapter Ten

Gianna tossed the salad she'd just made as Elio chopped up some chicken. After their less-than-healthy dinner last night, they'd decided to dine on something a little more nutritious tonight. She was a fan of big salads with all the fixings, and Elio admitted he was the same. She'd thrown some rolls into the oven to accompany the meal.

Carrying their bowls to the table, they settled down, eating in companionable silence for a minute or two. It was crazy how quickly they'd established routines, both of them taking care of different things. From her making the bed, to him dealing with the trash, to her washing the dishes while he dried and put them away.

They'd spent the last few hours hanging out in front of the fire, making out, hot and heavy. And while they hadn't had actual sex, they'd both come, him in her mouth and her on his fingers. After that, they'd taken a shower, thrown on their comfy clothes, and made dinner together.

As they cooked, they'd talked about a bunch of silly nothings —the weather, different ways to make chicken, his favorite hangouts in Baltimore. The way Elio described his favorite bar, Pat's

Pub, had her dying to take a trip to the city just to try the Shepherd's Pie.

"You're an amazing skater. Who taught you?" she asked, as they ate.

"Bruno."

"Really?" Gianna hadn't expected that answer. Elio's oldest brother, Bruno, was a mechanic, married to his high school sweetheart, Vivian—who cut Gianna's hair. The couple had three rambunctious kids. Bruno was a bruiser from the word go, a huge man with a long, full *Duck Dynasty*-style beard, so it was hard to imagine him balancing on ice skates.

"He wasn't always the gruff-looking mountain man he is today. He played hockey in high school. I'm ten years younger than him. When I was six and he was sixteen, I went through a stage where I wanted to be one of the big kids. Followed him and Aldo, who was eleven at the time, fucking everywhere. I'm sure I drove them insane, emulating them, trying to dress like they did, talk like they did. The talking part got Bruno grounded for a couple weeks because it didn't take Mom long to figure out where I'd picked up my newfound love of the word 'motherfucker'."

Gianna nearly spit out the water she'd just taken a sip of. "I bet he wanted to kill you."

"Nah. Bruno's always been the type to take things in stride. Anyway, he played hockey, so I wanted to play. Got Mom and Dad to sign me up for a peewee league, and after that...I was bitten. Bruno's love of the game faded by the end of his junior year because he met Vivian, and from that point on, all he wanted to do was be with her."

Gianna knew about Bruno and Vivian's long relationship, through Viv, who'd clearly found her perfect profession. The woman was an entertaining storyteller and a world-class gossip, and by doing hair, she had a captive audience. Not that Gianna cared. Vivian was hilarious and she'd never given her a bad haircut.

"So you kept playing hockey?"

Elio nodded. "I decided at a very young age I wanted to go pro. Of course, a million kids dream of that, so I had plenty of well-meaning teachers try to convince me to choose something more practical, more achievable."

"What about your parents? Did they try to dissuade you?"

"No. Not at all. They're the reason I am where I am today. I told them what I wanted to do, and they found ways to help me get there, driving me all over the goddamn East Coast with my travel teams, paying for extra lessons with coaches, cheering me on every step of the way. They never told me to dream smaller. They just told me to work harder."

"Wow. Greatest parents ever," she said, her comment earning her one of Elio's full-fledged bright smiles.

"You still have all your teeth." She hadn't meant to make that comment, but the words flew out when she considered how gorgeous his smile was.

Elio laughed loudly. "Let's just say I have teeth. Not all these suckers are the ones I started out with."

"So, apart from your potty mouth, were you a good kid or a handful?"

Elio considered the question. "I'd say I was somewhere in the middle. Dad swears it was a good thing I stuck with the hockey because I've always had a devilish streak. Playing the sport kept me too busy to go too far down any bad paths. Plus, it gave me a good way to burn off frustration. I'm known as the enforcer on my team."

"That sounds very Arnold Schwarzenegger-like. What does that mean?"

"It means, if anyone messes with one of my teammates, I take care of it." He lifted his fists, boxer-style.

"I can't see you fighting anyone. You seem way too chill."

"Yeah. My family says the same thing. Everyone except Liza. She and I were closest in age, so the two of us were no strangers to fighting and tussling when we were kids."

"What was Liza like when she was little? I bet she kept your parents on their toes."

Elio shrugged. "You have to remember, by the time Liza came along, Mom and Dad already had three rowdy boys, all between the ages of eleven and one. It's safe to say by that point, they were a bit numb, desensitized."

"There's a big age gap between you and your brothers."

"Yeah. There's five years between Bruno and Aldo, five between me and Aldo. Then Liza came along a year after me. I'm pretty sure she was my mom's last-ditch attempt at getting her girl."

"Must have been nice growing up with brothers and a sister. Being an only child sucks."

"Yeah, it is cool, but sometimes I think I missed out on too much of the sibling stuff because I was always away, playing hockey. Daily practices, games, the travel I mentioned. And it's gotten worse since we've become adults."

"What do you mean?" Gianna asked.

"I'm the one who moved away. Hockey keeps me on the road and busy most of the year. Bruno's kids know me as Uncle Elio, but they're still shy around me. Meanwhile, Uncle Aldo shows up and they're dive-bombing him, begging him to wrestle and play with them."

Gianna sensed regret in Elio's voice, which was strange because she'd genuinely believed he loved his chosen life path.

"Aldo and Liza have the same group of friends, so they hang out together all the time."

"You're a part of that group," Gianna interjected.

"Part-time, at best. Apart from my relatives, I'm not exactly close to the rest of the friends in that circle, simply because I'm never around. I mean it was nice of Penny to invite me to her wedding, but I probably haven't spoken to her more than a handful of times over the years. And you and I...until this week..."

"We were acquaintances," she filled in for him.

"Yeah. That's exactly what we were."

"You know," she said, "hockey isn't forever."

He nodded. "I know that."

"Will you come back to Philly after you retire from the game?"

"Oh, hell yeah. Baltimore is great, but it's never been home."

"What will you do after you stop playing?"

He shrugged as he rose, grabbing her glass and his to fill up with more water. By tacit agreement, neither of them had had anything else alcoholic to drink since their tequila night. Her because there was a chance she was pregnant. And him...well, he didn't say it aloud, but she got the feeling he was eschewing alcohol as some form of support or camaraderie.

"Would you coach?" she asked, when he brought the glasses back, placing them on the table. She smiled her thanks.

He shook his head. "Not professionally. Maybe as a volunteer coach for the leagues I grew up in."

She pressed, curious about his future plans. "Would you go work for Moretti Brothers Restorations?"

"God, no. I'm a fair hand with a hammer, but I don't see me building anything."

"Would you go back to school?"

A small smirk crossed Elio's face. "I hated school. Did what I had to do to get my C's and got the hell out."

She huffed out a breath. "Do you have *any* plans at all?"

"Nope," he admitted. "I always thought I'd figure it out when I needed to."

Her eyes widened. "Zero plans?"

"Is that making your brain itch?" he asked, recalling her problem with their overflowing liquor cabinet.

"Yes."

"Will it help if I promise to give it some serious thought when I get back to Baltimore?"

"Yes. That would help a lot."

"You got it."

Several minutes passed as they continued eating.

"So what kind of kid were you?" Elio asked, tossing the question she'd asked back at her.

"I was a good kid. Boring, actually," she admitted.

"Never snuck out of the house to go to parties? Never snuck Sam in? No drunken frat parties in college?"

"None of that," she answered honestly.

"Seriously?"

"I told you, Grandma and I didn't have a lot of money. I knew I wanted to go to college, so as soon as I was old enough, I started working, saving as much as I could. When I got my first paycheck, I tried to give some to Grandma, but she said it was her job to pay the bills and my job to get into college. I wanted to help her because she worked so hard and because her life had been so difficult. So...since she wouldn't let me help with the money, I just made sure she never had to worry about my behavior."

Elio considered that, falling quiet for a minute or two. "Can I ask you something?"

"Sure."

"If it's too personal, you can tell me to butt out and mind my own business."

She grinned. "You've seen me naked more than dressed the last couple of days. I'd say we've crossed a line as far as getting up close and personal."

Elio brushed her argument away. "Sex is a different kind of personal," he explained before asking what he wanted to know. "You were raised by your grandma."

She nodded, even though that wasn't the question.

"Where are your parents, Gee?"

"Oh," Gianna said. "That's not personal at all, really. I don't know who my dad is. My mom got pregnant with me when she was still in high school. Sixteen. She was *not* the ideal child. My grandma was a single mother too, and, like I said, she worked two jobs, so she wasn't home a lot. My mom's one true talent was finding trouble, always running with a bad crowd. She'd been arrested for shoplifting three times before she was twelve. Anyway, one night, she got drunk and high at a party and the result was me. Grandma never told me who my father was, and I'm pretty sure it's because my mom didn't know."

Elio put his fork down. "I'm sorry."

She shook her head. "Oh my God, don't be. You can't miss something you never had. My mom told Grandma she was pregnant, and Grandma Mary put her foot down on my mom's behavior. Told Mom no more drinking, drugs, parties...and I think for the first time in her life, my mom listened. Until I was born."

Gianna hadn't talked about this in years. In fact, she hadn't told this story to very many people at all. Sam, Liza, and Keeley knew most of it.

And...that was it.

It wasn't because she was embarrassed or ashamed. The truth was she hadn't really had anyone else to tell.

"Let me guess," Elio said. "She started doing drugs again."

Gianna touched her nose with the tip of her finger. "You got it in one. Mom was one of those people who was her own worst enemy. She and Grandma never saw eye to eye, so if Grandma disapproved of something, Mom would go all in, just to spite her. I hated the way my mom acted, the way she constantly hurt Grandma. I was only young, but I could see how much Mom's actions and words hurt."

"Kids are very perceptive. I've seen it in my nephews. Billy is probably the most empathetic kid I've ever met. If someone is hurting, that kid can sniff it out and then he goes out of his way to make them feel better. Sounds like you were the same?"

Gianna lifted one shoulder. "I don't know if I make things better. I definitely couldn't help Grandma Mary when it came to Mom. I hated it when they fought, so I always hid in the closet in my bedroom until they stopped yelling. Usually, Mom would storm out and then Grandma would come find me, pull me out of the closet, and give me my favorite treat."

"Favorite treat?"

Gianna hid her face with her hand briefly. "God, you're going to think it's weird, but I love soft butter on saltines. Real butter. It was one of the few things Grandma and I ever splurged on."

Elio glanced toward the kitchen. "That actually sounds pretty good. And as always…"

"We only have half the ingredients. Butter, but no crackers."

"Yeah. So your mom lived with you when you were younger?" Elio seemed determined to hear the whole story. Not that she minded. His interest in her was sincere, and she couldn't recall the last time she'd had someone to talk to about herself, her life, her fears, hopes, and even her eccentricities.

"Grandma kicked her out more than a few times during the first five or six years of my life, but ultimately Mom would always come back, swearing that she was clean, that she wanted to turn over a new leaf. And Grandma would take her back."

"That couldn't have been easy for you," Elio said, reaching across the table to take her hand.

"I never liked it when Mom was home," she whispered. She'd never admitted that to another living soul, feeling guilty for feeling that way.

"What was your mom like?"

"She never had much time for me, and zero patience. She was a chain smoker, something Grandma would never allow in the apartment, so she spent most of the day sitting on a plastic chair on our tiny balcony, with an overflowing ashtray next to her. She'd leave the sliding door cracked, so the house always stunk when she was there. That's what I remember the most. The smell. I hated it.

"The last falling out she and Grandma had was when I was seven. Mom came home strung out on heroin. She'd been so wasted, she dropped all her shit by the door and passed out on the couch. I got up before Grandma. All the stuff in Mom's purse had spilled out, and her drugs were there. I picked up a needle—"

"Jesus," Elio murmured, gripping her hand more tightly.

"That was when Grandma Mary walked in. She saw what I was holding and freaked the fuck out. She knocked it out of my hand. Asked if I'd poked myself. I said no. I told her I knew the needle was bad. I don't know why I picked it up. I was just...curious."

"Christ," Elio said hotly. "You could have been hurt."

"Grandma woke my mom and kicked her out. Told her to not bother coming back."

"Did she try to come back?"

Gianna shook her head. This was the part she hated saying out loud because it was too hard to think about. Yet tonight, sitting in this peaceful cabin, in the soft lighting, with such an attentive, compassionate friend, the words came easily.

"No. When I was nine, I came home from school. Usually Mrs. Pasquet, the older woman who lived across the hall, took care of me until Grandma came home from work, but that day, Grandma was there. She sat me down on the couch and told me that Mom had died. I asked if it was because of the drugs and Grandma Mary said yes. I know she expected me to cry, and I even tried, Elio...but I couldn't."

He frowned. "I think it makes sense that you wouldn't cry. It sounds like you hardly knew your mother, and it wasn't like she was the one taking care of you. Your grandma was."

"I know that. I do. But I've *never* cried for her. Not once. In my whole life. When Grandma said my mom had died, all I could think was...that wasn't true, she hadn't died. Because Grandma Mary was my mom. She'd been the one to take care of me, read me stories, give me baths. Grandma wasn't exactly a warm and fuzzy person, and I'm pretty sure the word *strict* was invented to describe her—she was bound and determined I wasn't going to turn out like my mom. She never said it, but I know she blamed herself for Mom getting hooked on the drugs, certain that if she'd been home more, Mom wouldn't have strayed so far. It's why she took me with her to clean the apartments on the weekends."

"Gianna," Elio said, with something that sounded too close to pity. Which meant she was giving him the wrong idea.

"I never questioned her love for me," she hastened to add. "Even if she never said it."

"She never said it?"

Gianna wasn't surprised by Elio's shock. His family was the very definition of affection, with their constant hugs and double-cheek kisses. She'd heard his nonna tell every single one of her grandkids on Christmas Eve how much she loved them. "Grandma Mary told me she loved me twice."

"Twice," Elio repeated, shaking his head.

"The first time was after my high school graduation. She and my mom had both gotten pregnant when they were young and had dropped out. I remember walking off the stage with my diploma, sporting that godawful cap and gown, and going straight over to her. Grandma Mary had hugged me, really tight, like she didn't want to let go, then she whispered in my ear, 'I love you, darlin'.' It took everything I had not to cry right then and there."

"I bet that must have meant the world to you."

"You have no idea."

"Let's move somewhere more comfortable. Finished?" he asked, reaching for her bowl.

She nodded, and he took her dish and his to the sink. He stopped her before she could start washing them. "Later," he said. Then he added, "I promise," knowing how much she hated leaving dirty dishes in the sink. It was funny how quickly Elio had picked up on her quirks. Yet he didn't make fun of her—or get annoyed as Sam had—but instead accepted them.

He wrapped his arm around her waist and led her to the couch, sitting down next to her.

"You were lucky to have your grandma," Elio said. She'd thought the conversation was over, but Elio apparently wanted to know more. "What happened to her?"

Gianna blinked a couple of times, willing herself not to cry. "She died a few months after I graduated from college. I moved back in with her because we knew about the cancer at that point, and I wanted to be close to take care of her."

"That couldn't have been easy. You were still so young."

"Twenty-one. I was sitting with her the night she died. Hospice had been called in, and they were giving her morphine, so she wasn't suffering. She'd been out of it as a result, sleeping most of the time, her eyes unfocused, her mind distant when she was awake. One of the nurses said that sometimes a dying person needs reassurance that it's okay to go. So that last night, I held her hand, and I told her that I'd be okay. She opened her eyes and looked at me. *Really* looked at me. She said, 'I love you,' and...that was it. She passed away before I could say the words back."

She swiped away the tears, shaking her head. "God. I'm so sorry."

"Shit, Gianna," Elio said, wrapping his arms around her, pulling her close. "I didn't mean to make you cry."

She tried to pull away, intent on going to the bathroom for a tissue, but he held her tighter against his chest.

"Stay there," he demanded. "You gotta give me a minute, or else my stud status will be blown when you see what a blubbering mess I am right now."

Gianna laughed through her tears, then clung to him, taking the time he was giving her to pull herself together.

When she felt his arms slacken, she lifted her head and realized he hadn't been lying about his own emotions.

He kept one arm around her shoulder, the two of them nestling close, watching the fire.

"After Grandma died, I decided I was going to have a big family," she said, breaking the peacefulness of the moment.

"Oh yeah?"

"Yeah. I love listening to the way you and Liza talk about your childhood, and Christmas Eve was...God, I never knew a holiday could be like that. It was loud and crazy and fun and there was just...so much love. I want that for my kids. You know, maybe I'll have as many kids as your parents had. Four sounds pretty perfect to me."

"Four, huh? That might be culture shock considering your only-child status."

"That's exactly why I'm having four. When Grandma died, I wasn't completely alone because I had Sam. He moved in almost immediately and...he became my family. When he left, I lost more than my boyfriend and my best friend. I lost..." She swallowed heavily.

"Your family."

"I'm not doing that to my kids. They're always going to have lots and lots of family. A houseful of siblings, so they'll never be alone."

Elio leaned closer, placing his lips against hers. "You're incredible, Gianna."

Every time he said something like that, Gianna felt the heaviness that had been pressing down on her since Sam left lift a little more.

No, she decided. That heaviness had been there longer than the past few months. It had been there for years, weighing her down until the load felt normal.

Elio broke the kiss, standing, then reaching down for her. She took his hand, following him to the bed. He slowly undressed her, kissing every bit of skin as he exposed it. She did the same, stripping him, exploring, stroking, caressing all the beautiful parts of the man.

He was extremely handsome, but a few days ago, she would have used that word to describe him based on what she could see. His chestnut-colored hair that was long on top, so it fell over his forehead and brows in such a way that she constantly longed to run her fingers through it. His light brown eyes, strong jaw, the crook in his nose that told her he'd broken it a time or two, the cleft in his chin, his chiseled chest, muscular arms and thighs—all of it put together made him one of the most gorgeous men she'd ever seen.

But now, she knew that when she thought of him as beautiful, it had nothing to do with the way he looked on the outside.

He was beautiful because of who he was on the inside, and how he made her feel.

Once they were naked, Elio pulled back the covers, neither of them breaking the union of their lips. He pressed her down on her back, coming over her, kissing her for countless minutes.

"Please," she whispered, overwhelmed with the need to have him inside her.

Elio's gaze locked with hers, as he drew on a condom, placed his cock at her opening, and slid inside. Even as he began to thrust, he looked deep into her eyes, and she let him see every emotion, every feeling. Everything.

She lifted her legs, wrapping them around his waist, locking her ankles at his lower back. The shift allowed him to go deeper, and they groaned in unison.

Every time they'd come together, it had been a whirlwind, a tornado, a goddamn force of nature—powerful, heady.

This time was different, slower, calmer, yet just as potent. He was taking her down with gentle, soft strokes, and sweet words whispered in her ear.

"Gianna," he said at last, just as she felt herself about to go over. "Come with me," he said.

"Yes," she murmured. "With you."

Her back arched and her body trembled as her orgasm rushed through her, filling up every empty, dark corner of her soul, flooding it with light and warmth...and him.

"Happy New Year," he murmured.

She said the words back, though three different ones drifted through her head.

I love you, Gianna whispered to him in her mind.

She knew better than to say those words aloud. Not because they didn't belong here but because this wasn't the time, and that sentiment wasn't what he wanted from her.

So for now, she would take what he offered—his kind words,

kisses, hugs—wrap herself up in the amazing emotions, and then...well...

Then she'd take a page from his book.

She'd figure out what came next...

Later.

Chapter Eleven

Elio breathed in a deep breath, soaking up Gianna's citrusy scent, before opening his eyes. They'd slept in late. Again. It was going to take him a day or two to sort out his sleep patterns once he returned to Baltimore.

It was Friday, and most likely their last day together in the cabin. The weather forecast was calling for warmer temperatures today, which would accelerate the melting enough that the two of them could get their cars out. They only had to drive four miles of unpaved dirt lane before they hit the plowed roads.

Elio hadn't been completely honest with her when he told her he had zero plans for his future because he did have a ghost of an idea, but it was so vague it was practically transparent.

He'd gotten into a discussion with Gio and Rafe at the holiday party, interested in learning more about their inn. Elio thought he might like to invest in a business after retiring from the game, maybe a restaurant or even an ice rink, and he'd picked their brains about their process and the hurdles they'd encountered.

Of course, they hadn't exactly talked him into pursuing the idea. It became apparent very quickly they were both feeling stretched too thin, and they admitted they'd jumped into the project too soon. Rafe had inherited several businesses from his grandfather last summer, and he was still working to learn the ins and outs of those.

Gio, ever the carpenter, had loved the idea of renovating the mansion, but he was no fan of the business end of things, leaving too much to Rafe, who was quite simply overwhelmed.

Not that Gio wasn't the same. He confessed he felt like he was burning the candle at both ends, keeping up with his full-time job with Moretti Brothers—something made harder now that Joey was off filming *ManPower*—and the renovations.

The conversation had left Elio thinking that perhaps the investment idea would be more hassle than it was worth. Besides, he didn't have a clue what kind of business he even wanted to invest in.

Gianna lay on her side, facing him, though she was still sound asleep. Elio decided there was no better way to ring in the New Year than waking up next to her. He took a few minutes to study her face. He was amazed when he recalled his first impression of her, how he'd thought her wholesome. Jesus, he'd actually used that word to describe her, picking it over the obvious one.

Because while she was wholesome, she was so much more than that. Nothing short of gorgeous. With her wavy blonde hair, the cute little upturn of her nose, the delicate slope of her eyes, framed with long, thick lashes. Her complexion was pale, which only served to highlight her rosy cheeks. Her eyes were the lightest blue he'd ever seen, the color reminding him of glaciers he'd seen once in Alaska.

But it wasn't her appearance that had turned his head this week.

It was her.

He considered her childhood, with her absent dad, shitty mom, and overworked grandmother. How she had come from all of that with her good heart and sense of humor intact astounded him.

He'd taken his upbringing for granted, never having to worry about money. God only knew how much money his parents had invested in his interest in hockey. It wasn't a cheap sport.

He had tried to "pay them back" for all of that, now that he made very—*very*—good money, through expensive gifts and by footing the bill for their dream trip to the Bahamas a few years earlier.

But as a kid, he'd never spared a thought when it came to paying bills, and it would never have occurred to him to consider butter an extravagance the way Gianna did.

"You're watching me sleep," she said huskily, her dark lashes fluttering, then rising slowly.

"Creeping you out?" he joked.

She shook her head, still looking at him with drowsy eyes.

"Happy New Year, Freckles," he said.

"Happy New Year." She stretched out with a long, contented sigh, reminding him of a sleepy kitten as she slowly woke up. "I never sleep this good in Philly. Of course, I live in an eight-story apartment building with paper-thin walls, so it's safe to say it's never this quiet. Between the neighbors and the traffic outside, noise is just a fact of life."

"You ever consider moving out of the apartment, looking for something else?"

Gianna flipped to her back, yawning, as she tried to come fully awake. "I think about it, but I'd never find somewhere decent for what I'm paying in rent. Although I'm sort of hoping..."

"Hoping?" he prodded.

Gianna sat up, facing him. "Well, I haven't told anyone this... so do you mind if we keep it a secret just between us? For now?"

Elio sat up as well. "I won't tell anyone."

"You know that Gio and Rafe are opening that haunted inn, right?"

Elio had been amused by Keeley's assertion that Rafe's grandfather was haunting the place, but when she started telling him some of the strange things that had happened since the three of them moved in there, he had to admit she might be right. "I know about their plans."

"One of the perks for the person they hire to manage the place is free lodging in the guest cottage behind the mansion."

"That's a pretty good perk."

"I know," Gianna said. "I'm hoping to convince them to let me run it. My degree is in hotel management, but God knows I'm not using it much in my current job."

"Don't care for your job?"

She shook her head. "It's been beyond dull."

"Rafe and Gio know you well, Gianna. You and Keeley are good friends. I'm sure they would hire you," Elio said, certain all Gianna had to do was ask.

"Yeah, but...I don't want to just ask for the job. I want them to know I'm the right person for it. I've been cleaning up my resume and creating a business plan to show them my ideas for running the inn. I don't want to say anything to them until I have everything in place. It's like you said, Keeley and I are friends, so I don't want to put them on the spot or make them uncomfortable by asking them to hire me out of obligation. So my plan is to lay out everything—staffing, reservation policies, scheduling, even some ideas for possible special events. I want to play up the haunted idea, and I've even started generating a list of names for the inn, too, since Gio admitted the three of them can't come up with anything they like."

"Damn. That's a lot of work," Elio pointed out, though he was impressed by her efforts.

"Well, I probably wouldn't do this much if it was a usual job interview. If it wasn't Gio and Rafe, because it *has* been a lot of work for a job I don't have. I just want them to feel confident that if they hire me, it's for what I can do, not who I am. Running that inn would be my absolute dream job."

"You dream of working with ghosts? And I'm the creepy one for watching you sleep?"

Gianna giggled. "You're still the creepy one," she joked. "If they hire me, I'll only be two years late on achieving that particular goal."

Elio tilted his head, confused. "There's a timeline?"

Gianna flushed slightly, which he'd learned was a tell for her. She blushed whenever she confessed what she considered one of her obsessive-compulsive quirks.

"I had a Great Life plan I've been working toward for the last few years. Dream job at twenty-four, engaged at twenty-six, married at twenty-eight, first baby at thirty. Of course, that's all shot to hell now. I'd intended to use my time here this week coming up with a new plan."

Elio fought not to laugh, but in the end, he couldn't hold back his grin. "Yet another plan."

She rolled her eyes. "I know everything I just said probably makes me sound like a crazy person."

He shook his head. "No, but that original plan is oddly specific. Was there any reason for the ages you picked besides the fact they're all divisible by two?"

Gianna picked up her pillow and swung it at his head. He dodged in time so all she hit was his upper arm. "Those ages just felt right to me," she replied, though Elio didn't think she sounded convinced.

Then he said something that had been bothering him for a while. "You know, eleven years is a long time to date someone. I'm curious why you were putting the engagement and marriage off for so long."

Gianna pulled the pillow she was still holding to her middle, wrapping her arms around it. "Sam was the one who came up with the list originally. He's an architect, and he was determined to land a job with his dream firm by the time he was twenty-four."

"Did he?"

Gianna nodded. "Yeah. One night, shortly after Grandma died, we were lying in bed, talking about the future. He'd moved in a few weeks before that and I remember thinking it felt so right, being in that apartment with him. It was like the next part of my life—the adult stage—had begun, and I was happy."

"Did Sam feel the same?"

"I thought he did," Gianna answered. "But I'll admit that since September, I've thought about that conversation more than a few times, and I'm seeing some of the things differently."

"Like what?"

"Sam was the one who insisted we wait until we were twenty-six to get engaged. He said that by then, we'd be established in our jobs, with steadier income. That made sense to me, so I went along with it."

"Did you agree with the rest as well?"

"At the time, yeah, I did. Though now, I'm wondering why. I mean, why in the hell would we wait two more years after we were engaged to get married? What on earth would we learn about each other in years twelve and thirteen that we hadn't discovered in the first eleven?"

"You're not wrong about that," Elio agreed.

"But at the time, we were still young, and truthfully, it just felt like words, you know? Not a real plan. Until twenty-four came and went. Then twenty-five. Then...my twenty-sixth birthday arrived, and I thought..."

She didn't finish her comment, but Elio could figure out what she'd thought without the words. "No ring."

She shook her head. "He got me a Roomba."

"Jesus Christ."

Her eyes widened with amusement, and she snorted. "Worst gift ever, right? Even for a clean freak."

"Worst. Hands down."

"Of course, hindsight is twenty-twenty. My birthday was in August. Which was after Sam started dating Emma."

"Sam is an idiot." Elio had made similar statements about Gianna's ex a few times this week.

"God," she said, smacking her hand over her mouth dramatically. "I swore to myself I was going to stop talking about Sam and then, boom! Another whole conversation about the asshole. I'm sure you're sick of hearing about him."

Elio considered that. With any other woman, he would have hit his limit on talk about the ex long before now, but with Gianna, he found himself wanting to hear more. It offered him insights into her past, and who she was as a person, because that relationship had probably defined her as much as the way she'd been raised. He wanted to know her, so that meant hearing about Sam.

Rather than respond to her comment, he changed the subject. "So you intended to come up with another life plan this week?"

She nodded.

"You probably won't like hearing this, but I think you should skip the plan altogether. Life doesn't work like that. No one can plot out the big moments in quite that kind of detail because life happens, takes twists and turns you don't expect. Maybe it's enough to just say you want to find your dream job, get married, and have kids."

Gianna considered that, a soft smile crossing her lips. "You're right. That *is* enough."

He bent forward to steal a quick kiss.

"How do you do that?" she murmured against his lips.

Elio leaned back. "Do what?"

"Simplify things for me in such a way that all the things I thought I needed to do to keep my brain from exploding don't seem necessary anymore."

"Like what?" he asked.

"I haven't vacuumed this cabin since Tuesday. We left the dinner dishes in the sink last night. You've just convinced me not to make a list. I always make lists...for everything. And none of that is bothering me. Not even a little bit."

"Have you considered it's not me? Maybe it's this place and the fact we're on vacation."

Gianna dismissed that suggestion immediately. "I've gone on vacation before and trust me, usually I'm *more* stressed because my daily routines are disrupted."

He stole another kiss, this one lingering. "I think the reason is pretty simple."

"Oh yeah?"

"It's all the great sex."

Gianna shifted closer, running her lips along the side of his neck. "You know what? I bet that's it. So really, it has nothing to do with you at all. I just need to make sure to keep a hot guy in my bed at all times."

Elio knew she was teasing him, but the idea of Gianna taking another man to her bed didn't sit well with him. In fact, it pissed him off, made him feel...

What the fuck was this?

Jealousy?

He dismissed that idea immediately. He'd never been jealous a day in his life, and he didn't intend to start now.

"It must be nice to be you," she mused, falling on her back on the mattress.

"Why do you say that?"

"Because you've already gotten where you want to be. You wanted to play professional hockey and you worked your ass off until you got there. I feel like I'm still a million miles away from everything I want from life."

"I wouldn't say I'm exactly where I want to be." Elio hadn't meant to say that aloud. He'd only told Aldo about the idea of retiring from hockey.

Gianna's gaze focused on his face. "What do you mean?"

Elio considered whether or not he wanted to continue the conversation. He could brush her off, feed her some lie, but he liked talking to her. Liked sharing the parts of himself he'd never shown anyone else.

Besides, he wasn't making a bit of headway on coming to a

decision one way or the other. Maybe talking it out with Gianna would help.

"You said it yourself last night. Hockey isn't forever."

Chapter Twelve

"**W**ait." Gianna sat up once more. "Are you thinking about leaving the game?"

He fell silent for a moment, trying to figure out how to explain his thoughts, his feelings. However, he gave Gianna too long to put two and two together.

Her eyes widened. "That's why you came to the cabin, isn't it? To think about your future."

"I've been debating whether or not I want to keep playing. Some days I can't imagine leaving. Some days I can't stand the thought of going back."

"That's a big decision."

"Yeah. It is. And one that I need to make soon. The thing is, I have a lot of good years left in me, and there are things I haven't achieved yet, professionally, records I could break, stuff like that. But I've been off the road the last two months, home more with my family than I've been in over a decade, and I liked it."

"Has your time here helped you figure it out?"

Elio grinned. "I've been a little distracted. In a good way. But no. I'm no closer to deciding. I suspect perhaps it will come clear once I'm back on the ice. Either the spark will still be there, or it won't."

"Well, if you decide to leave the game, I know Liza will be delighted to have you home to stay. She misses you like crazy."

"I miss her too. Though she might not like having me around as much as she thinks once it's a reality."

"Oh God," Gianna groaned. "You're not going to be like Aldo, are you? Always showing up at the clubs to check on her?"

Elio knew all about Aldo's protective streak when it came to their sister. "No. Liza's an adult and she's perfectly capable of taking care of herself."

"Said no Moretti man ever."

Elio laughed. "Liza and I are very close in age, so growing up, we were basically playmates. Aldo, on the other hand, has six years on her, and he takes his big brother role very seriously. It doesn't help that his best friend is Kayden, the cop, who tells him way too many horror stories about the crimes he investigates."

"Excellent points. So, what exactly *are* you planning to do that might drive Liza insane?"

Elio hadn't voiced his suspicions about Liza and Matt Russo to anyone, but he was interested in getting Gianna's opinion.

"I'm starting to think she might have a thing for Matt Russo."

Gianna barked out a loud laugh that died quickly. "Are you being serious?"

"I am."

"But she hates Matt, calls him the bane of her existence."

Elio had heard that particular complaint. "She calls him a great many things...constantly and frequently."

He watched as his suspicions soaked in, Gianna's expression morphing. Her outright disbelief replaced by something that looked perilously close to thinking he might be onto something.

"Yeah," she finally said, "but he's a Russo." It was clear she thought that would be the end of any wayward feelings his sister might have.

"I know," Elio said. "Which is the problem."

"Can I ask you what the deal is between the Russos and the Morettis? I've only ever heard bits and pieces."

"We better get comfortable for this story." Elio propped his pillow up against the headboard, leaning back.

"Long one, huh?" Gianna asked as she followed suit.

"It could be, but I'll try to give you the abridged version. It started with our great grandfathers, who at one point in time were business partners and friends. That ended when Mattia Russo had an affair with my great-granddad Lorenzo's wife."

"You're all still pissed about that?"

Elio decided to tell the story faster. "No. But let's just say that history has repeated itself a couple of times. Matt's grandfather, Riccardo, hoped to win my nonna's heart. Nonno did."

"I'm not surprised," Gianna said. "Even in his eighties, your grandfather is a looker."

Elio chuckled. "Oh yeah, Nonna said there was never any competition. She took one look at Giovanni Moretti and knew he was hers forever. Gio is named after him."

"What did Riccardo do?"

"He took his revenge by ruining Nonno financially."

"How?"

"The rumors surrounding the Russos claim they acquired their wealth through dirty means. Some speculate they're connected to the Mafia."

"No way!"

"It's just gossip, rumors, but there's no denying they have a great deal of pull with politicians and city officials who have less-than-savory reputations. Nonno lost his business after a lot of trumped-up citations and false allegations, and his health suffered from the stress. He had a pretty serious heart attack."

Gianna frowned. "I hate to know he suffered like that, and I can see why your family would be angry. But aren't Matt and Gage's grandfather *and* father dead? I mean, you can't exactly blame them for the sins of their ancestors. Gage is a really nice guy."

"I've only met Gage once, at the holiday party, and I agree with you. He was very likable. But he's not Matt."

Gianna plumped her pillow, turning sideways. She was clearly enjoying the story. "Okay. So what did Matt do?"

"The Russos seem to covet things that aren't theirs. He and Tony are the same age, and there was some rivalry between them in high school. Tony won senior class president and the position of quarterback on the football team, both things Matt had wanted. So...he retaliated."

"How?" Gianna asked.

"He slept with Tony's girlfriend. Had sex with her in the backseat of his car, parked in a place where he knew Tony would catch them."

"Holy shit. What a dick," Gianna said.

"Exactly."

"Does Liza know that story?"

Elio nodded. "She does."

"Hmmm." That was all Gianna offered, though he could see his stories were still swimming around in her head.

"But I don't want to spend the day talking about my family's ancient history. It's our last day here and the first day of the new year," he said softly. "We need to make it count. So what should we do?"

Her reply was simple and one word. "Everything."

Elio chuckled. "What does everything involve?"

"We eat all the leftover food, finish putting the puzzle together. We ice skate again, take one last shower together, cuddle by the fire, and use up the rest of the condoms. How many are left?"

"Three," he replied without bothering to look in the box.

Gianna's eyes twinkled with delight. "Been keeping track, I see."

"Fine. I agree to all the repeats and completes, but," he drawled. "There is still one thing we've left undone."

She narrowed her eyes suspiciously, clueing him in to where her thoughts had gone.

"Not the butt stuff," he said quickly, trying not to laugh. "Though you're making a mistake discounting that out of hand."

"I'll take your word for it. What have we forgotten?" she asked.

"Your toys. You haven't shown me what you brought."

There was no denying the definite interest in her eyes as her gaze traveled to her suitcase, tucked in the corner.

"You didn't even unpack them?" Elio rose from the bed, crossing to her case.

"I put them in the suitcase on a whim. The truth is, I probably wouldn't have pulled them out at all, even if I'd been here alone."

Elio opened the suitcase, shaking his head. "Freckles. They're still in their wrappers."

She sighed heavily. "I'm aware of that, though in my defense, I got that bullet vibrator for Christmas. It was a gift from Penny. She gave one to all of us girls. Said it was her favorite."

He studied the two toys. Neither was particularly scandalous, despite the fact her cheeks were flushed bright red at the moment. The bullet vibrator was ideal for clit play, and while the dildo was larger than he might have expected, it wasn't outrageous.

Clearly nervous, Gianna kept talking. "I think Penny ordered like a case of those little vibrators. Said she was worried Walmart was going to stop selling sex toys and she needed enough backups of her favorite to last her for the rest of her life."

Elio chuckled. "Are these the only two toys you own?"

"Yes."

She needed to up her toy game, and Elio made a mental note to send her a little gift once he returned home. He was going to jazz up her masturbation routine with a proper vibrator, a butt plug, maybe even some nipple clamps.

"Batteries?"

She pointed to the suitcase. "They're in there."

"Good girl," he said, when he found the AAAs she'd included.

Unwrapping the toys, he threw away the packaging, then headed to the bathroom to wash them. Gianna followed his progress but remained in bed.

When he returned, he tossed both toys on the mattress near her feet, then retrieved the last three condoms from the box.

Crawling back onto the mattress, he tugged Gianna down until she was on her back. He climbed over her, caging her beneath him, stealing a long, hot, passionate kiss. He'd never kissed any woman as much as he'd kissed her in the past few days, and if he was being honest with himself—something he was trying *not* to do—he was going to miss her lips.

Hell, he was going to miss *her*.

Which was why he was kicking honesty to the curb.

He was a go-with-the-flow guy. Footloose and fancy-free. A confirmed bachelor who preferred a no-strings lifestyle. He wasn't the type of man who longed for a woman's kisses or sent her naughty presents or felt jealous.

Yet, Gianna was drawing out all of that, and while it should be uncomfortable as fuck, it wasn't.

"Elio," Gianna whispered.

God, he loved the sound of his name on her lips.

He forced himself to push away, coming up on his knees. He picked up the bullet vibrator and pressed the button. It was a simple toy, just two speeds.

Gianna remained on her back, watching him with interest. Especially when he pressed the vibrating toy against her clit. Her back arched and she cried out loudly.

"Holy shit! Penny was right." Her hands flew to his wrists, something he was getting accustomed to. Gianna always struggled with the things that felt "too good."

"Hands on your pillow," he said, his tone commanding, letting her know he expected her to comply.

She released him instantly, giving him that surrender pose that had his cock thickening even more. He didn't consider himself an overly dominant lover, but there was something about Gianna submitting to him that drove his arousal to heights he'd never achieved with anyone else.

He kept the vibrator against her clit as she thrashed her head from side to side, her body undulating from the sensations. He didn't doubt he could make her come the first time this way, with nothing more than the tiny vibrator. He considered it but decided against it. There was something else he wanted from her more.

Elio turned the toy off and placed it on the mattress beside her. He saw the question in Gianna's gaze as he leaned over her again.

"Sit up for a minute," he ordered.

She did so, waiting as he piled their pillows up, placing them against the headboard.

"Lean against them." Elio put her in the position he wanted, half-lying, half-reclined. Then he returned to his previous spot, kneeling between her legs. This time when he picked up the vibrator, he handed it to her.

Her brows creased. "El?"

"Use it on yourself, Gee. I want to watch you."

She glanced at the remote, pushing the button. "I don't know if I can keep it in place. It feels so good, it's overwhelming."

"Do it," he said. "For me."

Gianna pressed the vibrator against her clit, her eyes drifting shut in instant bliss.

He tapped her under her chin. "Open your eyes. Look at me."

She blinked a few times, trying to focus on him as the vibrator worked its magic.

"Don't let up on the pressure," he said, when he felt her grip loosening.

"I'm...it's..." she gasped. "God, El. It's so good, but..."

"Not enough?"

She shook her head. "Need you."

He picked up the dildo. "It doesn't have to be me." He considered her choice of toy, recalling her comments about his size intimidating her the first time they had sex.

She must have noticed his expression. "Keeley texted me the link to that toy after Sam dumped me. Said that until I got a new boyfriend, I'd have to improvise. One night, I drank too much wine and bought it. When it showed up, I thought Keeley must have sent the link as a joke. I mean...it's huge."

Elio gave her a crooked grin, not bothering to call her to task when she turned off the vibrator and her eyes narrowed.

"And yes, I'm aware that it's pretty much the same size as you," she begrudgingly admitted, her words provoking a full-fledged smile.

Because he couldn't resist, he held the dildo next to his erection. "Not quite as big," he teased before sobering up, recalling that this was it for them. In less than twenty-four hours, they would be driving away from each other, him to Baltimore and her to Philadelphia.

Neither of them had offered anything more than the here and now.

Because they couldn't.

He still hadn't made his decision about his future with the team. Hell, about his future in general. And Gianna was still trying to find her feet again after Sam knocked her down.

"Here. Show me, Gianna. When you're home again and you wake up in the middle of the night, hot and needy, show me what you're going to do."

She trembled slightly at his request but took the dildo from him. Then—she gave him so much more than he asked for.

"I'm going to close my eyes," she whispered, doing just as she said, lowering her eyelids. "And think of you. Of your kisses. Of the way you cup my cheek just before your lips touch mine. How you drag the backs of your fingers along my neck, over my breasts."

As she spoke, she imitated the words, drawing her knuckles over her bare breast.

"I'll remember how you pinched my nipples, how you made the hurt feel so good." She pinched her own taut nipple, and he

153

fought not to push her hand out of the way so he could take over. "I love the way you suck them into your mouth, tease them with your teeth."

Elio took his cock in hand, slowly stroking it as she drew pictures of them in his mind.

Gianna placed the vibrator on her clit and turned it on the lower speed. She cried out, "God, I'm going to think about your lips and fingers here. How crazy you made me, how hungry, how needy."

She turned up the speed, but this time, she didn't resist the sensations, didn't seek to mute them by pulling the toy away. She held it there a few moments, but like before, it still wasn't enough, so she picked up the dildo.

Elio held his breath as she placed the head of the toy at her pussy. She pushed it in, only the flared head of it, then pulled it out again. The tip of the dildo was shiny with her juices. She was so wet, so ready.

He'd never felt an arousal like this. He gripped his dick harder. It was that or throw that fucking dildo across the cabin and take her so hard, she'd have no choice but to feel it until...

Gianna moaned, and he watched as more of the toy slipped in. She was offering him the unique opportunity to see what it looked like when her body accepted him inside her.

She seesawed in and out, her pussy stretching around the thickness.

"Does that hurt?" he asked softly, thinking it must. She was so tight, and the toy, like him, so much bigger.

She shook her head. "No. It feels full. It feels..." He got the sense she was struggling for the word, though he couldn't tell if it was because she couldn't think of it or because she was too distracted by her pleasure.

Elio watched, spellbound, as inch after inch of the dildo disappeared, going deeper with each return. Her breathing was labored, but she forged on. The vibrator had drifted away from the sweet spot, so he reached out, taking it from her. He placed it back over her clit, putting it exactly where she needed it most.

"God!" she yelled, her head coming off the pillow in response to the stimulation. The dildo sank in the final inch, and Gianna's hand fell to the bed beside her.

"Gianna," he said, but she shook her head, waving him away. She took the vibrator back from him, her eyes still shut tightly.

He was forced to move his knees to the outside of hers when she fought to close them around the toy.

Elio shifted to her side, watching Gianna's hips rise and fall as she fucked herself with the vibrator, the dildo lodged deep. She didn't seem to need the thrust, just the pressure on her clit and the full feeling.

Elio had never seen anything so enthralling. His grip on his cock tightened, but he didn't stroke as quickly, as forcefully as he might have. Instead, he mimicked her motions, tightening and loosening his grip as he imagined the way her pussy muscles were likely clenching against the dildo.

Gianna's hips moved faster, and he recognized the second her orgasm struck. She thrust her hips up one last time and held there, suspended several inches off the mattress, a look of almost-pain on her face.

"Elio!" she cried out.

His name.

Gianna hadn't fully come down when he lost what little control he had left. He took the vibrator and turned it off. Then he gripped the dildo, pulling it out, even as her body resisted the departure, her orgasm lingering, clinging tightly to the toy.

"God," she gasped, when the flared head cleared. "Elio." She reached out for him, almost blindly. "Please."

She didn't need to beg.

Fuck. He was the beggar in this bed. The one ready to lay himself at her feet if only to steal scraps of her time, her attention, her.

He drew on a condom, shoving into the hilt, belatedly aware

that she had taken the dildo in slower, giving herself time to adjust.

Elio forced himself to hold there, fighting the need to take her like a rutting beast.

Gianna's nails scored his back and she—honest-to-God—bared her teeth. "Don't stop. Prove that I'm yours. Make me feel it!"

If she intended to say more, to up the ante on her demands, he didn't give her the chance. Her words not only dared him, they freed him, body and soul.

Elio thrust hard and fast, his climax striking a split second before Gianna came again.

The two held steady, the only sound in the cabin their gasping breaths and the crackling fire. He remained above her, his weight held up on his elbows by her shoulders. Her gaze locked with his, and while neither of them said anything, Elio felt as if they spoke volumes.

They might be separating tomorrow, but there was no way he would be leaving her behind. He was going to carry her with him, back to Baltimore, back out on that ice, on the road, everywhere. She was there now, burrowed deep. In his thoughts and, God help him, his heart.

Because while he had zero experience with the emotion, he knew without a doubt, this was it.

He was in love.

Chapter Thirteen

G ianna stood next to her car, watching as Elio locked the
door to the cabin.

She fought hard to give him a cheerful smile, not
wanting him to know how hard this goodbye was going to be
for her.

They'd spent the morning packing their things and tidying
up. Gianna had lived in the same apartment her entire life, but she
didn't think she'd miss the place when she moved out as much as
she would this cabin.

She and Elio had remained in bed a little later than either of
them had planned because they'd both agreed it would be silly to
leave just one condom in the box. So she'd grabbed it, put it on
him, then climbed on top, riding him as he stroked her clit.
Gianna had thought herself in the power position, but Elio had
proven that wrong the second he gripped her hips, driving her
pace, her depth, her angle. They'd come much quicker than she'd
wanted, the interlude ending far too soon for her, considering it
was the last.

"All good?" she asked when he approached her.

He nodded.

She held up her hand, revealing the key dangling there on a chain. "I'll return Liza's key to her when I get back to the city."

Liza had texted her nearly every single day of her stay, yet she hadn't told her friend about Elio's presence. He hadn't asked her not to, nor had he seemed upset that she hadn't. When Aldo called on Wednesday, Elio had pretended to be back home, in Baltimore. No mention of the cabin...or her.

For Gianna, it felt as if they were holding tightly to this escape from the real world, keeping it their own special secret, something that was just for them, that they didn't want to share with anyone else.

"I'll follow you off the mountain," Elio said. "Make sure you get to the highway alright."

"Okay. I'll grab a pregnancy test on my way back to Philly," she promised. "And I'll call you either way."

"Thanks," he said, glancing back toward the cabin almost wistfully. "I hate to leave."

"Me too. This week was..." There wasn't a word big enough, so she didn't try. Didn't have to.

"Yeah," he agreed, grasping her waist. His head lowered as he stole one last glorious, amazing kiss. Their tongues took their last tastes, and she drew in a deep breath through her nose, trying to memorize the smell of him, woodsmoke and his Old Spice bodywash.

When they parted, she gave him a smile.

"I guess I'll see you around. Sometime."

Fuck.

That was the lamest farewell in history.

Elio scowled, though it was one of those blink-and-you-missed-it looks. His expression cleared quickly. "Goodbye, Freckles."

He released her and she missed his touch in an instant. Then, he walked to his truck, waiting until she got in her car and turned it around in the driveway before starting his own vehicle.

True to his word, he followed her down the winding roads

until they hit the highway. He honked the horn, and she returned his wave, watching him in the rearview mirror. Then, he turned left as she turned right.

And that was that.

What a week. Despite the sadness of leaving him, Gianna was surprised to realize the stronger emotion right now was happiness.

The loneliness that had lingered for too long seemed to be gone. She hoped for good.

After what felt like a lifetime of Gianna wandering around in shadowed rooms, Elio had turned on the lights, and she vowed to herself that she was never going back into the dark.

Turning on the radio, she shuffled through the stations until she found Neil Diamond, singing along to "Sweet Caroline" loudly and off-key, as she grinned like a fool.

It was late afternoon when Gianna dragged her suitcase to the fourth floor of her apartment building. The damn elevator was on the fritz again. The trip from the Poconos to Philadelphia shouldn't have taken more than a couple of hours, but she'd hit traffic, due to the fact the roads were still slick. Plus, she'd treated herself to a long lunch at a restaurant Liza had suggested, and then, she'd lost a couple more hours wandering around an indoor flea market.

She'd skipped the grocery store upon pulling into town, deciding to put it off until tomorrow. All she wanted to do tonight was unpack, start some laundry, and veg in front of the television. She planned to throw the frozen pepperoni pizza in her freezer in the oven for dinner.

Unlocking the door to her apartment, she'd only taken a few steps inside before getting the sense that she wasn't alone.

She started to back toward the hall, reaching for her phone to call 9-1-1, when Sam stepped out of her kitchen.

"I thought I heard the door open," he said.

"What the hell are you doing here?"

Sam rubbed the back of his neck uncomfortably, having enough sense to feel guilty for being in her apartment without permission.

Then she changed her question. "How did you get in? You don't have a key anymore."

Sam cleared his throat. "Mrs. Pasquet."

Gianna glanced over her shoulder at her neighbor's closed door. "She let you in here?"

"She has the spare key."

"And you asked for it?" She couldn't keep from raising her voice, her ire growing more with each passing second.

"No, no," Sam quickly replied, waving his hands as if to erase that thought from her mind. "I was waiting for you, out in the hallway. I'd been there about an hour when Mrs. Pasquet opened the door and saw me. We chatted for a few minutes."

Mrs. Pasquet had adored Sam, and in some ways, it felt like her elderly neighbor had taken their break-up harder than Gianna had, always asking her if she'd seen Sam lately.

"I told her I was hoping to talk to you. She told me you'd gone on vacation, but she seemed confused about when you were getting home."

Gianna had told Mrs. Pasquet she'd be back on Saturday, but her neighbor was getting more and more forgetful, something that had been worrying Gianna lately.

Which made the fact that Sam took advantage of the beloved woman even more infuriating.

"So you somehow convinced my ninety-two-year-old neighbor to give you the spare key?"

Sam shook his head. "She offered it. Said she didn't think you'd mind if I waited for you inside the apartment rather than hanging out in the hallway."

Gianna lifted her hand. "Give me the key back, then get out. And don't bother trying to get it from Mrs. Pasquet again. She won't have it."

Sam dug into his jean's pocket and handed it to her. "Gianna, please. I...can we talk for a minute?"

She snorted derisively. "We already had that talk. Back in September, remember? I think it started with 'this isn't working for me' and ended with 'I don't love you anymore.' Of course, you somehow missed the part about Emma, which was probably the most import—"

She stopped mid-rant when she caught a whiff of something. "Are you *cooking* something?"

This time, Sam's guilt was nearly palpable. "I brought food. Thought I'd make your favorite dinner. Lasagna and garlic bread."

Her temper flared hot and fast. "Are you fucking serious right now?! You have five seconds to get the hell out of here or I swear to God, I'm calling the cops."

"No!" Sam said hastily. "You don't have to do that. I'll leave. I just..." He ran his hand through his hair. "Fuck. I'm sorry. Okay? I wanted to tell you I'm sorry. For all of it. I was a grade-A douchebag, an asshole, a gigantic dick."

"Keep going," she said, crossing her arms.

She hadn't meant her words as a joke, but Sam gave her a ghost of a smile, clearly taking them that way.

"I never meant to hurt you," he said softly.

She stared at him, at this man who'd been the center of her universe for eleven years, and she knew he was telling her the truth. He wasn't a bad guy. He'd just done a very stupid, hurtful thing.

"I know that, Sam," she said. "But you *did* hurt me."

"I keep looking back, trying to figure out why I did it. But no matter how hard I try, I can't find an answer."

"You're obviously not trying that hard because the answer's pretty fucking obvious if you ask me. You let your dick do the thinking." Gianna recalled Elio saying as much to her, then she realized he'd been right about Sam coming back. She didn't know if Sam's plan with this dinner had been simply to apologize or if he was trying to win her back, but Elio had told her he'd come groveling. And here he was.

Sam sighed heavily. "Yeah. I did. It's just we'd been fighting so much, never managing to get through the week without some blow-up. And then, the firm took on Emma's family as a client, designing their new office building, and—"

Gianna held up her hand. "Let me stop you right there. I have no desire to hash out any of this. It's ancient history. Water under the bridge and all that shit."

"I was just trying to explain where my head was. What was driving my actions."

She shrugged. "I don't care about any of that. I've moved on, Sam. None of this matters."

Gianna wasn't sure what he'd expected from her, but it was obvious he hadn't foreseen this. Which pissed her off. Did he really think she was so weak or needy or stupid that she'd accept his apology, talk it out with him, and then...what?

They'd get back together?

Then she considered their past—brief—breakups and realized that was exactly how things had played out. Of course, there was a big difference between breaking up over petty fights about money or her cleaning issues or him staying out too late with the guys. He'd cheated on her and lied about it.

This wasn't the same thing at all.

"Gianna, please. I need to find a way to make this right."

She shook her head. "That's not possible."

He looked at her as if waiting for her to change her mind. Oh my God. He really *did* think she was a pushover.

"You need to leave."

Sam stood there, hesitant to go. She knew why. It was finally starting to sink in that she was serious, and this was his last chance to change her mind.

She gestured to the still-open apartment door, but he didn't move. "I need to...I have some things I need to grab."

She followed him to the kitchen, watching as he grabbed his

cellphone from the counter. "I set the timer on the lasagna," he said. "Should be ready in another forty minutes."

She didn't reply except to give him a single nod of her head. She was dumping the food in the trash the second he left.

Then he walked to the living room and grabbed his coat. For the first time, she looked around her apartment and noticed several things were amiss.

"When did you get the key from Mrs. Pasquet?" she asked, when she noticed the throw blanket on the back of her couch was balled up in one corner of the cushions, rather than folded and laying over the back.

Sam sighed. "Yesterday."

Gianna narrowed her eyes. She was so angry, she couldn't find the ability to speak. Every part of her felt poised to explode. "Are you fucking *kidding* me?" she asked through gritted teeth.

"I didn't mean to..." Sam realized he was on shaky ground. "I was sitting on the couch, waiting for you. It got late and I fell asleep."

"You had no right." There were so many furious words piling up in her head, she couldn't get them out. "Why didn't you leave this morning?"

"I did. But I saw on your calendar that you were coming back from your trip today, so..."

That was when she recalled the dinner in the oven. "You went to the grocery store and came back?!"

He didn't bother answering. He clearly didn't want to. He knew every word was only digging his grave deeper.

The fucker had looked at her calendar.

"Get out!" she yelled. "Get the fuck out and don't ever come back here."

Sam grabbed his stuff and quickly walked to the door. She followed him, intent on slamming it behind him and locking it. He turned to look at her, standing just in the threshold.

"For what it's worth, I really am sorry."

She scowled. "It's worth nothing."

Sam left, but she didn't slam the door. She refused to give him the satisfaction. Instead, she closed it gently, threw the dead bolt, then walked to the couch and picked up the blanket, her hands trembling in anger.

"Motherfucker," she cursed as she folded the throw and put it in its normal place over the back of the couch.

She dragged her suitcase to the washing machine, threw a load in, then grabbed the vacuum. She felt violated. He'd slept in her apartment.

Two hours later, the entire apartment was clean, sparkling. Rather than dump the lasagna, she let it finish baking, then took it down to the two homeless men who slept at the end of her block.

"Just in time," she murmured as the oven timer went off. Her frozen pizza was ready.

She placed a couple of pieces on a plate and carried them to the living room, just as her cellphone rang.

She checked the caller ID, praying it wasn't Sam, and hoping it was Elio.

It was neither.

She answered. "Hey."

"You back?" Liza asked.

"Yep. Home again, home again, jiggety jig," she said, repeating the silly little saying Grandma had always recited whenever they'd been away from home for a few days.

"How was it? Clear out all the cobwebs? Ready to start the next big adventure?" Liza asked.

"The trip was great, exactly what I needed. That cabin is absolutely incredible. Heaven on earth."

Right, Gianna thought, it was the place, and not the company, that made her time away so perfect.

"Told you so. And your Sam issues?" Liza asked.

"Over. So fucking over." Gianna spent the next few minutes telling her best friend what she'd returned home to, as Liza raged and fumed on her behalf.

"What a fucking asshole. Jesus! Do you think you should change the locks?" Liza asked.

Gianna hadn't considered that, but it wasn't a bad idea. "I really don't think he has a key anymore—or he wouldn't have taken Mrs. Pasquet's—but I guess it couldn't hurt."

"What are your plans this week? I was thinking we could get together for dinner at my place with some Chinese food. Maybe discuss the possibility of setting you up on Bumble."

Gianna sighed, not wanting to commit to the dating profile until she'd taken the pregnancy test. Not that she could tell Liza that.

"My work schedule is pretty insane this week, thanks to the days off. How about the weekend? Friday night?" Gianna should know by then if she was or if she wasn't.

God only knew how she'd break the news to her best friend if she was.

"Sounds good," Liza said.

Gianna's phone beeped, another call coming through. Glancing nervously/excitedly at the screen, she was disappointed to see her boss's name. "Hey, Liza. I gotta go. That's my boss calling."

"Okay, I'll see you Friday. Later."

She disconnected the call with Liza to answer the one from her boss.

"Are you home?" her boss, Donna asked, instead of the usual greeting.

"Yeah. Got home a few hours ago. What's up?"

"Oh, thank God. We're dying on the vine here, Gianna. Both night managers called in sick. There's some virus flying around, and everyone is dropping like flies. I've been here for twenty-eight hours, and now...dammit, I'm starting to get a sore throat. I hate to call you since it's the last day of your vacation—"

Gianna was already on her feet. "Let me change my clothes and I'll be right there." She intended to go in armed with all the disinfectant cleaning supplies she had on hand.

165

"You are a lifesaver," Donna replied.

Gianna didn't mind helping because her boss was really awesome. It was that fact that had kept Gianna working at the hotel as long as she had rather than looking for something else.

Regardless, there was no room for advancement where she was, and with Rafe and Gio building her dream inn, it was time to move on.

"I can be there in half an hour."

She and Donna said their goodbyes, the relief in her boss's voice so evident, Gianna didn't mind missing the last night of her vacation.

She hadn't been looking forward to sleeping alone. Five nights snuggled up with Elio had ruined her for her own bed. At least by working tonight, she could put it off for another night.

Gianna wondered what he was doing right now. Part of her was tempted to text him, but she wasn't sure how he'd feel about that.

While they'd talked constantly this week, sharing so much of themselves with each other, it occurred to her now, there were a lot of important things they'd left unsaid.

It was early Wednesday evening when Gianna dragged herself home from work, weary to the bone. Donna hadn't exaggerated about the illness sweeping through the hotel staff. Gianna had worked double shifts ever since Saturday night. She had spent two days cleaning rooms when every maid but one called in sick.

Gianna had also covered for Donna, who had indeed gotten the killer flu, so in addition to serving as a maid, a desk clerk, and even a maintenance person in one instance, she also took over the position of manager, working herself to exhaustion.

Donna had returned to work this afternoon, taken one look at Gianna, and told her not to come back until Saturday, proclaiming she'd earned a couple days off.

Gianna had intended to go straight home, but halfway there, she remembered her refrigerator was completely bare, so she stopped by the grocery store. Placing the bags of food on the counter, she dug through them until she found what she was looking for.

She'd been too busy to grab a pregnancy test before today. Hell, she'd been so overworked, she hadn't had time to even stress over the possibility.

But now that she had it, she was anxious for the results.

Walking to the bathroom, Gianna opened the package, read the instructions, then pulled down her pants.

One glance down told her all she needed to know.

"Fuck," she whispered, her heart sinking.

Slowly, she placed the test back in the package and tossed it under the sink, before grabbing the tampons instead.

Sinking down on the toilet, she put her head in her hands, fighting the desire to cry.

What the hell was wrong with her? This was a good thing...right?

Then why did she feel this soul-crushing devastation?

For a few minutes, she just sat there, willing away the tears. Then, she took a deep breath, cleaned herself up, and headed back to the kitchen.

Her phone lay on the counter. She glanced at the clock. Elio had a home game tonight. In fact, he was probably in the locker room getting ready.

She now had the Baltimore schedule memorized, and she knew exactly what channel the games were on. He hadn't played since leaving the injured reserve list, but Liza had texted their entire friend group this morning, telling everyone Elio was in the starting lineup tonight.

Gianna had promised to call him, but she'd already made him wait three days for a response. So she opened her contacts list and clicked on his name, sending off a quick text, certain he wouldn't see it until after the game. He'd confided one night that he unplugged completely a few hours before game time to get in the right headspace.

I'm not pregnant.

Then she sent another text, lying about her reason for not calling, saying something lame about not wanting to make him wait. The truth was she didn't think she could say the words aloud without crying.

Once the two messages were sent, she unpacked her groceries, made herself some macaroni and cheese, the box kind, and dipped out a more than generous helping.

Walking to the living room with her bowl and phone, she sat down and turned on the TV, settling down to watch the game. They were singing the National Anthem, the camera panning the line. Her heart did a little flip-flop when Elio's face showed on the screen.

She glanced at her phone. There was no response, but—shit —she could see that Elio had read the message.

What did he think of the results?

Was he breathing a huge sigh of relief? Or was he feeling like she was?

Disappointed.

Chapter Fourteen

Elio laughed as Tank and Blake got into a tussle, trying to one-up each other on who was going to score the most goals tonight. It was a common argument between the two competitive bastards. It was a good thing they were best friends or the over-the-top insults about receding hairlines, sloppy stickhandling, dick size and function, as well as the obnoxious "your mama" jokes, probably would have ended in bloodshed a long time ago.

In the past, Elio usually stepped in to break things up before they got hurt, telling them to grow up, but today, he just let them have at it.

It occurred to him how much he would miss this if he decided to hang up his skates. This time, just before the game, with all the guys getting ready, talking trash about the other team—and each other—was one of his favorite parts of the job. He still loved the competition, loved being out on the ice, loved that moment when the puck connected with the stick, and he just knew that fucker was going to hit the back of the net.

Since returning, he'd been making a concerted effort to come to a decision, instituting some of Gianna's list-making skills by weighing all the pros and cons. As such, he'd been paying closer attention to things that he had taken for granted or forgotten to notice at all because they had become second nature after so many years.

He pulled his jersey on, anxious to finally get back out on the ice. He was in the starting lineup after too many fucking weeks away. He'd gotten back to Baltimore early Saturday afternoon, heading to the rink rather than his apartment, anxious to return to his workout routine.

He'd been practicing with the team—and on his own—nearly twelve hours a day since then.

"Good to have you back, El Train. I missed you out there on the ice."

Elio smiled at the nickname as Preston sank down onto the bench next to him.

His old teammate, Alex Stone, had dubbed him the El Train, playing on his name and the fact that, according to Alex, Elio had a tendency to fly in and take their opponents down with the force of a speeding train.

As he'd told Gianna, it really was a source of amusement amongst the Moretti family that Elio's mild-mannered personality didn't translate on the ice. As the enforcer on his team, he never hesitated to step in with fists flying, ready to defend any teammate he'd deemed wronged.

"It's good to be back. That sling sucked ass."

Elio and Preston played on the same line, the two perfectly in synch out on the ice. Coach Fields had remarked more than once that it was like they shared a hive mind. Preston seemed to know where Elio was going to end up before Elio even started heading that direction.

"Tonight's the night," Tank said. "With the El Train back, we're gonna ride Carolina hard and put 'em away wet."

"Sort of like I did with your mom last night," Blake joked.

Tank took the obligatory swing, and the two men were right back at it.

Elio shook his head. "Can't believe I'm going to say this, but I missed you idiots."

Coulton, the goalie, placed a hand to his heart. "Idiots? Jesus, man. Have you been away so long you've forgotten your pet name for us? What happened to *fucking morons*?"

Elio snorted. "I'm trying to clean up my language," he lied.

"Yeah right," Tank said, calling him out. "Five bucks says you're dropping the F-bomb two minutes after the puck drops."

"I'll take that bet," Blake said. "I'm betting he cuts loose with a string of motherfuckers within the first thirty seconds."

"You guys aren't giving our boy enough credit," Preston said, slapping Elio on the back. "My money is on him losing his shit when he realizes Paula The Relentless managed to score herself a season ticket last week and her seat is right behind our bench... near a few of the other girlfriends and wives."

Elio whipped around on Preston. "Are you fucking kidding me?"

Blake and Tank both groaned, claiming Preston had played dirty. Regardless, they promised to pay up after the game.

His teammates had taken to calling her Paula The Relentless several months ago, when she managed to "run into him" for the sixth time.

One perk to breaking his collarbone was that it had disrupted his schedule enough that he hadn't been hitting the usual stomping grounds. He hadn't seen her in months, and he'd thought that separation would break the chain once and for all.

"Tell me you're kidding about her and the fucking seat," he said to Preston, who gave him an apologetic look.

"I wish I could. She sort of doubled-down after you went on the injured reserve list, showing up at our after-game celebrations at the pub, hanging out at Max's around lunchtime, even going to some of the closer away games. It's driving her nuts that she can't predict where you might be. I *told* you when you made that girl your booty-call that she was in it for a ring and that nice fat checking account of yours. Girls like that don't go down easy. They come back swinging."

Preston *had* offered that warning, but Paula had always played it so cool. Cool enough that he let himself enjoy the sex without strings, the hookups without effort.

"She wears your jersey to every game," Blake added, though he looked much less apologetic than Preston and a lot more amused.

Elio had participated—gently—in practices and attended club meals and meetings, but on the Baltimore team, it was considered bad luck for an injured player to sit on the bench or travel with the team. And if there was one thing a hockey player never did, it was fuck around when it came to luck.

"Shit," Elio muttered. He was going to have to pull Paula aside at some point and tell her—*again*—that they were over. The fact that he'd had that conversation with her a half dozen times before didn't give him much hope that he'd be successful this time.

"Game time in five, boys," the assistant coach yelled.

Elio turned around to close his locker when his phone pinged. Typically, he turned it off before a game, but since returning from the Poconos, he couldn't make himself silence it. Gianna's face flashed in his mind. He'd been waiting for her call for three days, and the more time that passed, the more anxious he became, nervous about the results, and worried that perhaps she had fallen back on old habits. He could just imagine her scrubbing her apartment to within an inch of its life.

He reached for it, his chest tightening when he saw her name, and he clicked to open the text.

> I'm not pregnant.

Just three words—but they took him down.

He sank to the bench, feeling like he'd just been checked into the boards.

Elio had expected to feel relief. After all, he and Gianna

weren't a couple. Despite the fact they'd been acquaintances for years, they'd only really become friends last week.

They didn't know each other well enough to become parents together. And neither of them was in a place career-wise where a baby made sense. He was still on the fence about his future in Baltimore, and Gianna was on the verge of going for her dream job.

So, this was a good thing.

Or at least that was what he was trying to convince himself.

Because good or not, he was...God...he was disappointed.

And it was a heavy disappointment, one that sank deep.

Another ping and he glanced back at his phone.

> Wanted to call, but knew you had the game.
> Didn't want you to wait any longer.

And that was it. Gianna hadn't added anything else, hadn't given him a single clue to her own feelings about the results. Was she relieved? Happy? Sad?

He considered her stories about her grandmother and mother, how they'd both been single mothers, how they'd struggled. Never once when she talked about them did Gianna allude to how she would feel in that same situation.

Goddammit. That had been his fault. He'd pushed off all talk about the pregnancy and the two of them had held firm to it. At the time, he thought he'd been saving them from stressing out about an unknown, but now, there was too much he didn't know. Things he desperately *wanted* to know.

Like how she was feeling.

He'd replayed their time together over and over since leaving her, the memories on auto-repeat. It felt as if they'd been at that cabin for years, not a mere five days, the two of them sharing a lifetime. A wonderful lifetime.

"Game time!" Tank called out. "Look alive, El Train."

Elio was surprised to discover most of the team had already

filed out, so he was forced to put the text and Gianna out of his mind, something that was surprisingly difficult to do.

He'd never had a hard time shutting the world out when it was game time. Because in the past, the game, the competition, and winning was all that mattered to him.

That wasn't true anymore.

Now there was something that mattered even more.

And it was her.

"What a game," Preston said as he took a swig of Guinness. "We fucking kicked ass."

They had. They'd shutout Carolina, winning soundly four goals to nil. Preston had scored, as had Elio. He should be in high spirits, like his teammate, but he was struggling to get there, Gianna's text still rattling around in the back of his brain.

He hadn't texted or called her back yet, not sure what he was going to say.

Preston glanced around Pat's Pub and grinned. "Big crowd here tonight. Wonder if they've got music planned for later."

Elio gestured toward the stage where a guitar and amp were set up. "I think that's a good bet."

Preston's eyes lit up. "Wouldn't it be cool if Hunter Maxwell was in town? I wouldn't mind hearing him perform. Or even Aubrey Summers."

The best/craziest part about the pub was the fact that the Collins family, who owned it, included not one, not two, not three, but *four* famous musicians. Like, world famous.

And while it was rare, it wasn't unheard of for Hunter or Aubrey, or even Sky Mitchell and Teagan Collins, to perform there when in town.

Elio had been introduced to Pat's Irish Pub during his first year playing for Baltimore. His teammate, Alex Stone, had taken him around the city shortly after Elio had signed. Alex, team captain at the time, had lived in Baltimore for several years, long enough that he'd determined what bars were popular with tourists and which were local favorites.

Pat's ranked at the top of both lists, serving drinks to a steady crowd of regulars while serving up meals that had the tourists planning return trips just for another bite of Riley's, Shepherd's Pie.

Over the years, Elio had brought quite a few of his teammates to the pub, much to the delight of the sports-mad Collins family. Add in the fact his cousins, Layla and Erin, had both married into the Collins clan, it had become a home away from home, the place he came when he felt homesick.

"Hey, guys," Alex Stone said, approaching their table. "That was one hell of a game."

Preston and Elio stood up, offering handshakes that morphed into guy hugs, both happy to see their old teammate.

The Baltimore team had changed quite a bit from the early days, enough that Elio was starting to feel his age. He wasn't the oldest on the team, but he wasn't far from it. Preston was only a couple years younger, which meant he and Elio had been teammates the longest.

Most of the guys on the team were a decade younger than him, and Elio felt the disconnect. These days, he typically opted to head home after a single celebratory beer or two, letting the young bucks party until the wee hours.

"It's about time you got your ass back to town." Elio had been looking forward to this reunion with his old teammate. "Miss your ugly mug."

"Same," Alex said, as they sat down. "And I'm glad this first round—which I'm buying—is for a win, and not to drown our sorrows over a loss to fucking Carolina."

"Well, look what the cat dragged in." Padraig Collins, the bartender, walked over to take Alex's drink order and chat for a few moments.

Elio and Alex had shared hotel rooms together whenever they were on the road during his early days with Baltimore.

Then, at the end of one season, Alex had headed to Vegas to attend the wedding of a friend and returned with a bride of his own.

Alex's wife, Charley, wrote children's books and for the first year of their marriage, she'd traveled with the team a good bit, able to write on the road. Of course, that was before she got pregnant and had a daughter. After that, Alex hung up his skates, opting to become a full-time husband and father.

When Elio had learned his old teammate and friend was going to be in Baltimore this weekend, one of the stops in Charley's latest book tour, Elio invited him for a drink after the game. Sitting here with Alex, listening to him and Padraig chatting about hockey, felt like old times.

Originally, Elio's invitation had sprung from the desire to talk to Alex about life after hockey, curious to see if his friend was happy with the decision he'd made, if he had any regrets.

Now...there were other things he wanted to discuss as well. The problem was, he didn't want to show his hand in front of Preston, who'd invited himself along at the last minute when he found out Alex was in town. Until Elio made a solid decision about his future with Baltimore, he wasn't saying a word to anyone on the team. Preston was trustworthy, but Elio wasn't willing to test it. Hockey players gossiped more than a bunch of old women.

"How's life going? Those two girls of yours keeping you hopping?" Elio asked, when Padraig returned to the bar to get Alex's drink. Alex and Charley had welcomed daughter number two a year earlier, and Elio had enjoyed giving his friend shit about his looming future, about all the boys who were going to come sniffing around during the teen years.

"Charley and I were just saying yesterday that we should have stopped with one. Because while the parent/kid numbers are even, we're still outnumbered. Badly. Of course, it doesn't help that Olivia was the perfect baby. Our expectations were definitely ill-formed when Katherine came along."

Elio chuckled. "She still giving you a run for your money? Last I heard, she was resistant to the car seat."

"Car seat?" Preston asked curiously.

Alex gave their friend the short version of the story he'd regaled Elio with during a phone call a couple months earlier. "She scream-cried in the car for six hours straight when we were driving home from a trip to Niagara Falls."

"Six hours?" Preston sounded as horrified as Elio had felt when Alex told him about the trip.

"Without a single break," Alex added. "We kept thinking she would fall asleep, but nope. My girl is made of stronger stuff. And her stuff hates the car seat. Now that she's started walking, I can't remember the last time I've managed to relax in my recliner for more than five minutes in a row. She's into everything. I had to repaint the upstairs hallway when she escaped the crib and got her hands on a Sharpie marker."

Despite everything he was saying, Alex was grinning from ear to ear, and it occurred to Elio, he'd never seen the guy happier. Ever. And they'd won the Stanley Cup together.

"Better you than me," Preston said, rising. "Hey, give me a minute. I gotta go see a man about a horse," he joked, walking to the restroom.

"So no regrets on the Mr. Mom gig, huh?" Elio asked, deciding to make the most of these few minutes alone with Alex.

Alex shook his head. "Not a single one. Marrying Charley and having those girls was the best thing I ever did."

"And you don't miss the game?"

Alex lifted one shoulder, shrugging casually. "Sure, there are times when I'm watching and wishing I was back out there. Then Olivia comes over, crawls in my lap, lays her head on my chest, and I realize I'm exactly where I'm meant to be. Besides, you've met my wife. If I feel the need to get my ass handed to me on the ice, I just head to the rink with her and let her remind me why it's probably a good thing I retired."

Elio chuckled. Charley had apparently been quite a tomboy

when they were growing up, she and Alex playing on the same youth hockey leagues. According to Alex, she could still give him a run for his money on the ice.

"So it was the right decision?"

"One hundred percent. You know, I'd ask about your collarbone, but I saw you score that goal tonight. That puck was flying fast enough, it should have had a flight attendant on board."

"I feel great. Back in fighting shape. Although, I must admit I didn't mind not being on the road with the team the last couple of months. Gets old traveling with a bunch of smelly-ass men, snoring, farting, and adjusting their junk every five seconds."

Alex's eyes widened. "What? Did Elio Moretti just say life on the road was getting old? Never thought I'd see the day you'd ever say a negative word about our beloved hockey."

The old Elio would have picked up the challenge his friend laid down, insisting that there was nothing on earth better than the game. This time, he simply remained quiet.

And because Alex had always been a very good friend, he noticed. "Hang on a second. Are you thinking about retiring from the game?"

Elio nodded. "I've been giving it some thought lately."

"Wow. That's big. I always figured you'd play until you got too old to bend over and tie up your skates." Alex leaned back against his chair, letting the news sink in. When it did, he asked, "Why now?"

Elio frowned. "Why now?"

"What's driving this? Is it the injuries?"

Aldo had asked him the same thing over the holidays. Elio shook his head. "No. I meant what I said. I feel fine." He glanced toward the restroom. Preston emerged, but he detoured, striking up a conversation with a pretty brunette.

Alex followed his gaze. "Looks like we're about to lose our drinking buddy. Preston's got his Mr. Charming face on. Guy still cherry-picking the hot girl on guys' night out?"

Preston was famous for finding the prettiest girl in a bar or party—the one all the guys noticed—then laying on the charm until he wooed her to his bed for a night or two. And if another teammate got there first, it only increased Preston's interest in her because the guy was a competitive bastard.

Elio nodded. "He is. Loves the challenge of it."

Alex turned, focusing on him. "There was a time I accused you of the same."

"You always forgot to protect the five-hole," Elio joked, perfectly aware he was the pot calling the kettle black, that he'd stolen more than a few rink bunnies away from his teammates as well.

Alex snuck one more glance over his shoulder as if to confirm they wouldn't be interrupted. "I assume you haven't told anyone on the team."

"I haven't, so I'd appreciate it if—"

Alex raised his hand, waved him off. "You don't even have to ask. Mum's the word. So...is it your family?" Alex looked concerned. "Your parents doing okay?"

"They're great. Although I think it's safe to say my family's playing a part in this decision. I've been away eleven years, Alex. Missed a shit-ton of birthdays, holidays, weddings. I got to do some of those things while I was on the injured reserve list, and I enjoyed it, realized I was tired of always being on the outside, hearing about all the fun stuff my family and friends were getting up to secondhand."

Alex nodded. "I get that. I mean, shit, at least you could hop in the car and drive home for a few hours if you ever felt the desire to reconnect with them. My family was halfway across the country in Wisconsin. And I was okay with that. Until I wasn't. If that makes sense."

It made perfect sense. This was why Elio had invited Alex out. His friend, better than anyone else, knew exactly what he was going through because he'd lived the same life.

"There's nothing wrong with wanting to go home, but I

think you need to ask yourself if this is just a fleeting case of home-sickness or if this is a genuine desire," Alex added.

Elio took a drink of his beer. "That's what I've been asking myself for months. I kept thinking after I'd healed, after I'd returned to the game, I would hit the ice and the answer would just appear...like magic."

"Let me guess...no such luck tonight?"

Elio sighed. "Nope. Of course, it doesn't help that I muddied the waters a bit after Christmas."

Alex leaned forward. "What's that mean?"

Elio hadn't told another living soul about his time with Gianna. Primarily because everyone he wanted to talk to was related to him and knew her. He didn't want to betray Gianna's confidence if she preferred they keep their...fuck, she would probably call it an *affair*, a secret. Elio couldn't attach such a casual term to what they shared. Of course, he didn't dare call it anything else either. Not even in his own head.

"I spent a few days in the Poconos at my family's cabin," Elio started. "I thought the time away would help me clear my head, come to a decision. I didn't realize my sister had loaned the cabin to one of her best friends, Gianna."

"Ah...muddied the waters. I see."

Elio continued. "There was a blizzard, and we were snowed in together for five days."

Alex whistled, low and slow. "Damn, guess that wreaked havoc on your fuck-and-run routine. So now you've pissed off your sister and the friend? Liza threatening to cut your dick off?"

Elio shook his head, though it made sense that Alex would assume he'd led with his cock and fucked things up with Gianna. "No. You're the first person I've told about Gianna, and while I don't know for sure, I'm assuming she hasn't told anyone either. Because I haven't heard from my sister."

Alex's brows furrowed, and Elio could see his friend trying to make sense of what he was telling him. If it wasn't so fucking sad, it would almost be funny to see Alex struggling. Because his old friend wasn't even considering the most obvious answer—the possibility that Elio had fallen for Gianna.

"I'm going to need you to explain what you mean by muddied the waters. I'm not getting it."

"We hooked up."

Alex snorted. "Yeah, that part goes without saying."

"The condom broke."

Alex sobered up fast. "Jesus. Is she—"

Elio raised his hand, waving it quickly to shut down that line of thought. "No. No. She texted me tonight before the game. She's not pregnant."

Alex's shoulders dropped in obvious relief. "Well, that's a good thing." Then he paused, studying Elio's face close enough that he knew he wasn't shielding his emotions or thoughts at all. "That *is* a good thing, isn't it?"

Elio tried to find a way to respond. "It is. Or, at least, I should think it is, but the truth is..."

Alex gave Elio plenty of time to finish his comment, but Elio didn't make the attempt. Wasn't sure what to say.

"Elio, are you in love with Gianna?"

"Yes." There was no point in denying the truth. Not to his friend. Not to himself.

"Holy. Fuck."

Elio narrowed his eyes. "You know it's not *that* far out of the realm of reality."

Alex gave him a know-it-all grin. "Bro. Me getting Katherine in her car seat without a meltdown of epic proportions seems more likely than the idea of Elio Moretti falling in love. I have got to meet this girl."

Elio grimaced. "There's no way in hell I'm introducing her to you. As of right now, and by some miracle, she seems to like me. Thinks I'm a nice guy."

Alex barked out a loud laugh. "Oh yeah, the introduction is vital. I need to save the poor woman."

"Asshole," Elio muttered.

It took a few moments for Alex to compose himself and once he had, Elio saw exactly what he needed in his friend's face. Not only understanding but delight.

"I'm happy for you, Elio. Truly."

"Thanks, but like I said, the water is still muddy as fuck."

"You didn't tell her how you felt, did you?" Alex asked.

"No," Elio admitted. "Kept thinking I needed to sort out the career decision first."

"You can't put shit like that in boxes, pulling one out at a time. Take it from me. I played a similar game with Charley and almost lost her. When you fall in love, especially for the first time, you need to tell the woman. So...you said she likes you? Is that it?"

Elio shrugged. "Gianna and I approached our week in the cabin like a casual affair, and then, after the condom broke, I sort of made some stupid comment about us not 'borrowing trouble,'" he air-quoted, "and after that, a lot of the discussions we should have had about our feelings never happened."

"So you tell her now." Alex made it sound so damn simple.

And that was when Elio realized...it was.

"Okay. I will, but first..." When Elio went to Gianna, it was going to be with his future free and clear.

"First," Alex finished for him. "You have to let management know that you're hanging up your skates at the end of the season.

"Exactly." But that wasn't all he needed to do.

He needed a life plan too. Because his girl loved a plan.

And he knew exactly who to call.

Gio.

Chapter Fifteen

Gianna wiped her palms on her dress pants and hitched her laptop case more securely over her shoulder as she entered the mansion, following Rafe to his office. She'd finally gotten up enough nerve to call Gio and ask if she could meet with him and Rafe. She suspected Gio had known what the conversation was about because he hadn't asked but had instead set a date and time, then told her they were looking forward to seeing her.

She hadn't said a word to Keeley about her ambition, but it was no secret amongst her friends that she was dissatisfied with her current employment situation. She had a degree in hotel management. Rafe and Gio were soon to have a hotel. It didn't take a genius to put two and two together and figure out why she wanted to talk to them.

The fact Gio had been willing to meet—and so soon—did very little to calm her nerves. She'd been so stressed out this morning, she'd gotten sick. She was used to experiencing anxiety, but it had never reached the level to where she'd thrown up.

"Hey, Gianna," Gio said, rising from the seat behind Rafe's desk. While both men lived in the mansion with Keeley and were working to renovate it, Rafe was the only one who worked from here on occasion. Gio's full-time job was with the restorations business he ran with Tony and his twin, Luca. Before he got his gig hosting *ManPower*, Joey had been their fourth.

"Hi," she said, placing her laptop case on a nearby chair. "I really appreciate you guys taking the time to meet with me."

"We were glad you called," Rafe said, gesturing to one of three chairs that had been set up together in a cozy seating arrangement. "In truth, you beat us to the punch."

"The punch?" Gianna asked as she sat.

Rafe and Gio claimed the other two. "Yeah. As you know, we're getting close to finishing our renovations on the mansion, and it's time to start looking toward staffing, as we're hoping for a June first opening."

"Keeley told me." What Gianna didn't say was that she'd hung on every word Keeley had ever said about the inn preparations, and when her friend had dropped the opening date, Gianna realized it was time to, as Grandma had always said, "piss or get off the pot."

Rafe leaned forward, his elbows on his knees. "Keeley's been yelling your name in our ear ever since we decided to turn this dusty mausoleum into an inn."

That was what Gianna had both hoped and feared. Suddenly, she was glad she'd gone the extra mile. There was no way in hell she wanted anyone to say she was hired simply because of nepotism.

"You *are* here to talk about running the inn, right?" Rafe confirmed.

She nodded. "I am."

Gio smiled. "Great. Then we'd like to look at your resume and talk to you about your previous work experience. Rafe's been coaching me on interviewing. This is the first one I've ever done... from either side of the desk. My dad basically had to hire me at Moretti Brothers or risk me living in his basement until I was in my thirties, drinking beer and playing Kario Mart with this yahoo." Gio crooked a thumb toward Rafe.

Gianna was aware of Gio's love of the epic Mario Kart-style drinking game, since he'd roped her into playing it more than a few times.

Rafe rolled his eyes. "Obviously, I didn't do enough coaching. Thought we agreed we were going for an air of professionalism."

Gio snorted. "Yeah. That was never gonna happen."

Gianna laughed as she opened her laptop case, silently acknowledging that simply running the inn wasn't the only thing making this her dream job. Working for two men like Rafe and Gio, who were kind and supportive and fun, would also add to her workplace happiness.

She pulled out two copies of her resume and handed one to each of them. Then, she pulled out her computer and opened it, standing to set it on the edge of the desk so they could both see the screen easily. "In addition to the resume, I've created a portfolio that will give you an idea of my plans for the inn if you decide to hire me."

She watched as Gio and Rafe exchanged a look, one that she understood in an instant. It was why she'd gone the extra mile, preparing for this meeting. Time to address the elephant in the room.

"We're friends, but this isn't personal. It's business. I know that. I don't expect you to hire me just because of my friendship with Keeley, or even *our* relationship," she added, gesturing to herself and them. "I want to prove to you that I'm the best person for the job because of my education and my experience."

For the next two hours, she shared her plans for reservations, staffing, special events, and even her list of potential names for the inn. She realized that somewhere in the last thirty minutes, the conversation had drifted away from the standard interview and had turned into a staff meeting, the three of them chiseling out a lot of the finer details as if she was already the manager.

"Jesus, Gianna," Gio said at last, glancing at Rafe, then gesturing to her laptop. "I can't believe this. It's...incredible."

"You've got the job. Of course, you've got it. And this hire doesn't have a damn thing to do with the fact we're all friends either." Rafe reached for a file folder, handing it to her. "Here's the job description—though given what you've just shown us—it's clear we missed a few bullet points as far as duties. We're going to have to defer to you, since neither Gio nor I have any experience running a hotel. Something you've just made painfully clear."

Gio nodded emphatically. "We need you. No doubt about that."

"That file also includes the salary and benefits package," Rafe added. "But it's negotiable."

Gianna opened the file, her eyes widening. Holy crap. This would be a huge pay raise.

"We were hoping you could start February sixteenth. That would allow you to give two-weeks' notice at your current job. Of course, you don't have to tell us right now. Take some time to look that file over and if you have any ques—"

"I'll take the job," she interjected.

Gio laughed, then stood up, reaching out to give her one of those big bear hugs the Morettis were so famous for. It reminded her of Elio, and her heart panged. She'd missed him more than she thought possible these past few weeks. The only thing that kept her going was her current job and the preparations she'd made for this interview. Well, that and reorganizing her closet...for the twelfth time.

"Thank God," Gio said, when he released her. "If you'd decided to play hardball, I was fully prepared to start begging." He pointed to her laptop. "I can't believe how much work you've put into this already. You're ahead of the game."

Rafe, the more circumspect of the two friends, reached out and shook her hand. "I can't begin to express how glad I am that you're joining us on this venture."

They talked a little bit longer about everything in the benefits package, including the caretaker's cottage, a retirement plan, and one of the best health care plans she'd ever seen. Her current health care plan was crap, so Baros Corporation's plan in comparison, with its vision and dental, seemed too good to be true. She thanked them for the opportunity again, then they said their goodbyes.

As she left the mansion, she was shocked to discover that first, the sun was setting—it had been a very long meeting—and secondly, that her feet were still touching the ground. She would have thought for certain she was flying.

Climbing into the car, she turned her phone back on, after silencing it for the meeting. There were twenty-seven texts and four missed calls, all from Keeley and Liza. Gianna laughed. Of course, her friends had known about the meeting. In truth, Gianna was surprised to discover Keeley hadn't been there to crash the interview.

She fired off a quick text to them.

I got the job.

Keeley responded the way she always did. In a long series of emojis, including everything from six of the smiley ones to an array of fireworks, rockets, and dancing ones.

Then Liza texted,

We need to celebrate this weekend!!!

Gianna gave that comment a thumbs-up. Then her finger hovered over her contacts, as she considered texting Elio to tell him the news as well. She'd picked up her phone a thousand times to call him, simply because she wanted to talk to him. Not about anything big or exciting. Just...to talk.

Upon her return home, the time spent in the cabin reinforced how terribly quiet and lonely her apartment was. It was the best thing about taking this job. Within the next month or two, the caretaker's house behind the inn would be ready for her to move in. After that, she would be surrounded by people, and with any luck, the too-silent nights would be a thing of the past.

She clicked on Elio's name, pulling up their very sparse text thread. It only contained the two texts from her, the ones telling him she wasn't pregnant, and his very simple response that had come much later that same evening.

> Thanks for letting me know.

She'd read those words over and over, wishing he'd offered her some deeper insight. As for her, it had taken her several days to get over the utter and unexpected devastation. Even now, the idea of what might have been blindsided her, feeling like a sucker punch every damn time.

She put her phone back in her purse without texting and started the car, heading home. She and Elio had made no promises and no future plans. He'd been very clear about how his relationships—if she could call them that—played out.

Perhaps if the two of them hadn't slept together, she could have reached out to him as a friend, but they'd blurred the fuck out of that line. So much so, she didn't have a clue what they were now.

Was he expecting them to return to their "just acquaintances" status, the kind of people who only saw each other socially from time to time? Or would they find themselves more solidly in the good friends camp the next time they met?

Or...

She didn't finish that part, didn't let herself long for something Elio didn't want. She'd indulged in what had begun as "casual sex," reassuring Elio that she wasn't ready for anything more because she was still trying to get over Sam and his deception. She believed it was that guarantee that had convinced him to continue the affair. If he'd had even a niggling suspicion that her feelings for him would drift out of the attraction range and into the affection one, she had no doubt he would have put the brakes on all sexy times the morning after Taco and Tequila Tuesday.

"Shit," she murmured to herself. She couldn't keep doing this, obsessing over what Elio may or may not feel for her. That way was sure to lead to madness.

All she could do was own up to her emotions, admit that she'd let herself fall head over ass in love with Elio...with Liza's brother...with the playboy NHL star who would never return her feelings because he'd fallen in love a long, long time ago...with hockey.

"Let it go," she muttered to herself.

She pulled into the parking lot behind her building, then walked upstairs to her apartment. Dropping her laptop on the dining room table, she headed for the kitchen but stopped halfway. She didn't feel like cooking tonight.

She should be elated, ready to paint the town red. After all, she had just landed her dream job. That called for a celebration.

But she was just too damn tired. She'd been sluggish for the better part of the last two weeks. At first, she'd thought she was coming down with the killer flu bug that had run rampant through work, but no other symptoms appeared. Then she chalked it up to stress over the meeting with Gio and Rafe.

Now she was concerned that perhaps it ran much deeper than that because the feeling wasn't going away.

Depression? Maybe.

Loneliness? Less likely but possible.

Heartbreak? *Ding ding ding.* We have a winner.

She'd gone to the cabin to sort herself out, not jump from the frying pan into the fire, trading one broken heart with Sam's name on it for another with Elio's.

Liza had been trying—unsuccessfully—for weeks to get Gianna to set up an online dating profile. Something she'd been resistant to do. Now, she was thinking perhaps it was time to take the leap.

Besides, she was running out of excuses. No one would ever accuse Liza of being a quitter because she just kept coming back.

Gianna eyeballed her couch, debating skipping dinner. Her stomach vetoed that idea by rumbling hungrily.

Back when she and Sam had dated, Wednesday nights had been pizza night, when they would walk the two blocks to Sal's and split a pie. She had continued that tradition without Sam for a few weeks after their split, always hoping she'd run into him. Looking back now, she could see just how pitiful she'd been.

"Ugh," she muttered. "Enough."

She didn't want to think about Sam any more than Elio. Although, while thoughts of Elio made her sad, memories of Sam no longer made her feel anything—no more anger, sadness, nothing.

"Hmmm..." she mused. "Maybe you're celebrating more than one thing tonight," she suggested to herself, when she realized that in addition to landing her dream job, she was finally over Sam.

"Go me," she said, offering herself a little cheer.

Grabbing a warm jacket and her purse, she walked the two blocks to Sal's, smiling to herself when she got close enough to smell the garlicky pizza sauce, pleased she'd decided to make the effort. The crisp, chilly air was perking her up and she didn't feel so exhausted anymore.

She made a mental note to add "take a walk" to her daily routine.

"You're late," the owner, Sal, called out cheerfully to her when she walked in.

Gianna frowned, confused.

Late for what?

Glancing around, she suddenly understood when she spotted Sam, sitting alone, a whole large pizza on the table before him. From his chagrined expression, she realized he wasn't here by chance.

"Sam," she said, walking over to him. "Let me guess, large pepperoni, mushroom, and onion?"

He nodded. She could see she'd taken him aback with her civil tone. Their last meeting had been a hell of a lot more contentious. Of course, he had broken into her apartment—two days in a row.

"I haven't been here since..." He fell silent, not bothering to say the rest.

"Since we split up," she finished for him. She didn't mention she knew that, that she'd come here too many Wednesdays hoping to see him.

"At the time, I was worried about running into you," he admitted.

"Yeah. I guess it could have been awkward bumping into me with Emma by your side. Oh, wait..." She laughed at her own joke, and Sam gave her a curious look, aware that the anger that had been there when he'd broken into her apartment was gone.

"Emma didn't know about you until that night at the mall."

Gianna nodded. She'd figured that out on her own.

"It was why she dumped me," Sam continued. "Kicked me out of her apartment. She was pissed I'd lied to her, said that I'd been cheating on both of you."

"I'm suddenly feeling some respect for Emma."

Sam sighed sadly. "I shouldn't have come here. I don't know why I did. I'll get Sal to box up the pizza and go."

Gianna waved him off. "You don't have to do that. I don't own Sal's. You can eat here whenever you want." She looked down at his pizza, wondering how many hundreds of that exact same pie they'd shared over the years.

"If you wanted...you could...sit with..." He gestured at the food. "I mean, it is a large."

She should say no. She knew that, but loneliness is an invasive thing, preying on a person. She was tired of eating alone, tired of talking to herself.

Tonight was a celebration. She got the dream job. And she had turned the corner on Sam, once and for all.

Gianna pulled out the chair across from him, raising one finger in warning. "This doesn't mean anything," she said. "To quote Taylor Swift, 'We are never ever getting back together.'"

Sam laughed. "Yeah, I can see that. You're different. You've changed."

His words weren't an insult. Instead, he was looking at her with something resembling respect.

They both grabbed a slice of pizza, and Sal came over with her standard drink order, a glass of Diet Coke. The entire moment felt completely familiar yet totally strange at the same time.

"So you were living with Emma?" she asked.

Sam nodded. "Yeah."

"And what about now?"

He grimaced. "I've moved back home with my parents."

She understood that probably wasn't where any twenty-six-year-old wanted to be, but it wasn't a terrible thing. His parents were cool.

"Things with me and my mom have been rough."

"Why?" she asked.

Sam looked at her like the answer should be obvious. "Because of you. She loved you, and she never really warmed up to Emma. She's still pissed at me for being such a dumbass."

Gianna grinned. "Your mom is the best."

Sam rolled his eyes. "Yeah, yeah. Rub it in. You know how she is, Gee. She's determined to make my life a living hell."

"What's she doing? And don't leave out any of the good stuff."

Sam shook his head. "You're a heartless woman." But then, he gave her the list she'd requested, and it made her very happy. "She's treating me like I'm sixteen again, bitching about my messy room, the dishes I leave in the sink, the times I come in too late. I gotta find my own place. And soon."

She didn't bother to hide her smirk, then helped herself to another slice. The least the bastard owed her was some pizza. They fell silent for a few minutes, but it wasn't awkward. There was too much history between them. Too many years as best friends, roommates, lovers.

And yet, as she sat here, all she could think about was that she'd never missed Sam the way she had missed Elio these past few weeks.

"So how are you? How's work?" Sam asked.

Gianna told him about the new job, and he lifted his glass of soda, the two of them toasting her success. He told her about his latest project. It was an easy conversation between two old friends.

Right up until he said, "I miss you."

"Sam," she said, sighing.

"I know it's over," he quickly added. "I know I fucked up beyond all repair. It's just..."

"Over," she said, stressing the word. "It's just over. We weren't heading in the same direction. If you open your eyes and really look at the last couple of years we were together, it's obvious. Some people grow together. Some grow apart. I turned left."

He gave her a sad smile. "And I turned right."

"I've moved on, Sam, and you will too."

"Moved on? Does that mean you're—"

She narrowed her eyes and cut him off. "My personal life is none of your business."

He sighed. "Yeah. You're right. It's not. I shouldn't have asked."

They finished most of the pizza, Sam asking for a doggy bag for the last two pieces. Sal boxed them up and Sam handed her the box after paying. "Here," he said. "For your lunch tomorrow. I know how much you love leftover pizza."

"Thanks." They left the restaurant together. She stopped on the curb to say goodbye, but Sam gestured toward her apartment. "My car is parked your direction, on the next block."

They walked together. Gianna stopped when she spotted his car, surprised she hadn't noticed it on her way to Sal's.

"I'll walk you the whole way," he said.

"It's just a block, Sam. You don't have to do that."

"I know, but I'm going to anyway."

She knew what this was. Felt it as strongly as he did.

This was it. The end.

They stopped outside her apartment building, and she turned to face him. "So..." she started.

He gave her a smile. "You know I'm always going to love you."

She blinked a few times, determined that she wasn't going to cry as she looked at his sad, beloved face. Sam had been her first love. They'd been children when they met, and they'd grown into adulthood together.

"I know." Perhaps if more time had gone by, she could have offered him those same words back, but the wounds, though healing, were still too fresh. "Goodbye, Sam."

"Goodbye, Gianna." He opened his arms, but he didn't reach for her. He let the decision be hers.

She stepped forward, accepting the hug, happy for this closure, even as her thoughts turned to Elio...and how much better his hugs were.

Then she pulled away, gave him a small wave, and walked inside.

Elio sat in his truck, watching Gianna and Sam embrace. He'd driven to Philly right after practice this afternoon, anxious to see her and share his news.

Yesterday, he'd signed the paperwork on an investment, one that he'd thought was the perfect plan for his future.

Today, he'd told management that this was his last year. He was hanging up his skates.

Plus...it was his birthday.

Elio had picked up the phone to call her, to share all of it, then decided a trifecta like that was worth a two-hour drive. He'd wanted to see her, talk to her. He was tired of the distance between them. In just a few short months, he would be home for good and he'd hoped...

Elio sighed. Well, he had hoped the two of them could pick up things right where they'd left them in the cabin.

Now...

It was clear Gianna and Sam had been on a date. And while the man hadn't kissed her good night, Elio could tell he'd wanted to.

In his mind, Sam had made an unforgivable mistake, but everyone's threshold for forgiveness was different. Eleven years was a long time to date someone. Elio had told Gianna that very thing one morning as they'd talked about her life plans.

She'd shared nearly half her life with Sam. That was a lot of history, a fuck-ton of memories.

All he'd had with her was five days in a cabin. In comparison, it was nothing. Though God knew, to him, it felt like everything.

He'd been a fool to drive here, to think...to think she'd be waiting for him, pining for him. He'd promised her nothing, told her nothing about his feelings.

Meanwhile, Sam had been standing there, right in front of her, wearing his heart on his sleeve. Elio was all the way across the street and even he could see that.

So he couldn't be angry or hurt that Gianna was back with her ex because at least the jackass had figured out what he'd lost and somehow found a way to make it right.

Elio rested his forehead against the steering wheel and closed his eyes, overwhelmed with a pain he'd never experienced.

Gianna had been the first woman to teach him about falling in love.

And now, she was the one to introduce him to his first broken heart.

He remained there until he found the strength to force himself to move.

Then he started the truck and drove back to Baltimore.

Chapter Sixteen

"Hey, man. Just called to see how it's going and to thank you for the tickets to the game on Sunday. Fucking awesome seats, bro. Everybody flipped. You got us halfway up the lower dome, right between the blue lines."

Elio smiled at Aldo's enthusiasm. He typically got his family and friends tickets to the hockey games whenever Baltimore played in Philadelphia, and while the seats were usually pretty good, this time he called in some favors to get them the best seats in the stadium.

"Wanted to make sure you could see all the action. Since..." He paused. He hadn't told anyone in his family about his decision to leave the game yet. He intended to break the news to everyone this weekend, while he was home for Penny and Gage's wedding.

"Damn. You did it, didn't you?" Aldo asked.

Elio sighed. "Yeah. I did. Hanging up my skates. I'm moving back to Philly at the end of the season."

"I know you said you were thinking about it when we talked over Christmas, but I have to admit, I didn't think you'd go through with it. Hockey's been such a huge part of your life, ever since you were a little kid."

"Hockey's been my *whole* life," Elio amended.

"Yeah. You're right. It has. So...any regrets?"

It was a fair question and an easy one to answer. "Not a single one."

"Seriously?"

Aldo's surprise made sense, mainly because Elio had expected a feeling of "what the fuck did I just do?" to hit him ever since telling management about his intentions. Maybe it would come at some point, but the second he'd pulled the trigger, all the stress he had been suffering while trying to make the decision had just vanished. *Poof.* Gone.

When he considered moving back to Philly, he was excited by the prospect of doing something new, something different. And if he simply focused on his future from a career point of view, he would even say he was happy.

But that happiness wavered and faded every time he thought about Gianna. He'd spoken to Liza three times since he'd spied Sam and Gianna returning from their date, but she hadn't mentioned Gianna getting back with her ex. Elio hadn't been able to figure out a way of asking without revealing his feelings for her, so he'd just let her fill him in on all the gossip, just like she always did, while praying she'd reveal the information he desired.

No such luck.

"No regrets," Elio reassured his brother. "I plan to tell the family this weekend."

"Cool," Aldo said. "I'm glad I won't have to hold on to that secret for long. It's a doozy."

Elio chuckled. He'd told Aldo, perfectly secure in the knowledge that his brother wouldn't say a word.

His cousin, Joey, was the one they all went to if they wanted to spread news throughout the Moretti family without having to do it themselves. Joey had never kept a secret in his life.

"Yeah, no worries there. I'll tell the gang at the wedding, then break it to Mom and Dad on Sunday morning."

"I should tell you Mom will be thrilled you're quitting. She never worried about you until these last few years when the injuries hit. She was watching the night you got clocked and broke your collarbone. I don't think she's seen a game since you've gone back."

Elio didn't know that, and he appreciated Aldo sharing it with him. It merely reinforced that he'd been right to quit.

"Only a couple more months," he said. "Our chances of getting into the playoffs are slim to none this year. The team, overall, has just suffered too many injuries."

"It's a shame you're going out like that," Aldo observed.

Elio didn't bother to say he didn't mind either way. He'd been with the team the year they'd won the Stanley Cup, and while he would have loved to end his career that way, it didn't matter so much to him that he was tempted to stay longer to see if that lightning would strike twice.

"Liza will be glad to have you back too. Since you don't seem to fall under the same heading as Kayden and me—kings of the overprotective brothers—she'll no doubt start dragging you out as her wingman."

Three phone conversations with Liza without a single opening and now, here was Aldo, handing one to him on a silver platter. "I thought Gianna was supposed to fill the space left open when Keeley started dating Gio and Rafe."

"Yeah, that's what Liza thought too, but Gianna's been pretty resistant to putting herself back out there. Liza's invited her over for dinner several times so that she can help Gianna upload her profile on those stupid online dating sites."

"She won't do it?" Elio asked, his curiosity piqued.

"Nope. Gianna just keeps pushing her off, claiming she's too busy at work, or sick, or wrapped up in planning Penny's bachelorette party, or helping with the wedding prep."

Elio had thought it strange that Liza hadn't mentioned Gianna getting back with Sam, but now it appeared his sister didn't know. Which made sense. While Gianna had found a way to forgive Sam's sins, Liza was made of sterner stuff, and there was no way she'd be able to keep her opinion to herself. Obviously, Gianna was trying to put off the inevitable explosion that news would detonate for as long as she could.

And Elio couldn't blame her for that. Liza was a force to be reckoned with.

"Liza told me a little bit about the bachelorette party the last time she called. Sounds like it was a wild one."

"Yeah. Kayden, Gio, Rafe, and I all followed their progress on Find My Friends. They hit four bars, and I can only imagine the state they were in when they stumbled out of the last one around three a.m."

The old Elio would have laughed at Aldo's grumpiness over their sister's wild ways, but this time, he knew Gianna was out there too, and he didn't like the idea of her being out so late and so intoxicated.

"I'm surprised the four of you weren't there, shadowing their every move."

Aldo laughed. "Oh, believe me, we would have been if not for Gianna."

Jesus, Elio thought. His brother was two for two on the Gianna goods today.

"What's that mean?"

"Apparently, she's been fighting some sort of stomach bug, so she offered to be DD. She texted me all night with progress reports and assuring all of us that everyone was fine. She made us promise not to rat her out to the rest of the gang because she was sure her texts would have annoyed Keeley and Liza to no end. But Gianna's also clever enough to know that by appeasing us, she was keeping us from crashing the fun."

Elio felt a strange sense of pride in Gianna's actions, while simultaneously worrying about her being sick, but before he could ask Aldo about her illness, his brother continued speaking.

"Without her texts, we totally would have broken up the party early, especially when they kept venturing deeper into South Philly."

"South Philly?" Elio asked, scowling. Gianna might have been sober and providing updates, but she was hardly qualified to keep them physically safe on her own.

"Relax. Penny's bachelorette party wasn't just for women. Penny—being Penny—has two attendants in her bridal party. Jess is her maid of honor, while her buddy at work, Toby, is serving as her bridesman. He and another guy, Rich, were invited to the bachelorette."

Elio remembered both men from the holiday party. They were nice guys, but he wasn't sure he'd exactly call them "the muscle," when it came to keeping the women safe. He and Toby had spent the better part of a half hour talking video games, the man bragging about the fact that he was what he referred to as a "virtual weapons expert."

"Even so," Elio started, but Aldo just chuckled.

"Kayden's buddy, Seth, was on duty that night, and he did more than a few drive-bys of every club they went to, patrolling the general vicinity, so he was never more than a few minutes away if trouble broke out. We're not new to stalking the kid sisters. You sure you don't want a piece of that action when you get back home to stay?"

Elio laughed. "I'll let you guys handle the heavy lifting. I prefer to keep my weekends free."

"I bet you do," Aldo joked. "You get back on the horse yet? Now that you're all healed up?"

Elio didn't like to lie to his brother, but he also knew if he told Aldo the truth, that he hadn't had a date since losing the sling, it would rouse his suspicions.

"I'm getting there. So is Gianna better now?" Elio asked, unable to shake his concern.

"What?"

"You said she was the DD because she was sick."

"Oh, yeah, I suppose she's better," Aldo said. "Liza

mentioned the two of them went out to lunch a few days ago. The flu's been running rampant around Philly the last month or so, just like it does every year at this time."

"Yeah, I guess." If she was out for lunch, she must be feeling better. He tried to let that set his mind at ease.

"Well, I'll let you go. Just wanted to thank you for the tickets. Looking forward to seeing you in a couple of days."

"Same," Elio added, as he and Aldo said their goodbyes. He hung up the phone and drifted toward the kitchen. It was getting late enough that if he didn't start making dinner, he'd declare it too late and order a pizza.

Glancing at the refrigerator door, he noted that tonight was soup and sandwich night. He grinned as he looked at the scribbled menu hanging there. He'd started the weekly menu right after leaving the cabin, and he hadn't forgotten to buy a damn thing from the store ever since.

Gianna was a genius.

He sighed as he opened the fridge and pulled out the fixings for a grilled cheese. After assembling the sandwich and putting it in the skillet, he poured a can of tomato soup into a bowl and popped it into the microwave.

Elio had never minded eating alone. In truth, he'd never even thought about it. He'd just prepare his meal, carry his plate to the living room, and eat while watching sports or the news on TV.

Now, he longed for someone to eat with, someone to talk about his day with. Cooking and sharing meals with Gianna had been some of his favorite times at the cabin. After sex, of course.

He missed her.

Those words drifted through his mind at least fifty times a day.

Then, he realized there *was* one reason he regretted quitting the team.

Because as hard as it was to be here in Baltimore, knowing she was with someone else in Philadelphia, it would be a thousand times harder living in the same city and seeing her with Sam.

Seeing her with another man knowing...

She should be with him.

Gianna sat on the examination table, numbness sinking in.

"But...I can't be."

She'd been throwing up off and on for three weeks, ever since the day she'd accepted the job running Rafe and Gio's inn. She'd thought it was a stomach bug, figured she'd finally come down with the same plague everyone had been passing around work.

But then it occurred to her that the nausea was fleeting, coming and going, so that while she had moments when she felt like utter dog shit, she had just as many moments where she not only felt great, but she was a bundle of energy.

During one such bout of vigor, she was cleaning out the bathroom cabinet. She found the pregnancy test she'd bought, and a light went on. After some quick math, she realized she was late.

She'd taken the test, hands shaking. When it had shown her a positive result, she'd been certain it was wrong. After all, she'd had her period since returning home from the cabin and she sure as hell hadn't had sex. So she called her doctor and made an appointment.

"Gianna," Dr. Blake said. "You are most definitely pregnant."

"But I've had my period since...well...since I've had sex."

"Was it a normal period?" her doctor asked.

Gianna considered the question, then shook her head. "No, but to be fair, none of my periods have been normal since I stopped getting the birth control shot. One month heavy, the next light. I thought it was just my system trying to work itself out. This one was," she sighed, "very light." Something she hadn't thought about at the time because she'd been pissed off at Sam for breaking into her apartment, missing Elio so much it hurt, and exhausted from too many days of working double shifts and preparing for her interview with Gio and Rafe.

And now that she had the job, the groundwork had only

gotten more intense because she was thrilled by the opportunity she'd been afforded, excited by the tasks. Gio and Rafe were encouraging her to make the inn her own, to follow through with her vision, and she didn't want to let them down.

"Most likely what you experienced was spotting, not a real period."

"Is that bad?"

Dr. Blake shook her head. "Very common, actually. Do you know when you conceived?"

Gianna nodded, her shock quickly giving way to genuine excitement. "December twenty-ninth."

The doctor consulted her iPad, and said, "Then we're looking at a September twenty-first due date. That also means you're around six weeks pregnant. I'm going to give you a prescription for prenatal vitamins. If you smoke—"

"I don't," Gianna said quickly.

The doctor smiled. "Or drink, you need to stop now for the remainder of your pregnancy."

Gianna had never been much of a drinker, so that wouldn't be a hardship. In fact, she hadn't had any alcohol since tequila night at the cabin. That hadn't been intentional—rather a combination of too busy and too queasy. She was grateful she'd volunteered to be the DD for Penny's bachelorette party because that night had been wild, to say the least, and her friends had probably broken some sort of world record for the most blow job shots consumed in a single evening.

"Would you like to hear the heartbeat?" Dr. Blake asked.

Gianna nodded eagerly, barely breathing as the doctor placed an ultrasound probe on her stomach, running it around until... there it was. A steady beat.

"It's so fast." Gianna sniffled and quickly wiped her eyes.

Dr. Blake smiled. "Sounds nice and strong. Congratulations, Gianna."

"Thank you," she said, her voice breaking slightly as she was overwhelmed by emotion.

The doctor handed her a prescription and her checkout papers. "Stop by the desk and hand this to the receptionist. She'll set up your next appointment and we'll do an ultrasound. Give you a first look at this little love. If you'd like to bring the father...or a friend, you're welcome to."

Dr. Blake had been her doctor for years, so she was aware Gianna wasn't married. And they'd started today's conversation discussing why Gianna had missed the shot, which meant her doctor also now knew that she and Sam were history.

"An ultrasound," she whispered. It was incredible how real that one word made this feel. There was a life inside her. And in just a few weeks, she'd be able to see her baby.

"Thank you, Dr. Blake."

Gianna set up her next appointment, then walked to her car.

Her initial happiness became muted as the rest of the dominos fell, one by one in her mind.

What the hell do I do now?

She'd told Elio she wasn't pregnant. What would he say when she called to say, "Oops. My bad. I'm totally knocked up."

She tried to imagine his face, his reaction, as she dropped that bomb. She'd basically let him off the hook and his texted reply—just a simple thank you—hadn't given her a single clue how he'd felt about it.

How would he respond when he found out he was going to be a father?

As she drove home, she practiced at least twenty different versions of the conversation, forcing herself to play out every possible ending...imagining Elio angry or upset, but also seeing his face light up with joy, with happiness.

That was the ending she prayed for.

Climbing the stairs to her apartment, she recalled his promise that they would figure this out together, that he wouldn't leave her to do it alone. She'd taken comfort in that at the time, but that wasn't exactly how it was going to play out...because she'd already made the first decision without him.

This was her baby, and she was keeping it.

She'd just taken off her coat and kicked off her shoes when her cell rang. Glancing at the screen, she saw Liza's name.

What the hell was she going to tell Liza? Her best friend didn't even know that Gianna and Elio had been trapped together in the cabin. Or that they'd had sex.

Gianna wasn't sure why she hadn't shared that information with the girls. It wasn't like she hadn't told them every detail of her relationship—and breakup—with Sam. Hell, she'd spent the better part of an hour on a three-way call with Liza and Keeley a couple weekends ago telling them about the closure she and Sam had found over pizza, how she'd said goodbye and meant it. Her friends had cheered her on, called her courageous.

She'd never kept secrets from them, but this...this she hadn't known how to share.

She took a deep breath and answered the phone.

"Hey, chickie," Liza said cheerfully. "Feeling better?"

"Yeah. I am." Gianna had foolishly mentioned her stomach was still bothering her a few days earlier when Liza tried—once again—to invite her over for dinner so they could set up her profile on the dating apps.

Jesus. That wasn't happening now.

She could just imagine her profile.

Gianna Duncan, 26. Slightly neurotic and very OCD.

Loves vacuuming, making lists, and due in about eight months.

Only men interested in an instant family need reply.

"I'm glad because you don't have time to be sick," Liza said. "Tomorrow's the wedding!"

She, Jess, Keeley, and Liza had been helping Penny prepare for her wedding for months. Gage had crashed Penny's birthday party back in September and dropped the bomb that he wanted to be her boyfriend.

And then, because Gage was Gage, he'd rushed them to an engagement, and now to the altar. It was like the man was so in love, he couldn't function in a world where Penny wasn't his wife, his forever.

Gianna couldn't imagine what it must feel like to be loved so completely and passionately. Which proved once more just how wrong she and Sam had been for each other.

"There's no way I'd miss Penny's big day," Gianna reassured Liza.

"What the hell are we going to talk about once this wedding is over?" Liza joked. There was no denying they'd all gone wedding mad, the preparations consuming every conversation she'd had with her girlfriends.

Regardless, Gianna knew exactly what they were going to start talking about next.

The baby.

Gianna was going to have a baby and Liza was going to be an aunt. While Gianna wasn't sure how Elio was going to take the news, she knew without a doubt how Liza would respond. Once the shock wore off, Aunt Liza, as well as honorary aunts Keeley, Penny, and Jess would rally around her. Knowing her friends, the theme for the nursery would be figured out and the entire thing decorated before Gianna hit her third trimester.

She grinned at the thought.

"This weekend is going to be a blast," Liza gushed, "between the wedding tomorrow, the kickass reception tomorrow night, and Elio's game on Sunday."

Elio had gotten their whole gang of friends—her included— great seats for Sunday's game against Philadelphia. Gianna wouldn't have understood or even cared about stadium seating before the cabin, but now that she was basically the world's biggest Baltimore fan, she knew Liza's excitement was justified.

"I'm glad he's going to be able to come to the wedding," Gianna said, measuring her words so as not to give anything away.

"I told him it was amazing luck, but Elio swears the chances of Baltimore playing Philly the day after Penny's wedding were so miniscule, that when partnered with the fact the coach was okay with him driving himself up the day before instead of riding the bus with the team, it technically classifies as a miracle, not luck."

Gianna had been surprised when Penny mentioned Elio had RSVP'd as a yes for the wedding because, as Liza said, it was unusual for him to make it home for any events during the season.

She was grateful now for that miracle because it meant she could tell Elio about the baby in person. The moment Dr. Blake confirmed the pregnancy, she'd known she didn't want to tell him over the phone. She wanted—needed—to see his face.

She'd pull him aside, drag him somewhere private during the reception, and then...God...then she'd say the words she'd been playing on repeat.

Elio. I was wrong. I am pregnant. We're having a baby.

She would tell him first. And after that, well, despite being only six weeks pregnant, she felt as if she had to tell Gio and Rafe. She was as nervous about telling *them* as she was Elio. Because she was going to be very pregnant when the inn opened and having a baby a couple months after that. What would they say? Would they be angry at her? Would they feel deceived?

Don't borrow trouble.

Those words, spoken in Elio's deep, soothing voice, drifted through her mind and, surprisingly, they calmed her.

Monday was her first official day as hotel manager, so she wanted to tell them before she started. In case they wanted to fire her ass.

But Elio first.

"Okay. I'll see you tomorrow," she heard Liza say.

Shit. Liza had been talking about the wedding the last few minutes, and Gianna hadn't heard a word of it, too lost in her own thoughts.

"See you tomorrow," Gianna said.

She set her phone on the coffee table and dropped down on her couch, aware she was grinning like a lunatic.

Because while there were so many unknowns looming in her future, she wasn't stressed out about it. Instead, she was happy.

So happy, she could explode.

She twisted, lying down, staring at the ceiling, running her hands over her stomach.

A baby.

"I can't wait to meet you," she whispered, aware that she wasn't talking to herself anymore. This time, there was someone else there to listen.

Chapter Seventeen

Elio stood at the doorway to the ballroom, giving himself a second to calm down, aware his temper was riding too close to the surface. It had been one hell of a fucked-up day, and if he had any sense of self-preservation, he would have just called the night a wash and headed to his room in Aldo's apartment. He was in a foul mood and not fit company for anyone.

He was more than fashionably late for Penny's wedding. In fact, he was so late, he was going to look like an idiot walking in now. Today's practice had taken longer than it was supposed to, so he was already an hour behind schedule when he walked out of the stadium.

Only to find Paula waiting for him by his truck. She'd picked the wrong day to hit him with her attempts at seduction. When her come-ons failed, she turned on the waterworks, expecting her tears to sway him.

They didn't.

Instead, he told her—again—it was over. When she insisted she was fine with reinstituting their previous booty-call arrangement, he'd gone the extra mile and been honest, telling her that wasn't what he wanted anymore.

He confessed that he'd fallen in love with someone else, and that was when her crocodile tears turned into genuine tears of jealous outrage. It had taken him a full half hour before he could get away from her and finally get on the road.

Then a major accident set him back two more hours. He'd spent most of that time stuck in traffic, telling himself to turn around and go home, but apparently, he was a glutton for punishment because he'd kept pushing forward.

He'd RSVP'd yes to Penny's wedding a couple days after returning from the cabin. At the time, he'd seen it as an opportunity to spend more time with his family, and if he'd managed to claim a dance or three with Gianna, so much the better.

However, as more time passed, he'd been forced to acknowledge that his feelings for Gianna were way stronger than he realized, and they weren't going anywhere. He'd been tempted to cancel after spying Gianna and Sam together outside her apartment three weeks earlier, certain he didn't have it in him to let her cheating ex steal those dances from him.

A decorative board outside the entry displayed the table seating chart. After a quick scan, he saw that he'd been placed at a table with Aldo, Kayden, Luca, Bruno, and Vivian. Glancing across the room, he spied his brothers, saw the empty seat saved for him.

Then he kept scouring the room until he found her. Gianna was sitting with Liza, Keeley, Gio, and Rafe. He frowned when he realized there was an empty chair next to her. Was that Sam's place?

Most everyone was seated, finishing up their meals, though there were a few stragglers—including Gage's brothers, Matt and Conor—lined up by the open bar. Penny and Gage were doing their newlywed couple duties, walking from table to table to greet and chat with their guests.

The ballroom was large, filled with huge bouquets of deep red roses, as one might expect from a Valentine's Day wedding.

Taking a deep breath, he stepped into the ballroom. Aldo saw him first, raising his hand to wave, then pointing to the empty chair next to him. Elio nodded and started to head that way, then held up one finger. There was another table he needed to visit first.

"Elio! You made it!" Liza leapt from her chair when he approached, giving him a kiss on the cheek. "Oh my God, you're so late, I'd given up on you."

He nodded, though his attention was locked on Gianna. She was giving him one of those sweet, guileless, gorgeous smiles of hers. She was happy to see him. It was written all over her face. He started to return the smile, but then his gaze traveled to the empty chair, and he found himself searching the room for Sam again.

"Dude, you missed the ceremony, happy hour, *and* dinner," Gio pointed out.

"Is the bar still open?" he asked gruffly.

"Yep," Gio replied with a grin.

"Then I'll be fine."

"Where have you been?" Liza asked.

"Let's just say it's been a rough afternoon...evening...fuck it... day." Elio took a moment to list all the reasons for his tardiness, before wrapping up with, "So basically, the interstate was a parking lot for a couple of hours."

"Jesus. I would have turned around and gone home," Rafe said.

"I thought about it," he admitted. "More than a few times. But that felt like an even bigger waste of time, considering I would have been right back on the interstate tomorrow in the team bus, heading this direction for the game."

Unable to resist any longer, he pointed to the extra chair. "Are you missing someone?"

Liza sighed. "Yeah. My date. I invited a guy from work, but he canceled on me this morning. He took a tumble while he was jogging and sprained his ankle."

"No date for you?" Elio asked Gianna, who shook her head.

Interesting. Why hadn't she invited Sam?

"I think your seat is with Aldo," Gio said, "but since dinner is over and we have an extra place, I'm sure no one will care if you join us."

Liza glanced around the room. "Let me grab one of the wait-staff and see if they can bring you a plate. You must be starving."

"That's okay," Elio reassured her, claiming the chair they'd offered. "I'll just steal Gianna's piece of wedding cake."

Gianna laughed. "You might try."

Unable to resist, he subtly shifted his chair a bit closer to hers, drawing in a deep breath when he caught a whiff of her citrus shampoo.

God, she smelled good.

"You'd deprive a starving man an extra piece of cake, Freckles? You're a cruel woman."

Gianna laughed, but he could see his nickname had captured the attention of both Liza and Keeley.

Gio pointed toward the bar. "Want me to grab you a beer? Or something stronger?"

Elio shook his head. "I'll get something in a minute. Thanks for the offer. How was the wedding?"

"Perfect," Liza said, taking a few moments to fill him in on the ceremony, which, according to his sister, was the most romantic thing she'd ever seen. The women teared up, recalling the vows Gage had written for his bride, much to Rafe and Gio's chagrin.

"The guy really set the bar high for the rest of us poor bastards," Gio grumbled, while Keeley narrowed her eyes.

"If you're worried, maybe you should start working on yours now," she joked.

Gio wrapped his arm around her shoulder. "Nah. Figure I'll leave the vow-writing to Rafe."

"Is that right?" Rafe asked. "And what's your contribution going to be?"

Gio gave his best friend and partner a "duh" look before saying, "I'll be in charge of planning the honeymoon sex positions."

Rafe rolled his eyes as the women giggled.

"I'm not complaining," Keeley said. "Sounds like you'll both be playing to your strengths."

Elio felt the tension of the last few hours melt away, relaxed and happy to be here, surrounded by his family and friends. The feeling reinforced his decision to leave the team once more.

Then, unable to resist, he stole another long look at Gianna. "You look beautiful tonight," he murmured, leaning toward her, wrapping his arm around the back of her chair.

"You don't look so bad yourself," Gianna said, her gaze traveling over what he knew was now a wrinkled suit. He'd gotten ready for the wedding in the locker room after practice to save time and he'd gotten a few playful wolf whistles from his teammates. He'd felt well-groomed leaving Baltimore. Now, too many hours later, he just felt disheveled.

"What am I?" Liza asked. "Chopped liver?"

Elio needed to get a grip, or he'd give himself—and his feelings —away. Forcing himself to look away from Gianna, he grinned at his sister. "You look alright."

Liza narrowed her eyes. "Oh, that's great. Gianna gets beautiful and I get alright."

If there was one thing Elio excelled at, it was pushing his kid sister's buttons. "What words would you prefer, sis? Okay? Pretty good?"

"Stunning," another voice chimed in.

Elio looked up, frowning when he realized Matt Russo was standing next to their table, listening to the conversation.

"You look stunning tonight, Ms. Moretti," Matt repeated, his compliment accomplishing something Elio had never witnessed before. Matt Russo had rendered his never-silent sister speechless.

Matt and Liza stared at each other for a moment or two, long enough for Elio to steal a glance at Gianna, who gave him a shocked look as she mouthed "you were right."

"I want to thank you for coming tonight," Matt said, clearing his throat, looking around the table at each of them. "Your presence here means a lot to Penny and my brother."

The Russo brothers had lost both their parents, so it appeared Matt, the eldest, was stepping into that role tonight, welcoming their guests. It couldn't have been an easy task for him, considering the sheer number of Morettis in the ballroom. Then Elio spotted Conor standing next to Tony's table, and he realized the brothers appeared to be splitting the duty.

"We wouldn't have missed it for the world," Keeley said, speaking for the table, since Elio and Gio were both scowling. Elio tried to school his features, but a lifetime of anger and horror stories from his dad and Nonno ensured his animosity ran deep.

Rafe didn't talk. Rather, he just looked at Gio, amused by his partner's furrowed brows and crossed-arms pose. Meanwhile Liza...well...Elio couldn't quite decipher her mood. She looked at Matt like he was a rattlesnake poised to strike, but she wasn't afraid. Nope, she was ready for it, shovel raised and ready to chop off his head the second he made one wrong move.

"It was a beautiful wedding," Gianna added, when it was clear no one else was going to say anything.

Matt nodded, took one last look at Liza, and moved on to the next table. Before anyone could remark on the exchange, the deejay drew their attention to the dance floor as he called for Penny and Gage to come forward for the first dance.

The first strains of John Legend's "Conversations in the Dark" began as Gage pulled his bride into his arms.

Elio watched the couple swaying to the music and saw the way Gage looked at Penny like a man who'd just gotten everything he'd ever wanted. Until Gianna, Elio had precious little experience with jealousy. Now, as he watched Gage, he knew he wanted what that man had.

A future. A forever with the woman he loved.

He wanted to be able to look at every person in this room, point to Gianna, and say, "This beautiful woman is mine."

His gaze shifted to Gianna. She truly did look lovely, the pale blue of her dress matching her eyes perfectly. There was a pink hue in her cheeks that gave her a healthy glow, and it set his mind at ease. He'd hated hearing that she'd been sick, but whatever ailed her had clearly passed.

"Mr. and Mrs. Gage Russo," the deejay said, partway through the song, "would like to invite other couples in attendance to come up and join them on the dance floor."

Elio didn't hesitate for a moment, rising and offering a hand to Gianna. She accepted, placing her hand in his, and his heart began to beat a little bit faster. Out of the corner of his eye, he saw Rafe leading Keeley to the floor, Gio offering to dance with Liza. The six of them made their way to the floor, but once they were there, he swung Gianna into his arms and his vision shrank to just her.

"I'm glad you made it," she said softly. "I was afraid you might have to cancel."

"Believe me, I was worried about that as well after two hours in standstill traffic."

"Elio, I was hoping that...maybe..." Gianna seemed nervous, and he didn't like it. After everything they'd shared at the cabin, he thought they'd passed the point where she felt uncomfortable or shy around him.

"Maybe what?"

"Do you think it would be possible for us to find a few moments to speak in private?"

Elio sighed, suddenly understanding her anxiety. He'd expressed his opinions regarding her getting back together with Sam, and apparently, she was nervous about telling him she'd forgiven the cheating bastard.

"Gianna. What you and I shared at the cabin...it was special. But you don't owe me an explanation about Sam. If you want to get back with him, that's your decision and yours alone."

Gianna frowned in confusion. "Get back with Sam? What are you talking about? He cheated on me, Elio. The relationship is over."

Now it was his turn to be perplexed. "But...I thought..."

"You were right about him coming back," she started. "The day I got home from the cabin, I found him in my apartment."

"He still has a key?" Elio asked, his voice angrier than he'd intended.

Gianna shook her head. "No. Of course not. The asshole got the spare key from my neighbor."

Elio's temper flared. Earlier, he'd hoped her ex wasn't here. Now he was sorry the man was absent because he'd like to show Sam up close and personal why Elio was known as El Train, the enforcer. "What the *hell*?"

Gianna laughed. "That's what I said when I found him there. I told him to get out or I was calling 9-1-1."

"Good for you." Then he realized her story didn't match what he'd witnessed a few weeks ago.

"He left when he realized he'd majorly overstepped."

"And that was it?" he asked, knowing it wasn't.

"No. I ran into him one night at the pizza parlor where we use to have a standing Wednesday date."

Elio recalled the small leftover pizza box Gianna had been carrying. "He'd gone there on purpose? Hoping to see you?"

She nodded. "Yeah. I was a bit calmer that time. He offered me half his pizza. We sat and talked about what happened. It was just as you said. He wanted to get back together. I told him I'd moved on."

"You have?" Elio asked, every word of her story filling him with hope.

She tilted her head up, their faces so close he could feel the heat of her breath. "I have. It was a good talk. I think we both needed the closure. He walked me home, we said goodbye, and that was it. I haven't seen him since, and I don't plan to."

Elio smiled, then before he could think better of it—considering they were surrounded by family and friends—he gave her a quick, hard kiss.

If she was embarrassed or uncomfortable by the kiss, she gave no indication. Instead, she looked pleased. "Why would you think I'd gotten back with Sam?"

Elio would come clean about his single night of stalking later. Right now, he was more curious about her initial request. "It was just a misunderstanding. What do you want to talk to me about?"

"I don't want to do it here." She looked around the room as the song began to come to an end. Her anxiety concerned him enough that he decided to take matters into his own hands.

"Come with me."

The two of them left the dance floor. He placed his hand on her back, guiding her past their table and out of the ballroom. He took a quick scan of their surroundings. The grand hotel was large with lots of small, cozy seating areas. He took her hand, leading her down the wide hallway until he found what he was looking for. Around a corner was an alcove complete with a love seat, two chairs, and a large palm. It was out of sight of the ballroom entrance, so they could sit in relative seclusion.

"Okay," Elio said, once they were settled, both of them opting to share the love seat. Now that he was with her again, and he knew she was single, it was going to be difficult for him to keep his hands off her. "It's obvious something is bothering you. The sooner you say it, the sooner we can move on to the good stuff."

"Good stuff?"

He wiggled his eyebrows suggestively, letting her know without words exactly where he hoped this night would lead.

She tried to smile, but the effort was weak at best, and his eyes narrowed with concern. Something was seriously upsetting her.

"What is it, Gianna?"

"I'm pregnant."

Chapter Eighteen

Gianna prayed Elio couldn't see her hands shaking. She'd managed to keep her nerves at bay most of the night, genuinely enjoying the reception, the meal, the company.

The problem was, every now and then she'd recall the conversation looming, and her stomach would clench, her chest growing tight.

"I was wrong, Elio," she started, hating how thin her voice sounded. She was struggling to take a deep breath. She'd practiced this damn conversation nonstop since discovering she was pregnant. This should be easier than this, but it wasn't.

"*What?*"

She swallowed, her mouth suddenly dry. "I'm pregnant," she said again.

Gianna closed her eyes. That wasn't the way she'd planned to tell him at all. She'd intended to explain about the mistaken period, and the stress at work, about Sam, and then...

"Gianna. Open your eyes and look at me," he demanded. "You're pregnant?"

She'd wanted to do this face-to-face, thinking it would give her an advantage. She'd thought seeing his expressions would help her understand how he was feeling. She'd been wrong.

Elio's face told her no more now than his damn "thanks for telling me" text had back in January.

"I...God...I'm so sorry I told you I wasn't. I—"

"You're pregnant."

She could understand his shock. She'd experienced the same, needing to say those two words, "I'm pregnant," over about a million times before she could make them sink in.

She nodded, words escaping her. She clenched her hands together in her lap, trying to stop them from trembling.

Not that it mattered. One second, Elio was sitting there, stoic, still as a statue—the next, the biggest, most enormous smile she'd ever seen split his face and he was standing, picking her up, and giving her the most incredible Moretti hug in the history of Moretti hugs. Then he took it further by lifting her off her feet, holding her even tighter.

"Elio," she said, trying to pull away, though the man was showing no indication of letting her go. "You're not mad? You're...happy?"

"Jesus Christ, Gianna! Why would you think I'd be mad?"

"Because we had a four-night stand that wasn't supposed to be anything more than casual sex. Then the condom broke. And then I told you I wasn't pregnant because I'm an idiot."

"Was the test wrong?" he asked.

"No. I never took the test because I got my period. Or...I thought I got it. The doctor said it was most likely spotting."

His smile faded. "Wait. What does that mean? Is the baby okay?"

"It's fine," she reassured him quickly. "I realized this week I'd missed my period. And I've had this damn stomach bug, but it kept coming and going. And that was when...well, I started to think it might be morning sickness, even though for me, it's been morning, noon, and night sickness—so I took a test. Even when I saw the plus sign, I thought it had to be wrong, so I went to the doctor yesterday and she confirmed it. I heard the baby's heartbeat."

"You heard…" Elio's eyes widened. "No more doctor appointments without me."

She laughed as she shook her head. "It's still hockey season. You can't just—"

"I can and I will. I mean it, Gee. I want to be there for every appointment. I want to hear the heartbeat."

"The next one is the ultrasound. I have the appointment set, but I can change the date if it doesn't work with your schedule," she offered.

"Ultrasound," he said, and it was clear the word impacted him just as strongly as it had her. "So we're going to see our baby?"

"Yes. God, El, I'm so sorry for—"

"Don't say you're sorry. Ever again. It was an honest mistake." She closed her eyes. "I was so afraid you'd be mad or upset."

Elio cupped her cheeks, tilting her head upward. "Look at me."

Her eyelids lifted, her gaze connecting with his.

"I've never been happier in my life," he said. "This is a gift, Gianna. A *gift*. Are you happy?"

She smiled, blinking back the tears in her eyes. "Oh my God, yes. So happy. Like deliriously so. Which only proves we're both crazy," she said with a watery laugh.

"Why crazy?"

"Elio. We aren't a couple. Hell, we aren't even dating."

His scowl was so pronounced, she closed her mouth instantly. But Elio didn't speak, just kept looking at her.

When the silence drifted too long, she gathered her courage enough to say, "Well, we aren't."

"We weren't," he corrected. "But now we are."

"Are what?" she asked stupidly.

"Are dating. Exclusively. We're going to be a couple."

"You can't just say we're a couple."

He smirked. "Of course I can. I just did. We're a couple.

You're my girlfriend." Then, because it felt like he was still trying to wrap his head around it all, he added, "We're going to be parents, a family." He dropped down until he was sitting on the love seat, his face even with her stomach.

She tried to blink back tears when he placed his forehead against her belly, his large hands gripping her waist.

"A baby," he said once more, before placing a kiss there. "You're having my baby."

Gianna tried to rearrange everything she'd ever heard about Elio from his sister, from his family and friends, even from him. This wasn't the anti-commitment, relationship-resistant man everyone believed him to be.

He lifted his face to hers. There was no mistaking the joy, the wonder in his tone. "Thank you," he whispered. Then he leaned closer, placed his lips to her belly again, and whispered, "I can't wait to meet you."

"Oh God. I can't either," she said, the words thick. "You're going to make me cry." She waved her hands in her face to dry the tears forming there. She, Liza, and Keeley had spent a stupid amount of time on their hair and makeup this afternoon. If she cried now, they'd know it and she would have no way to explain.

Elio looked up at her. "I quit the team. This is my last year."

It took a second for his words to process, and when they did, she sank down next to him once more. "You quit? Already? Or... you're going to now? Because, El—"

"It's a done deal. My contract is up at the end of the season, and I've already told management I'm not going to renew it. The season ends in the middle of April, and after that...I'll be home for good."

"Home," she breathed. "Philadelphia."

"What we had at the cabin, Gee...it hasn't run its course. Hasn't come close to that. It was one of the main things that convinced me to hang up my skates. I knew weeks ago that I wanted more time with you. The afternoon I quit, I left the stadium, got in the car, and drove all the way here to tell you."

She frowned. "But I never saw you."

"I know. I had just parked outside your apartment and was about to get out of the truck when you and Sam walked down the sidewalk, with your leftover pizza. From where I was sitting, it looked like—"

"We'd gotten back together," she interjected. "Oh my God. That's why you thought we were dating again."

He nodded.

She sighed, remembering that day so well. "I wish you hadn't seen that. Wish you'd come upstairs. Because I wanted to talk to you so badly that day. I'd even picked up the phone to call, but didn't."

"Why did you want to talk to me?"

"I got my dream job. I am now the manager of a haunted inn!"

Elio grinned. "I know."

Gianna laughed. "Of course you do. Liza…" she began, stopping when he shook his head.

"Gio. He called me the day they hired you."

That surprised her because she couldn't understand why Gio would think Elio cared about her running the inn. Regardless, she forged on, trying to explain what had been her number two concern, prior to breaking the news about the baby to Elio. Now that she'd come clean, and he'd—thank God—responded so much better than every single one of the scenarios she'd played out in her mind, the Gio/Rafe worry had shifted to top spot.

"I've been working every spare minute to get ready for the opening because it's something that's all mine. Rafe and Gio have basically given me carte blanche on how to set things up, the staffing, everything. I've been so excited. Or…" She paused. "I was."

"You aren't excited anymore?" he asked.

She lifted one shoulder. "My first day is Monday. I can't start without telling Gio and Rafe…"

"That you're pregnant."

She nodded. "I wouldn't feel right." Then she opened up, all her fears falling out. "What if they change their mind? I mean, the timing is less than ideal. I'll be six months pregnant when we open the inn and then I'll need maternity leave. Plus, I accepted the job when I was pregnant."

"But you didn't know you were."

"Still, I'm afraid they're not going to be happy with me."

"You're kidding, right? This is Gio and Rafe we're talking about. They won't mind. If I know Gio, he'll start begging to be godfather. They're going to be happy for you, for us. Besides, how they feel doesn't matter overly much."

She frowned. "Of course it does. They're my bosses and I—"

He shook his head. "They're only two of your bosses. There's a third one, and he's the controlling shareholder."

"What are you talking about? There's no one else."

"That was the other thing I drove home that night to tell you. I figured out my future, and I wanted to let you know. Just in case the back of your brain was itching," he teased.

She laughed and shoved his shoulder lightly. "Very funny. What's your plan?"

"The night I made my decision to leave the team, I called Gio, asked if he and Rafe would be interested in a third investor for the inn."

Gianna's eyes widened. "You?"

"Yeah. Me. Gio put me on speaker so I could present my case to him and Rafe. It didn't take much convincing, both guys are stretched thin. They'd admitted to me over the holidays that the inn was turning out to be much more work than they'd antici- pated. I'd been trying to think of a business to invest in, but the inn didn't occur to me until you started telling me why it was your dream job. You planted the seed, and suddenly owning part of a haunted mansion sounded cool. I've stashed away a fuck-ton of money over the past decade," he admitted.

"You professional athletes," she joked.

He winked at her. "I'm loaded. Truth is, I have enough put

away that I wouldn't have to work again if I didn't want to."

"So you invested in the inn?"

"I bought fifty-one percent of the business."

"You're the boss," she whispered. "So I got the job because—"

"No." He raised his finger, pointing at her, not giving her time to finish that thought. "You got the job because you were the best candidate. Gio told me before I even signed the paperwork that they were interviewing you for the job. He asked if I wanted to sit in on it. I told him no. Told him I trusted him and Rafe to make the decision, and that if you were the right person for the job, they should hire you. I had zero impact on you getting that job. You earned it all on your own."

She considered that for a moment, then smiled. "Okay." Then she added, "Thanks for telling me that. But why didn't *they* tell me you'd bought in?"

"I asked them to keep that between us until I had a chance to break it to my family that I was leaving hockey. So...what do you think about the two of us working together?"

Gianna couldn't imagine anything better. She was excited about the job, but she also knew that once the baby came, she was going to need help. Knowing Elio would be there, carrying part of the load—at work and with the baby—was a huge relief. "Honestly, I love the idea."

He leaned forward and gave her a kiss.

When they parted, Gianna sighed happily. She'd been too afraid to let herself dream of this moment, certain nothing this wonderful could ever happen to her.

"I did a bunch of research on pregnancy last night. Most people wait until the end of the first trimester before they tell people."

Elio gave her a quick kiss on the forehead. "Fine. We'll wait a month, then I'll come home, and we'll tell everyone together."

"You're sure Gio and Rafe—"

"I'm sure," Elio said, "but if you're worried, we could tell them. Swear them to secrecy."

She considered that, then shook her head. "They'd want to tell Keeley. No matter what vow they take. I swear, those three share a hive mind these days."

He agreed. "She'd kill them if they didn't."

Gianna giggled. "Keeley does like to know everything about everyone. And if Keeley finds out before Liza..."

Elio chuckled. "Total social circle breakdown. So, we wait a month, then start making the rounds, telling my parents, grandparents, siblings, the aunts and uncles, cousins... Shit," Elio mused, with humor. "Might be easier just to have a big party and tell everyone at the same time."

Gianna reached out and grasped his hand. "You know that's a wonderful thing, right? You have the incredible problem of having too many people to tell. I...I don't have anyone."

Elio gave her a sweet kiss on the cheek. "I'm your family now," he whispered. "Me and this little firefly in here."

They moved together as one, his lips finding hers, kissing her so softly, so sweetly, she feared she was going to start crying again. Every single thing he'd said tonight had been perfect.

"I should warn you, Freckles, my mom is going to freak out when we tell her," Elio said. "She's a very hands-on grandmother, always stopping by Bruno and Viv's house for cuddles and kisses from her grandbabies. She'll be out of her mind with happiness when she finds out about our firefly."

Firefly.

She loved that Elio had already given their baby a nickname, already found a way to make this seem even more real.

And while kisses and cuddles hadn't been the norm for her, after being exposed to all of the Moretti affection on Christmas Eve, and Elio's nonstop kisses and hugs, she was now a huge fan.

"I'm sorry Grandma Mary couldn't be here, couldn't..." Her throat clogged up as she remembered her beloved grandmother, the woman who'd raised her.

"I'm sorry too," he murmured.

"I'm glad this baby will have your mom as a grandma."

"Noni," Elio corrected. "That's what my mom likes to be called. Since there could only be one Nonna in our family, my mom goes by Noni."

"Noni," Gianna repeated. "I like it."

"Liza and Aldo are going to flip," Elio added, his excitement growing as he started thinking about the long-reaching effects of her pregnancy.

"This baby is going to have a huge family," she said, smiling, so grateful for that. Her childhood had been too quiet, too lonely. She'd never wanted that for her child.

Elio wrapped one hand around the back of her neck, pulling her forward until their foreheads touched. "Our baby is going to be the most loved, the most spoiled, the smartest, best-looking, most athletic..."

"Our baby," she whispered, trying out the new pronoun. Since yesterday, she'd been thinking in terms of "my baby."

Her throat tightened with unshed tears, her happiness growing too big to keep inside. This baby was going to have a loving, wonderful, supportive father—a foreign concept to the girl who'd been raised by a single grandmother and abandoned by a single mother.

Elio placed his cheek against hers, the two of them simply holding each other, sharing each other's space and air. "I don't know how I'm going to make it two more months in Baltimore," he admitted. "All I can think about is how I want to be here, back home in Philly, with you and the baby."

She kissed him. "I know. It's going to be a long eight weeks." She looked back toward the hallway. She could hear the faint strains of the music thumping, laughter coming from the ball-room. "I guess we should get back to the wedding."

He sighed. "Yeah. But beware—we're only keeping the pregnancy secret. If I can't go in there and scream from the rafters that you're having my baby, you're going to have to let me tell the world you're mine."

"Yours," she said. "So, so yours."

Chapter Nineteen

Gianna couldn't wipe the smile off her face as they reentered the ballroom. Even though it was apparent their absence had not gone unnoticed.

Their group of friends was standing at the edge of the dance floor, looking in their direction as they approached.

"Where did you two disappear to?" Liza asked.

"Just taking a breather," Elio replied.

"You only danced one dance," she pointed out.

"Excellent point. We haven't even really started to work up a sweat. Come on, Gianna. Dance with me." Elio reached for Gianna's hand and gave her a quick spin before pulling her body close to his. "I'm in the mood for a little bumping and grinding."

Liza watched them curiously for a moment before allowing Keeley to draw her into a small circle of dancers, the two women standing close, talking as they moved. Liza continued to glance in their direction, her eyes narrowed suspiciously.

"You're a terrible tease. You know Liza's not going to give up until we explain why the two of us are suddenly so close. She can tell something's going on between us," Gianna said, her hands gripping his shoulders.

"I know. We'll put her out of her misery later. For now, I need you in my arms, and since dancing is the only acceptable way to do that at this wedding, that's what we're going to do." He bent his head lower, his cheek pressed against hers. Every few seconds, he gave her a soft kiss that had her body shifting into overdrive. She groaned quietly when his hands drifted from her back to her ass.

Two could play that game, she thought. Gianna gave as good as she got, her hands gliding beneath the lapels of his jacket, stroking his pecs through his shirt.

Elio lifted his head slightly to look at her. "I'm going to have to revise my previous statement. There's absolutely no way I can dance with you and keep it appropriate."

He backed that proclamation up by squeezing her ass and drawing her even closer, something she wouldn't have thought possible. A single piece of paper wouldn't fit between the two of them.

"I think it's safe to say we're a couple thousand miles away from appropriate," she acknowledged.

"Too much more of this and I won't be able to let you go. There will be too much physical proof. God, I can't wait to get you back in my bed."

This wasn't the first time he'd talked about the two of them resuming their sexual relationship, but she'd been so certain he would change his mind once she dropped the bomb of her pregnancy on him. Now, the seed he'd planted hadn't just taken root, it had grown to full height and bloomed.

It occurred to her she probably should have realized she was pregnant way before this week because her hormones had been off the charts. And while there had been plenty of "exhausted" nights after long work hours, she'd had just as many nights where she'd pulled out her toys, closed her eyes, and created a whole array of red-hot Elio fantasies.

She felt the slight bulge in his pants that told her he was

speaking the truth. He spun her, clearly seeking a way to put some distance between them before things got too hot and heavy.

As for her, her thoughts were traveling the same path as his. All she could think about was wrapping her legs around his waist and begging him to carry her out of this ballroom. She wondered if he would be up for getting a room in the hotel. Preferably right now.

And if not...

"I know you've had a hell of a day, but I was wondering if you would want to stop by my place tonight on your way home. Or if you're too tired, maybe tomorrow before—"

"Tonight," he interjected. "I'm going home with you tonight."

"Okay."

Elio leaned down until his lips were by her ear. "I've had way too much time to think of all the ways I want to take you, Freckles, so I hope you're well-rested, ready to expand on that wild and wicked concept."

Gianna's body clenched with hunger, her eyelids heavy with desire. "God, please."

Elio stared at her, and she saw the desire she felt reflected in his eyes. "Gianna, if you keep looking at me like that, I'm going to drag you out of here before they cut the damn cake."

"I wouldn't complain," she assured him.

He bent his head to give her a kiss that was too short for her taste, but given they were surrounded by family and friends who had no clue their status quo had changed, she understood his attempts at restraint, though they were weak at best.

"I didn't tell anyone about us at all," she told him. "None of my friends. They all think I was at the cabin alone."

"Yeah, I figured as much. Otherwise, my sister would have been blowing up my phone. Why didn't you tell anyone?" he asked, curious.

She shrugged. "I wasn't sure you wanted me to. And, the

truth is, it felt like our own special secret. I didn't want to share it."

"I understand that. I felt the same, though I did talk to an old teammate, Alex, about it."

"Why him?"

Elio gave her a charming, self-deprecating grin. "I needed advice in the romance department, a place where I have zero experience. Alex is my only married friend."

She giggled. "Given everything you've said and done so far tonight, I'd say he's an excellent counselor."

"He is."

"You know, I picked up my phone about a million times a day to text or call you, wanting to just talk to you about anything, everything, nothing," she confessed.

"Why didn't you?" he asked.

"I didn't know if you'd...we didn't exactly leave things in a place where..."

"Gianna," he said.

"Yeah?"

"I'm always going to want you to text and call me. I don't care if it's a million times a day."

She smiled, wondering how he always knew the exact things to say to make her melt.

"Now that I have you in my arms again, it feels like the world is finally right."

She felt the same way. She'd spent a lifetime feeling slightly out of step, unable to make the pieces of her puzzle fit together. Then she stepped under the mistletoe with Elio, and everything just slid into place.

"I can't resist you," he murmured, pressing his lips against hers, firmly, passionately, and this time, there was no pulling away.

At least not until she heard Liza's voice right next to them. "What the hell are you doing?"

The two of them broke apart, and she could tell from Elio's amused grin, he'd expected the interruption.

"It's just like the mistletoe kiss but without the mistletoe." Keeley grinned, stepping up behind Liza, one song ending as another began. It was a popular line dance, so the floor began to crowd up, everyone moving in unison.

"Mistletoe?" Liza repeated, confused, even as she hopped three times before sliding to the left. Obviously, Keeley had forgotten to fill their friend in on the holiday kiss. "What are you talking about?"

Gianna might have laughed at the four of them in a line, discussing the kiss while managing to keep time with every single one of the steps in "The Cupid Shuffle."

"Gianna and Elio kissed under the mistletoe at the holiday party. And let me just say, it was a hot one. I don't blame you for going back for seconds, girlfriend." Keeley was, of course, under the mistaken impression that this was just their second kiss.

Liza, however, was too astute not to realize that things between them ran much deeper than that. But before she could call them out on it, they were absorbed into a throng of dancers, Gio and Rafe jumping in, guiding Keeley to a spot in front of them so they could follow her moves.

Liza laughed when Luca, who'd claimed a place next to her, slid left instead of right, bumping into her. "You're messing me up," she complained playfully.

The Morettis were no strangers to a good time, and they'd obviously hit that point in the night when everyone was ready to take things to another level when the next song started. They formed a big circle, everyone taking a turn in the middle, wowing the others with their wicked moves.

Gage and Penny took a long spin in the center of the circle as they all cheered them on. Gage, after much encouragement, dipped Penny, giving her a long, passionate kiss.

The deejay did a great job keeping everyone on the floor as the crowd "Uptown Funked" it, got "Footloose," split up with guys on one side, women on the other for the standard, "You're the One that I Want" duet.

Elio serenaded Gianna with "My Girl" as he old-school, sock-hop spun her around the floor. The women scream-sang "I Will Always Love You" so ear-piercingly that poor Whitney was most definitely spinning in her grave. By the time they'd finished grooving to "Can't Stop the Feeling," Gianna was ready for a break.

Elio went to the bar, grabbing a beer for himself and a glass of water for Gianna, before heading back to the table. She thanked him for the drink, taking a long swig before setting it on the table as the rest of their friends returned, fanning themselves and dropping exhaustedly back into their chairs.

Then Aldo, Kayden, and Luca drifted over from their table, shaking Elio's hand and giving him shit for being so late.

Aldo teased his brother. "You know, I noticed you've adopted a Hollywood attitude since becoming a professional athlete, always needing to make a big, splashy entrance."

"Asshole," Elio muttered, then he took the opening his brother provided. "Guess I'm going to have to invest in a good watch, since I won't be a professional athlete much longer."

Gianna let her gaze scan the faces of everyone around the table, amused by how quiet they'd suddenly gotten. For a split second.

Then they all erupted at once.

"What are you talking about?" Liza asked, managing to make her question the loudest.

Elio tugged his sister's hair playfully. "I hung up my skates. Let my contract lapse. I'm moving back to Philly at the end of the season. You up for one more brother shadowing your every move?"

Elio had claimed he wouldn't do that, but like Aldo, he liked to poke the bear when it came to his siblings.

"Shit," she groaned, though from the smile on her face, no one was buying the fact that she was upset. "You're really quitting?"

"I'm really quitting," he said.

Liza reached out, giving him a big hug. "I figured you'd hang in there at least five more years. Having you home...it's going to be so awesome!"

Luca and Kayden offered their congratulations, but Gianna noticed Gio and Rafe just smiled, unsurprised by the announcement. Which made sense considering Elio had contacted them to buy into the inn business.

Gianna still couldn't quite believe they would be working together, and it occurred to her that *now* it was her ultimate dream job.

"You can't get back soon enough for us," Gio said. "You gonna be okay answering to this hard-ass, Gee?"

Luca frowned. "Why would Gianna be answering to Elio?"

"Because, as part of my retirement-from-hockey plan, I've invested in the haunted inn. Gonna run it with Gianna."

Keeley squealed. "Thank God that secret is out! I was literally about to pop."

Liza scowled at her friend. "You knew?"

"Only for a week." Keeley jerked her thumb at her guys. "These guys didn't tell me for two whole weeks."

"And the only reason she got the goods early was because she stumbled across the paperwork on Rafe's desk," Gio explained.

Keeley pointed her finger at both her guys. "And that's the last secret you ever keep from me," she repeated. "You promised."

Rafe gave Keeley a kiss on the cheek. "We promise, Kiwi."

"Well, since we're on a roll as far as coming clean, why don't we keep the party going," Liza said, never missing a beat. "When did the two of you start kissing?"

Elio looked at Gianna, who gave him the one-shouldered "go for it" shrug.

"The first kiss was under the mistletoe, like Keeley said," Elio started.

"And the second was on the dance floor just now?" Liza asked.

Elio shook his head. "No. It was at the cabin in the Poconos after the holidays."

"We got snowed in together," Gianna added.

"No. Way!" Keeley squealed. "Why are we only just hearing about this now?"

Kayden gave his sister an exasperated look. "Why do you think you need to know everything about everyone?"

"Because I do," Keeley replied, prompting the rest of them to laugh.

"So you got snowed in," Liza prompted, clearly not happy with the crumbs they'd offered so far. "And you kissed and then you..." She paused for effect, letting them fill in the rest.

Gianna blushed. "Did other stuff."

Elio chuckled at her very PG response, knowing it was sufficient enough to send all their friends' thoughts to very X-rated places.

"Whoa. I didn't see that coming," Gio said, piping in. "Guess I'm suddenly starting to understand the interest in the inn."

"You should have seen that kiss under the mistletoe," Keeley said. "Serious sparks."

Gianna felt herself blushing. "We were trapped in that snowstorm, and then we sort of fell into the tequila—"

"And the vodka," Elio added with a wicked grin. "In an attempt to clean out the liquor cabinet."

"Anyway, we, um..." Gianna's words faded away when she realized she was about to come right out and admit that she'd had sex with Elio in front of his whole family.

"Had a one-night stand?" Aldo asked Elio softly, trying to make what he knew of his brother's past relationships fit with what he was seeing now.

Elio shook his head, wrapping his arm around her waist. He'd warned her he was going to say it and it looked like the time was now. "Nope. Gianna is my girlfriend."

The hockey announcement had shocked everyone to silence for a split second or two. This pronouncement struck harder, no one saying anything for *much* longer. Gianna got the impression everyone was waiting for one of them to add a "just kidding" to the end of his statement.

"We're dating," she added, when no one spoke.

"Exclusively," Elio stressed, specifically to his sister. "So she won't need your help uploading her profile to those stupid dating sites."

Liza sighed. "Another wingman down."

Luca chuckled, wrapping his arm around her neck. "No worries, cuz. I'll be your wingman if you want. Looks like you and I are starting to be in the minority here. All our rowdy, single friends and family are settling down."

"You're gonna be sorry you offered that," Liza warned. "Because I'm probably going to take you up on it."

"So to recap," Aldo said. "You're quitting hockey, moving home, dating Gianna, and running a haunted inn?"

Elio nodded. "In a nutshell."

"Maybe you should have chunked some of that information up. That's a lot to take in for one sitting," Aldo joked.

Elio's fingers tightened against her waist, and Gianna struggled not to laugh. They *had* chunked it up, unbeknownst to his brother. Because there was still an even bigger bomb to drop.

But the deejay saved them from having to say anything more when he invited the married couple to the floor. Penny sat on a chair as Gage "retrieved" the garter, his head disappearing under the skirt of Penny's wedding dress—staying there for a little longer than necessary, much to the amusement of the guests. He slipped the garter down her leg with his teeth, waiting as the single men in attendance lined the edge of the floor.

Elio, Gio, and Rafe stood amongst the other Morettis with beers in their hands. Keeley admonished Gio and Rafe, claiming they weren't even trying to catch the thing and that they should have left their drinks at the table. Gage sling-shotted the garter straight into Tony's hands. Tony swung it around on his finger before pointing at Jess, the maid of honor, as she laughed.

Then the deejay invited the single ladies to the dance floor for the bouquet toss. Liza and Keeley pulled Gianna from her chair, the three joining the throng of women gathered there.

Penny turned her back to them, tossing the bouquet with an impressive amount of loft. The bouquet flew high and far. Gianna had placed herself at the back of the crowd, which turned out to be the perfect spot to catch the bouquet.

Elio winked at her, laughing when she walked over and handed the bouquet to Jess.

"Chicken shit," he teased her when she returned to the table.

"I just think it's time for Tony and Rhys to propose to Jess," she replied, justifying her decision to give up the bouquet.

"I think they're struggling to figure out how to make that work. But given the way the three of them are looking at each other right now, I'd say this wedding has convinced them to come up with a plan sooner rather than later."

Gianna looked over at the trio, so wrapped up in each other, it took her breath away, and she couldn't help but agree with Elio.

"Come on," she replied, dragging him to the side of the room so they could watch Penny and Gage cut the wedding cake. "Thought you might appreciate being at the front of the line since you missed dinner."

They ate their cake, then returned to the dance floor when the deejay slowed things down, playing "Tenerife Sea," one of her favorite Ed Sheeran songs.

Elio hummed along, his lips next to her ears, lightly singing the line "all that you are is all that I'll ever need" to her. Gianna pressed more tightly to him, holding him like she'd never let go, and she knew in an instant they'd found "their song."

He kissed her—a long, slow, passionate one—when the song ended, and it appeared he was no longer willing to hide anything from their friends.

"This has been one of the best nights of my life," she said, as he led her back to their table.

"And it's not over yet," he murmured, kissing her on the cheek.

He was coming home with her. And there was no question what was going to happen when they got there.

"Want something to drink?" Elio asked.

"No, thanks."

"I'm ready for another," Luca said, rising. "Gotta take advantage of an open bar the Russos are paying for because God knows this lightning will never strike twice."

Elio and Luca drifted over to the bar as Gianna excused herself to go to the restroom.

Liza, in true female fashion, rose to go with her. Gianna figured Keeley would have been hot on her heels as well, but she was still on the dance floor with Gio and Rafe.

"You and I need to have a long talk, girlfriend," Liza said, following her into the ladies' room.

Gianna grasped her friend's hand. "I know we do. I hope you're not mad at me for keeping the Elio thing from you. I wasn't sure how to tell you at first and as more time passed, I thought, well, I didn't think he and I would..."

"You didn't think anything would come from it?"

Gianna shrugged, hating to admit that. "We didn't make plans or promises when we left the cabin. We just said goodbye. Given his disinterest in relationships..."

Liza grinned. "Trust me, he's not disinterested when it comes to you."

Gianna probably should have at least attempted to hide the smile her friend's observation prompted, but she couldn't do it. She smiled like a lunatic, her happiness shining through all the cracks.

"Jesus," Liza muttered. "Please, for the love of God, don't fill me in on all the great sex you had at my *family's* cabin." She stressed the *family* part, which had Gianna giggling. "I guess I understand now why you've been blowing me off. You don't need to venture into online dating hell. One of these days, you're going to have to tell me your trick for finding these guys who fall so fast and forever for you."

"Sam wasn't forever," Gianna reminded Liza.

"You dated the dude eleven years. To the woman who can't land a guy for more than a night or two, trust me, forever is the right word."

"Does it bother you?" Gianna asked, suddenly worried. "Me and Elio?"

"Holy shit, no. It's just…you're going to have to give me some time to get used to the idea. The two of you are very different people, but when I see you together… Damn, I can see it's working, and I'm blown away by it. But I'm also kind of worried."

"Worried?"

Liza sighed. "Elio's dating track record is nonexistent, so he's a dark horse, isn't he? And you had your heart dropkicked by that prick Sam." Liza reached over and grasped her hand. "I don't want you to get hurt."

"Elio won't hurt me." Gianna didn't hesitate to speak the words because she knew, all the way to the depths of her soul, that they were true.

Her utter assurance took Liza aback but not for long. She grinned, squeezing Gianna's hand tightly. "You're in love with him," she said softly.

Gianna nodded.

"And he's in love with you?"

She shrugged. "We haven't said the words yet. God, it's still early days. I just…I think…I mean, I hope."

Liza considered that, then grinned. "You don't need hope. And you don't even need to think about it too hard. Because I see the way he looks at you. If my brother hasn't already fallen hopelessly, madly in love with you, I'll eat my bra."

Gianna laughed. "I hope you're right."

"You know, if this works out, somewhere down the line we could be sisters."

Gianna didn't know how to reply to that. Not because she

didn't want it with all her heart but because she was still struggling to believe this was all real.

"Best. Thing. Ever," Liza said, as she reached out and hugged her.

And that was when Gianna realized the Moretti women were no slouches in the warm embraces either.

The two of them laughed happily walking back to the ballroom hand in hand.

Keeley scowled when they resumed their places at the table. "What the hell?" she complained. "Did you guys have the heart-to-heart without me?"

Rafe shook his head. "Everything is not your business." Of course, now like always, those words went in one of Keeley's ears and right out the other.

"Incorrect," she said to her boyfriend, her attention still locked on her and Liza. "Everything good?"

"Everything's great," Liza said, smiling at Gianna. Her gaze narrowed as Elio and Luca returned to the table. "You better not fuck this up," she warned her brother.

Elio took no offense. "I have no intention of fucking anything up."

Liza bounced back up from her chair. "Good. Now let's dance until we drop."

An hour later, Gianna was perilously close to that dropping point.

"You ready to leave?" Elio asked.

She nodded as they returned to the table. They said their goodbyes, retrieved their coats, then walked to the foyer of the grand hotel.

"Did you drive?" he asked.

She shook her head. "Rode with Liza."

"Good," he said, and she was glad they wouldn't have to separate for the drive back to her place.

He walked her to his truck, opening the passenger door for her. "You ready?"

She nodded slowly.

"Yeah," she said softly. "I'm ready."

He stole a quick kiss.

She was so ready.

Ready for tonight, for what lay ahead.

For the beginning of everything.

Chapter Twenty

E lio released her hand as they walked into her apartment, then he helped her out of her coat, hanging hers and his on the hooks by the door. He'd never been to her place, so she took a few minutes, showing him around before they sat down side by side on the couch.

"Do you want something to drink?" she offered.

"No. What I'd really like is a quick make-out session here on the couch, followed by really hot sex in your bedroom. Thoughts?"

She tapped her chin with her finger, pretending to consider his suggestion. "I don't know. I *am* pretty worn out from all that dancing."

Elio narrowed his eyes. "Freckles?"

"Hmm?"

"Find your second wind." That was all he said before he tugged her into his arms and kissed her.

Gianna found her second wind. And her third, fourth, eighth.

Elio's lips left no part of her face or neck or ears unworshipped, murmuring in her ear, "I missed you so fucking much."

Gianna's hands tangled in his hair, her lips doing a fair

amount of exploring as well. She loosened the knot of his tie, then drew it out of the collar with a quick flick of a hand before tossing it over her shoulder dramatically.

Then she went to work on the buttons of his shirt. She'd only tackled the top three before Elio laid claim to her lips once more. He hadn't been kidding about the making out. It felt as if he couldn't go a full sixty seconds without kissing her.

"Are you moving into the caretaker's cottage behind the inn?" he asked the next time they parted.

She nodded. "It should be ready in a few more weeks. Gio has been so sweet, letting me pick out the paint colors and the new cabinets for the kitchen."

"When the season is over, I'm moving in with you."

Her eyes widened. "That's a pretty big step for a man who'd never spent the entire night with a woman until he was forced to by a foot of snow."

"Very funny," Elio smirked, acknowledging the joke. "Just know that it's happening."

Gianna sobered up. "Seriously, Elio. I think we should take a teeny tiny step back, slow things down."

She recalled his pronouncement that they were going to be a couple, and it had thrilled her to the tips of her toes. She didn't have an issue with dating him. There was nothing she wanted more than to spend time with him, to see if that magical, wonderful time in the cabin could be recreated out here in the real world.

Optimistic Gianna was all in when it came to Elio, but realist Gianna, the one who'd just had her heart stomped by her last boyfriend, was skeptical, anxious.

"I want to date you, Elio. So much. But you have to admit, we don't know each other that well. There are things about me that might bug you after an extended period of time."

Elio narrowed his eyes. "Why do you say that?"

She shrugged. Not that her refusal to answer mattered.

"Are you saying that because of Sam? Because of things he said when he broke up with you?"

She never ceased to be amazed by how well Elio understood her. "I'm just saying, our time in the cabin was limited. My obsessive-compulsiveness might not seem so cute after a few weeks or months, but..."

"Let's break this down, Freckles, since you're stressing it out over it. You still vacuum every day?"

"Not lately, but I've been pretty distracted between the new job and...throwing up. I'm sure I'll get back to it."

"I can live with the vacuuming. And the Roomba. Still got the weekly menu?"

She nodded.

"Cool. Because I've started that habit at home, and it really works."

She was touched that he'd picked up her menu habit, but those were just a small part of a larger whole. "Those aren't the only idiosyncrasies I have," she said, feeling as if she owed him full disclosure. "Those are just the ones you've seen."

"So give me some others."

"I'm a little bit of a control freak."

"Are those your words or Sam's?"

"His, but it doesn't matter because they're true. I like things in specific places, like things done in specific ways. Plus, the clean freak component."

"Given what you told me about the apartments you cleaned with your grandma, I think that makes a lot of sense. Gianna, I'm not a slob. I like to think of myself as a pretty tidy guy. I'm also fairly adaptable. If there's something you want done a certain way and I don't have strong feelings about it, then it's fine."

"What if you *do* have strong feelings about it?"

"We'll play strip poker. Winner's way will become *the* way. And then we'll fuck like bunnies."

Gianna was pretty sure he was joking, but she couldn't help

but think it was an inspired plan. "I think I could get behind that."

"That's my girl. So what else?"

She grimaced. "I count steps in my head when I climb them. Like, every single time."

He laughed. "If it's in your head, why do I care?"

Gianna tried not to laugh but damn if he didn't have a point. "Fine. My closet and sock drawer are organized by color," she said, before adding, "this week."

"How about your panties?" he teased.

She huffed out a laugh. "Perv."

"I'm just saying if you're really concerned, maybe you should give me a peek at the panties' drawer. Or the lingerie one. Either one will work, so it'll give me an idea of what I'm signing on for here."

"You aren't taking me seriously."

Elio cupped her cheek, his expression growing more serious. "I'm taking everything you're saying very seriously, Gianna. But nothing you've said is anywhere close to a deal breaker for me. If Sam had hang-ups with that shit, that's on him. As far as I'm concerned, those things are just small parts of what make you *you*. And in case you can't tell, Gianna, I'm crazy about you."

"You are?"

"Crazy. About. You." He gave her a soft kiss on the forehead.

As always, he'd found the perfect words to make her anxieties fade.

Then he pulled away, still holding her face in his hands as he looked into her eyes. "So when I get home, we're moving in together," he said again, in no uncertain terms.

She couldn't come up with any other arguments against what he was suggesting. Probably because it was too good to be true.

"Promise me," he prodded, mistaking her silence as disagreement.

"I promise."

"Awesome. So we'll do the dating thing until April, until my time with the team is up. Maybe on weekends when we're not on the road, and I'm home in Baltimore, you can come down and stay with me, see the games."

She smiled. "I would love that."

"And I'm pretty sure there are going to be a lot of times when I sneak up here for a single night. Just because."

"Just because?" she asked, batting her eyelashes flirtatiously.

"Just because I'll be aching to hold you, touch you, kiss you. To cuddle with you, sleep with you in my arms while I let you steal all the covers."

"I don't steal the covers."

He chuckled. "Of course you do. I don't doubt for a second that I'm going to wear grooves in the interstate between here and Baltimore, simply to see the way your body is changing as this little firefly grows inside you. I don't want to miss a minute of it." He placed his hand on her belly as he said the last.

Gianna swiped at the tears that were flowing freely down her cheeks. There was no way she was stemming the flood, hormones and happiness were a powerful combination.

"Gianna," Elio said, pressing his lips to her cheek, kissing slowly down her neck.

"Hmmm," she hummed, tilting her head to give him better access.

"Where's your bedroom?" he asked, never lifting his head.

"Last door on the right," she said, her eyes closing in bliss.

Elio ran his tongue the length of her neck, not stopping until he reached her ear. "Get there."

She shivered at the dark, sensual command.

Rising together, she took the hand he proffered, then led him to her bedroom. He dropped her hand when they entered, twisting her away from him to lower the zipper on her dress.

His fingertips brushed her spine as he pulled the tab down, every soft stroke producing a shudder of need.

"God, I missed this," Elio admitted, pulling the dress off her shoulders, pushing it until it dropped to the floor.

Gianna stepped out of the fabric.

"Turn around. Let me see you," he demanded.

She spun to face him, lifting her hand to her stomach when his gaze slid down her body and stayed there. Elio reached out, covering her hand.

"I still can't believe it," he said. "When you told me you weren't pregnant, it felt like I'd lost the Stanley Cup. I've never known disappointment like that."

"I felt the same," she admitted.

Elio closed his hand over hers, lifting it, kissing it. "Gianna," he said, his lips brushing her knuckles as he said her name.

"Yes."

"Take off the rest of your clothes and get on the bed."

Finesse went out the window as the two of them quickly undressed. They'd left too much unsaid when they parted at the cabin, and they'd suffered for it. Forced to lock their feelings away, uncertain if their fondness, their affection, their desires were returned.

Even now, in the face of everything they'd said to each other, Gianna still struggled to believe this was all true. That it would last.

She'd been left alone by too many people she loved—abandoned by her mother, cheated on and dumped by Sam, and while her grandmother didn't choose to go, she'd felt the loss of Grandma Mary most of all, essentially orphaned at twenty-one.

Once they were naked, Gianna climbed on the mattress, Elio following. She turned, laying on her back, as he caged her beneath him, on his hands and knees.

Gianna ran her hands over his chest, taking the time to explore his body. Every time they'd come together in the cabin, there'd been this underlying sense of urgency, as if they knew their time was limited. As such, she hadn't truly taken the time she wanted to look at him, to learn his body. There was a thin scar on his shoulder she hadn't noticed before. When she ran her finger over it, he said, "Took a high stick during a pick-up game in high school. Split the skin enough that I needed a few stitches."

Elio gave her the time she needed to look, mainly because he was studying her as well. He stroked a spot just above her hipbone.

"Birthmark," she whispered.

His fingers drifted back to her stomach, and she smiled. She hadn't been able to stop rubbing her belly either, her hands drawn there as if she could feel the life that was growing inside her.

Elio lowered himself, resting his weight on his elbows, so he could kiss her. They took their time with this as well, their tongues touching playfully, a game of hide-and-seek. His lips were soft at first, but they soon grew hungrier, drifting away from her mouth to her cheek, her ear, her neck, then downward to her breasts.

She hissed when he sucked on her nipple, roughly.

"Yes." She'd loved his breast play at the cabin, but this time was different, more potent. Her breasts were more sensitive to his touch, every stroke of his tongue, pinch of his fingers, nip of his teeth more pronounced. "That feels so good."

Elio played with her, building her arousal slowly but steadily. Especially when he drifted even lower, his tongue finding her clit on the first swipe.

Her hips jolted upright, roughly enough that Elio had to grip her thighs, hold her steady for his passionate assault. His tongue left no part of her unexplored, and when he drove it inside her pussy, she had to clench her eyes closed tightly, the pleasure too intense.

"I think..." God, she thought she was going to come already. Then, she knew it.

Elio drove his tongue in faster, his thumb entering the game, stroking her clit with the same force, the same speed.

Her back arched as she came, calling out his name loudly. "Elio!"

He didn't stop, drawing out her orgasm until the last

remnants fell. Then he lifted his head, smiling at her like the cat who ate the canary.

She reached down, gripping his upper arm, pulling him back up her body. Once he was there, she lifted her head to kiss him, tasting herself on his lips. It was a rough, hungry, passionate kiss, and while she'd initiated it, Elio wasted no time taking control.

"Need you," she murmured against his lips. "Inside me. Now."

"Greedy girl," he said, and though his words were teasing, the dark look in his eyes told her she was going to get exactly what she wanted.

He shifted, reaching down to grip his cock. He placed the head at the opening of her body, then paused, glancing back toward his pile of clothing on the floor.

She laughed softly. "Elio," she said, capturing his attention. "It's not like I can get any more pregnant."

He snorted briefly, then...fuck...then he was there, pushing inside in one long, relentless, glorious thrust.

"Jesus Christ. You feel so goddamned good!"

She winced slightly, and while he saw it, he didn't stop.

"I can't—"

"I don't want you to stop. It's been too long," she whispered. "We can't go that long again."

He grinned and groaned simultaneously. "God, you're perfect. And you're right. Never again."

Words fell away as Elio slowly slid back out, his pace building with each return. What had begun as slow and steady soon morphed into nothing short of uninhibited, unrestrained madness.

Gianna, the epitome of the good girl, became someone else entirely in Elio's arms.

She was wild. She was wicked.

Lifting her head, she bit his pec, her nails scoring his back. Elio lowered, nipping at her shoulder hard enough that she suspected she would be wearing turtlenecks for a few days.

"More," she gasped, wanting him to leave his mark. Wanting to leave hers.

"Gianna," Elio said. "God. Yes. Missed. You." He pounded harder. "I'm there."

"Me too."

She closed her eyes as waves of pleasure bombarded her. Elio groaned, slamming inside with one last powerful thrust and then, she felt him coming, filling her.

They remained there, locked together, for just a moment or two. When Gianna opened her eyes, Elio's beloved face was there, inches from hers, looking at her with such wonder and...

Love.

She could see it. And she could feel it.

"I love you," she whispered, finally releasing the words she'd kept locked away for too long.

Elio didn't respond immediately.

"Gianna," he said at last, clearing his throat. Then he placed nothing less than a hundred kisses. On her lips. Her cheeks. Forehead. Even the tip of her nose.

"I love you so much it hurts," he said at last. "Being without you..."

"I know," she said. "I hated every second we were apart."

He shifted, both of them moaning softly as he pulled out of her, dropping down next to her on the bed. She turned to face him, only a few inches separating them.

Elio grabbed her right leg and pulled it between his, before gripping her waist and tugging her even closer.

"Two months feels like forever," she mused, wondering how she'd be able to say goodbye to him Monday morning when he returned to Baltimore. He'd warned her about leaving tracks on the interstate, but she was pretty damn certain she was going to be digging the grooves even deeper.

"The time will go quickly and then...we'll institute our new life plan. Dream job, engagement, marriage, baby. And this isn't going to be some eleven-year-long deal either, so put that out of your head right now."

"*Our* life plan?" she asked.

"Ours."

Gianna grinned. "You realize a couple of those things have already happened."

Elio laughed. "Yeah. I know. So now I'm hoping to convince you to go for the clean sweep."

"What's that mean?"

"I know you like to nail things down, set up a schedule, so how would you feel about dream job, engagement, marriage, and baby...all at twenty-six?"

"Elio."

"You can call me crazy, say I'm moving too fast, and it's true. But none of that changes my end goal."

"Which is?"

"Moving in together. A big-ass wedding. Four kids. Probably a dog or two. I'm also hoping to convince Gio and Rafe to sell the inn to us somewhere down the line."

Her eyes widened. "You've given this a lot of thought."

"I have, but that's not all. I have a lifetime of plans for us. You know what," he said, looking around her bedroom. "Maybe we should grab a pen and paper so we can start to make a list."

Gianna twisted, coming over Elio, her knees resting by his hips, her hands flat on his chest. "Life plans *and* a list?"

She shifted so that his cock, which was growing thicker by the second, rested along the length of her slit. Slowly, she slid up and down until he was rock hard and ready again.

Then, she lowered her head and kissed him. "God, I love when you talk dirty."

Elio laughed, but it turned to a guttural moan when she reached behind herself to cup his balls.

"Is that right?" He lifted her hips, pulling her down on his erect cock. They both gasped when he was seated to the hilt again. "Well then..."

Before she could react, Elio twisted until their positions were reversed, with him on top, his lips brushing her ear. "Get ready, Freckles. Because I've got a hell of a list for you."

Gianna groaned, her orgasm building quickly as Elio whispered the hottest list of sexual fantasies she'd ever heard, and that was when she realized she'd met her match.

Her perfect match.

Epilogue

Elio walked out of the stadium, grinning when he realized the whole gang had hung back to wait for him.

Gianna saw him first, and she dashed across the parking lot to hug him. Jumping up, she wrapped her legs around his waist and gave him one hell of a congratulatory kiss.

"What a great game!" she said excitedly.

Baltimore had trounced Philadelphia, four to one. As a hometown boy, he probably should have felt some guilt for the two goals he'd scored to ensure Philly went down.

But he didn't. Because his girl had been there, watching, and he wanted to make her proud.

He wrapped his arm around her shoulders after she lowered herself back to her feet. "Nice jersey," he said, kissing her on the cheek.

Gianna spun around for him, letting him see his name and number on her back. "I love it."

The two of them had spent the night wrapped up in each other's arms, and they'd had sex two more times before he'd begrudgingly dragged himself out of her bed this morning.

He'd made plans to go to his parents' house for breakfast to tell them he was leaving hockey at the end of the season. He had toyed with the idea of pushing it off, but Gianna had insisted he go, promising she would see him later at the game.

On his way to his parents' house, he'd called in yet another favor and had one of his jerseys delivered to her apartment for her to wear tonight. And while he loved seeing his name on her back, he wouldn't rest until it was *her* name too.

Gianna was convinced he was moving too fast, but it turned out his competitiveness wasn't restricted to the ice. He was in it to win it with her. The life plan he'd revealed to her last night. He wouldn't stop until he had it all.

Gio slapped him on the back. "Great game. I hate to see Philly lose, but watching you skate, and score those goals. It was a thing of beauty."

Elio looked around and realized they were missing a couple people. "Aldo and Kayden knock off after the game?"

Keeley shook her head. "They never made it at all."

"Three-alarm fire," Rafe added. "Sounds like a bad one. They were both at the end of their shifts, but when the call came in, they answered it."

"It's the Crossings Motel," Gio said. "Rocco's place."

"Oh shit," Elio said. His dad and uncles were buddies with Rocco, all of them part of a weekly poker game. The gruff, chain-smoking man had been a fixture in Elio's life since he was a kid. It was Rocco who'd taught him some of his more colorful curse words. "Rocco okay?"

Liza nodded. "Yeah. Aldo just texted. Said the fire was out, and no one was injured, but it was a total loss. Wanted me to tell you he was sorry he didn't get to see the game."

"Is he going to be able to swing by Divine?" Elio asked. The whole gang had made plans to go out for a late dinner after the game together, dining at the restaurant Rafe had inherited from his grandfather.

Liza shook her head. "No. Apparently something else came up that he and Kayden have to deal with, something to do with a woman who'd been staying at the motel."

253

"Damn." Elio was sorry he wouldn't get to see his brother before he returned to Baltimore, but then he remembered that it wasn't like he would be gone for long. Soon, he and Aldo would have plenty of opportunities to go out for dinner. Hell, they could even go to the hockey games together, both of them as spectators.

"Okay, let's load up the cars," Luca said as they crossed the parking lot. Everyone climbed into two different vehicles, as he led Gianna to his truck.

Luca honked the horn of the car he was driving when he and Liza pulled out, followed by Rafe, Gio, and Keeley in Gio's truck.

Gianna started to walk around to the passenger's side of his vehicle, but he grasped her wrist, pulling her toward him. Pressing her back against his truck, he stole a kiss.

"You were incredible tonight," she said, her hands wrapped around his shoulders.

Now that he had her back in his arms, he wasn't going to make the same mistake he'd made at the beginning of the year. It was time Gianna Duncan learned exactly what she meant to him.

Because he was going to take a page from Gage Russo's book, determined that before the year was out, she was not only going to be his fiancée but his wife.

"I love you." He'd said the words last night...for the very first time in his life. He'd been thinking them the entire evening, but Gianna, the brave, open-hearted woman, had been the first to say them.

And he'd been so moved by it, his throat had closed, so it had taken him a moment to be able to offer them back.

She kissed his jaw. "I love you too."

"I want you to think about something while I'm away these next couple of months."

"Okay," she said. "What?"

"Us."

Gianna laughed. "I don't think I'll be thinking of anything but."

"Gianna, I wasn't kidding last night. When I look at my future, all I see is you. I know you think I'm moving too fast. But the truth is, for my entire adult life, I haven't moved at all. Never taken one step. Never been tempted to. Then, I kissed you under that mistletoe, the fog lifted, and suddenly I was looking at the road to paradise. I'm impatient to get there. So take the next eight weeks and think about what I want. Because when I get home, I'm moving in and then, I'm proposing, and *then*, if I can convince you to say yes, I'm going to be waiting at the end of an aisle for you shortly after."

Gianna sniffed, wiping her eyes, despite the fact her smile was wide and bright. "You say the most perfect things." She stepped into his arms, and he held her tight. "And give incredible hugs."

She lifted her head as he lowered his, their lips meeting for the softest, sweetest, most perfect kiss of his life.

She sighed as they parted. "I needed that," she whispered, repeating the same words she'd said to him after their very first kiss. "I needed you."

"And I needed you, Freckles."

Ready for more Italian Stallions?
    Down and Dirty
    Hard and Fast
    Rough and Ready
    Wild and Wicked
    Hot and Heavy
    Naughty and Nice (a holiday novella)
    Tempted and Taken
    Steady and Strong
    Kiss and Tell

Want to see how Padraig Collins, bartender at Pat's Pub, found true love in the Wilder Irish series? Want to read more about

Elio's former teammate, Alex, and how he wound up married to tomboy Charley? Check out these books!

Wild Devotion

Wild Chance

Making His Play

Calling all fans of Mari Carr AND Facebook! There's a group for you. Come join the Mari Carr's Facebook group for sneak peaks, cover reveals, contests and more! Join now.

And be sure to join Mari's mailing list to receive a **FREE** sexy novella, Midnight Wild.

About the Author

Virginia native Mari Carr is a New York Times and USA TODAY bestseller of contemporary romance novels. With over two million copies of her books sold, Mari was the winner of the Romance Writers of America's Passionate Plume award for her novella, Erotic Research. She has over a hundred published works, including her popular Wild Irish and Compass books, along with the Trinity Masters series she writes with Lila Dubois.

Follow Mari:
www.maricarr.com
mari@maricarr.com

Join her newsletter so you don't miss new releases and for exclusive subscriber-only content.

Printed in Great Britain
by Amazon